The Queen's Margarine

The Queen's Margarine

Wendy Perriam

ROBERT HALE · LONDON

© Wendy Perriam 2009
First published in Great Britain 2009

ISBN 978-0-7090-8788-5

Robert Hale Limited
Clerkenwell House
Clerkenwell Green
London EC1R 0HT

www.halebooks.com

2 4 6 8 10 9 7 5 3 1

Typeset in 10/13½ pt New Century Schoolbook
Printed in the UK by the MPG Books Group

In memory of my beloved daughter,

Pauline Maria

1965–2008

Contents

1 Double M 9

2 Tulips 26

3 Repair 48

4 Margarine 58

5 Charmayne 70

6 Christmas Stocking 88

7 Turning Point 102

8 Thinking Without Thinking 117

9 High Speed 2 127

10 Travelling Light 150

11 Prickly Pear 160

12 River Heights 174

13 Pecking Order 195

14 On The Road 209

Double M

'Stop watching me!' Aubrey snapped. 'I can't stand the way you stare.'

The figurines continued to observe him with disapproving eyes, ignoring his instruction with their usual insolence. In truth, there was no escaping them, crowded as they were on mantelpiece and sideboard and every available surface, and ranged six-deep on the display-shelves, made specially in their honour, many years ago.

'OK, I know I should have dusted you, but that was *her* job and she's dead.'

The Spanish Beauty winced; the Queen of the May pursed her lips in shock. They preferred more tactful words for death: depart this life, pass over, meet one's Maker, join the angels, go to one's true home – all prissy, lying euphemisms.

'Anyway,' he continued, in a bid to be more amenable, if only for his dead wife's sake, 'you'll be glad to hear a cleaner's on her way – a pillar of the church, who'll sort me out in no time, or so the vicar says.'

People must be talking – parishioners and neighbours – if they were concerned enough to send someone round. True, the dirt was building up, but then he had never been one for housework – no need, with a wife like Pearl. As bright and shining as her name, she had kept the place immaculate; refusing to let him help with even minor chores. So, naturally, he was lost without her; had no idea how or what to cook; dithered in the supermarket because the place was just too vast and everything was sold in family-sized packs – nothing for a widower living on his own.

'I wouldn't call it living,' the Prima Ballerina sneered – one of Pearl's Royal Doulton range, poised eternally *en pointe* on the top

9

of the piano. 'You've allowed yourself to go to rack and ruin, like the house.'

'And what would your dear wife think?' the Broadway Queen chimed in. 'She'd be deeply shocked, if she saw you now.'

He fled into the kitchen and, slumping at the table, tried not to see the grease-encrusted cooker, the smeary windows, filthy floor, the larder shelves empty of all food. Perhaps he ought to scour the place before Marilyn, the cleaner, put in an appearance, so as to give a good impression. Or was that barking when you'd hired a dog? No point trying to decide, because actually he didn't have the energy to wash so much as a teaspoon. Grief had left him limp.

Instead, he made a cup of coffee – strong, to wake him up. Since the death, he had barely slept; missed the warmth of his wife's body curled neatly next to his. It was years since they'd made love – in fact, twenty-two years, four months and two weeks. He had kept a daily tally, although not knowing at the time that Christmas Day, 1986, would be the very last occasion. Nothing had gone wrong, nor had anything been said, either then or subsequently, apart from a few evasive excuses on her part: headaches, indigestion, wrong time of the month. He hadn't liked to force the issue, when she was physically so delicate, and so willing and co-operative in every other way.

Returning to his chair, he sipped the scalding coffee, not caring if it burnt his mouth. Physical pain helped distract him from the mental.

He jumped as the doorbell rang – a shrill, imperious peal. Marilyn was due at ten, and it was only a quarter to, but he shuffled out to the hall and opened the front door.

'Sorry I'm early, Mr Sadler, but better early than late, I always say. You are expecting me, I hope?'

He smiled politely. He certainly hadn't been expecting someone quite so ancient – *his* age, by the looks of it, which meant well past retirement and shambling towards dotage. The name Marilyn had led him to envisage a voluptuous young blonde, garbed in a low-cut evening gown – not this wrinkled, wizened figure in a navy nylon overall, with salt-and-pepper hair scraped up into a bun.

He ushered her in and offered her a coffee, which she hastily refused; horrified, no doubt, by the state of the cups, some of which were even sprouting mould.

'No, I'd better get on, Mr Sadler. There's a lot to do – that's obvious. Where would you like me to start?'

In his mind, he was still engaging with Marilyn Monroe. If it was a question of starting somewhere, well, would she kindly press her luscious lips fiercely into his, offer him her breasts to fondle, then, while he kissed the nipples, let her hands glide slowly down towards his—

'And where do you keep the cleaning things?' The other, breastless Marilyn was scrabbling in her bag for a pair or rubber gloves.

Cleaning things were Pearl's department, although he did vaguely remember seeing brooms and mops and suchlike in the cupboard under the stairs. As he led the woman there, he watched his private Marilyn remove her wispy undergarments and step naked from the shimmering folds of her seductive satin gown.

'My word! These dusters could do with a wash. And this mop's seen better days.'

He bristled in defence of Pearl. In the last months of her illness, it was all she could do to *breathe*, poor soul, so she could hardly be washing dusters or shopping for new mops. 'Start in the sitting-room,' he instructed, trying to sound authoritative, yet pathetically relieved when she followed in his wake. He'd heard tales of bolshie cleaners; tyrants in the home, who could hoover up an employer with the dust-mites, or sluice him briskly down the sink.

'Oh, what lovely little ornaments!' Marilyn exclaimed, her eyes darting here and there, as she surveyed the array of figurines. 'I've never seen so many all at once. They must have cost a bomb!'

Aubrey refrained from answering. It was ill-mannered, surely, for a virtual stranger to start discussing what things cost, the minute she arrived. Porcelain was, admittedly, expensive, but why begrudge his precious Pearl her one and only extravagance?

'Was it your late wife who collected them?'

He loathed the phrase 'late wife'. Well-organized, efficient and punctual to a fault, Pearl had never been late for anything.

'Oh, just look at that dear little mermaid!' Marilyn touched an admiring finger to the seaweed-like long hair. 'Every detail perfect, even down to the fish-scales on the tail.'

'She's called Ocean Beauty,' Aubrey informed her, as familiar with the figures' names as with those of his own friends. It had struck him sometimes that Pearl herself would have liked to be a mermaid – at least when it came to love-making. An enthusiast for kisses and cuddles, she preferred to call a halt before things moved – well, lower down. He had often felt a bit of a brute, wanting earthy, blatant sex, and wanting it so badly; not content with the flirty dalliance that meant so much to her.

'And those darling young lovers embracing! Aren't they just romantic?'

He nodded, unconvinced. The pair were called Love's Ecstasy, but to him their embrace was essentially coquettish, with no real depth of passion. And although Pearl had bought two similar pairs – Together for Ever and So In Love – none of the six lovers ever seemed to sweat or pant (as *he'd* done, long ago, in wild transports of desire), but made do with gentle squeezes and mere touches of the lips.

'I'd better be careful not to break them. Did your late wife have a feather duster?'

'She's not "late".'

'What, dear?'

So he was no longer Mr Sadler, but now 'dear'. It would be 'Aubrey' next, or 'Aub'. Surnames were going the way of typewriters and coal-fires, mincers, mangles, fountain pens – quaint, unnecessary items that had outgrown their usefulness. The bereavement counsellor had called him Aubrey without a by-your-leave. He'd had no wish to see a counsellor in the first place, let alone one who looked sixteen, and whose sole experience of death was probably that of a pet guinea-pig. She had told him he'd feel guilt and anger, as reactions to his loss. Instead, he felt bewilderment and loneliness. Anger got you nowhere – he'd seen that with his parents.

'I said I'm worried about breaking them,' Marilyn repeated, raising her voice and obviously assuming he was deaf. His hearing was near-perfect, in fact. He could distinguish a thrush from a blackbird when the little blighters began tuning up at half-past five in the morning. While Pearl was alive, he'd been blissfully asleep at half-past five in the morning; her small blonde head cradled on his shoulder.

Marilyn was still looking at him, clearly waiting for a reply. I don't care if you smash the lot, he had to stop himself from saying. Without their doting owner, the entire collection had become critical, judgemental; always pouncing on his faults and rebuking him for this or that. The hostility was mutual. He had never actually liked these schmaltzy figurines, but because they gave such pleasure to his wife, he had gladly shared his home with them. Now, however, they only served to emphasize her absence. The fairies he particularly detested, with their soppy faces, gauzy wings and self-satisfied expressions. As for the troupe of ballerinas, their fragility and elegance made him feel too big and brash; the proverbial bull in the china shop. And, when it came to the head and hair departments, *all* the figures shamed him. Bald as a boiled egg, there was no way he could compete with their elaborate coiffures, feathered hats, Easter bonnets, bridal veils, diadems, tiaras. The angels were the worst, of course, with cascades of ringlets rippling down their backs, and impressive china haloes. Although wasn't a china halo something of an oxymoron? Reflectively, he rubbed his bare pate, wondering if all balding men should be issued with a halo, as a form of compensation.

'Did you hear what I said?' Marilyn asked impatiently, perhaps beginning to suspect that he was not just deaf but demented.

Hastily, he switched his thoughts from the latest image forming in his mind: Marilyn Monroe, still bewitchingly naked, but now complete with wings and halo. 'I suggest you simply leave them alone and get on with the rest of the cleaning.'

'But they're covered in dust. They need a good seeing to.'

A phrase he hadn't heard in years. His mother had often given him 'good seeings to' – beatings with a wooden spoon – if his father hadn't hit him first, that is. A 'good seeing to', in the sense of sex, wasn't part of his parents' vocabulary – nor, he suspected part of their relationship. In fact, it had often struck him as extraordinary that he'd ever come to be conceived at all, and he'd concluded, in his early teens, that his mother must have picked him up cheap in the market, along with the usual cods'-heads for the cats.

'Look, do whatever you like,' he said, throwing up his hands in defeat and retreating to the bedroom. Happy as his marriage had been, he actually believed that men and women were two quite different species. Things had probably worked out better for the Hunter-Gatherers, when the men went out *en masse* to catch rabbit or hunt antelope, while the women stayed at home to clean the cave, mind the bairns, and pick the nuts and berries. He had always hoped to have a couple of sons, so he could do some hunter-gathering himself: take the wee lads camping, teach them how to snare a rabbit, dam a stream, tickle a trout. But no children had materialized – none of either sex. Royal Doulton had made good the lack, with a whole range of china bambinos; chubby-cheeked kiddie-winkies, with cutesy names to match: Bundle of Joy, Light of my Life, Precious Little Sweetheart. Pearl had tended her brood with true maternal devotion, although spared the dirty nappies, of course; the broken nights, the screams of colicky rage, not to mention the actual labour pains. He himself felt cheated. He had wanted the real thing, noise and mess and disruption notwithstanding.

Upstairs, he paced the bedroom, uncertain what to do with himself, and feeling a tad uneasy with a stranger in the house. Usually, he just sat and stared – or sat and wept – but both were out of the question with Marilyn around. Nor was he free from interference even here. Pearl's Disney range was watching him from the dressing-table: Snow White, Sleeping Beauty, Cinderella, Peter Pan. Well, at least Peter Pan was male. When it came to gender, he was outnumbered fifty to one. Some blokes would think themselves lucky with a crowd of so-called Pretty Ladies clustered around the bed. But their haughty faces and stylish frocks made him feel still more of a slob. He had never been one for dressing up and now wore the same old shabby cords every day of the week. And he kept buying shirts from the Oxfam shop, because the washing-machine was a mystery, and bound to break if he, the ignoramus, tried to pit his wits against it.

He glanced at himself in the mirror, attempting to assume the smug, refined expression of the Ladies. Futile. In place of their well-defined cheekbones, he had only jowls, whilst their rosy-pink, baby-smooth complexions made his own yellowed skin seem like an ancient piece of parched and cracking leather.

'Isn't it time you *did* something?' the Sleeping Beauty reproved. 'Instead of mooning around feeling sorry for yourself.'

'That's a bit rich,' he retorted, turning on the figure. 'What did *you* ever do except sleep for a hundred years?'

'She's got a point, though,' Cinderella remarked. 'I didn't meet my prince without putting in a lot of hard graft first – cleaning hearths, skivvying in the—'

'And *I* kept house for the Seven Dwarfs,' Snow White interrupted. 'You've only yourself to look after, yet you're making a total hash of it.'

'Look, cut it out! Marilyn's taking care of the mess.'

'Yes, but what happens when she's gone? She may be doing you a favour today, but she won't be here on a regular basis.'

'Thank God,' he muttered, *sotto voce*, already counting the hours until he was on his own again. However lonely he might be, the wrong company was worse than none.

'Are you all right in there, dear?'

The wretched woman had materialized on cue, hovering just outside the door; her voice rising in concern. If word got around that he was talking to himself, the social services might cart him off to a care home, and before he could say Alzheimer's, it would be bingo and incontinence pads.

'Yes, I'm fine,' he mumbled, gritting his teeth. 'In fact, I'm going to have a little nap.' Naps were actually more difficult than managing to sleep at night. If he lay down in the morning, in the hope of forty winks, he became miserably aware of just how long the day was, without Pearl to give it point and shape. 'So if you wouldn't mind getting on downstairs....'

'But I can't find any Windolene. And I'm not sure what you want doing with all them sympathy cards. It's difficult to dust, you know, with every surface cluttered.'

Burn them, he all but said. They'd been there a whole two months now – ghastly things, with lilies on the front, or disembodied praying hands. And the words inside were bogus through and through: 'sharing your sorrow', 'holding you in my heart', 'bringing a message of comfort'. There *was* no comfort, and no one could share his sorrow. Well, a son or daughter might have done, or perhaps a sister or brother, but he and Pearl were both only children, and, many of their genuine friends had, sadly, died already. Besides, despite the hand-written messages scrawled beneath the printed ones – 'don't hesitate to ring if we can help in any way', 'do count on us for support', etcetera, etcetera – no one had been near for the last few desolate weeks. The cards were so much flummery; a pertinent reminder that his old school motto, Actions not Words, still had force and point.

'Can I come in?'

Before he could reply, Marilyn had barged into his sanctuary, expostulating, as ever. 'Good gracious me! Those sheets look none too clean. Would you like me to start up here?'

'I thought you'd already started.'

'I need to get my bearings first,' she pointed out, ignoring his sardonic tone. 'See what's where, if you know what I mean. And, actually, I think I'd better pop back home and fetch a load of cleaning stuff. It's not just Windolene you're out of, but Cardinal Red, for the step, Fairy Liquid, Sparkle, and even …'

He closed his eyes. The products sounded like the names of yet more figurines. Pearl had never gone in for Cardinals, in fact, but Windolene was not that far from Gwendolene – one of the Pretty Ladies – and, as for Fairy Liquid, fairy liquidation was more what he had in mind.

'And if you want this bedding laundered, I'm going to need detergent, and probably some Vanish.'

Vanish, he thought – perfect word.

'In fact, while I'm about it, I'll take myself to Asda and invest in some new dusters and a decent mop and broom.'

'Yes, *vanish*,' he screamed silently. 'Vanish into the bowels of Asda and leave me in blessed peace.'

'I hope I'm not disturbing you.'

'Not at all,' Aubrey fibbed. Strange how bereavement sharpened up one's lying skills, whilst other talents atrophied. True, he wanted company, but not, repeat not, the vicar's.

'Come in,' he muttered listlessly, eyeing the black-garbed reverend with a mixture of distaste and apprehension. Everything about the fellow was skeletal and skinny, bar his bulgy eyes and prominent Adam's apple, which seemed all the more protuberant in contrast to his concave figure. He was never very comfortable around pious, churchy people – Pearl excepted, of course. But then

Pearl's religion had been rather like her figurines, with its emphasis on the positive and its mostly surface appeal. No Crucifixions for her or Agonies in Gardens; only simpering Madonnas and goody-goody saints. He himself kept well away from the church and, in fact, had never met the vicar until Pearl's demise had made it more or less inevitable.

'Do sit down.' He forced a smile. 'Can I get you a cup of tea?'

'No, no. I shan't stay long.'

Thank God, thought Aubrey – not that he believed in Him.

'I just wanted to see how you were.'

'Fine.'

'I hear Marilyn did a good job.'

'Excellent.'

'But she, er, said you seemed a little ... down.'

Down? His wife of forty-seven years now rotting in her coffin. Why should he be down?

'That's only natural, of course. But what you must remember, Aubrey, is that she's gone to a better place.'

He had a sudden vision of his wife surrounded by porcelain figurines – a whole heavenly host of cherubim and seraphim, with the usual fulsome names: Paradise Beauty, Celestial Bliss, Love Is All Around. 'Yes, just as you said at the funeral,' he muttered, shuddering at the memory. He had loathed that mawkish service – an overlong concoction of denial, hypocrisy and cant. 'I'm sure she's in her element,' he added, quickly tacking on a 'Reverend', to sweeten any sarcasm.

'Please do call me Frank.'

A vicar could never be frank. If doubts crept in (which inevitably they must), how could a Man of God admit to them without losing all respect and credence, not to mention his livelihood? Anyway, it was hardly frankness to suggest that, despite her marble-cold and waxen corpse, Pearl wasn't really dead, but had simply migrated to a Royal Doulton heaven, along with a myriad other Pretty Ladies, International Beauties and Princesses. He wondered about the Mermaids. Would *they* qualify for entry?

'Do mermaids have souls?' he asked the vicar, suddenly.

'I beg your pardon?'

'Mermaids. I mean, as far as God's concerned, do they count as human beings, to be damned in Hell or saved in Heaven, according to their vice or virtue, or should they be classed with fishes and thus barred from either place?'

The vicar was looking distinctly uneasy, although he did his best to rise to the challenge. 'Aubrey, my friend, I know from long experience that grief can manifest itself in many different ways. These sorts of speculations may point to the fact that you're beginning to doubt God's essential goodness, as a result of your present grief.'

He had doubted it since childhood, in plain, unvarnished fact. Would any halfway decent God have created parents like his – a violent mother and an alcoholic father? And the recent cyclone in Burma, earthquake in China, and rash of teenage stabbings had done nothing to shake his decades-long belief that one lived in a random world, with no benevolent deity to prevent disaster, pain and cruelty.

'Perhaps you could try to change your perspective and focus on that fact that your wife is now released from all her dreadful suffering.'

Yes, true enough, he conceded, gazing at their wedding photo. Pearl had never looked more beautiful in that white meringue of a dress, topped with the whipped-cream froth of the veil.

'And when the good Lord sees fit, you'll join her in that same happy realm.'

If there *were* a Heaven (a gigantic if), he knew he'd feel an intruder there. Tipping the scales at sixteen stone, he just wasn't the right size or shape to be deemed appropriate company for ethereal angels and lean, ascetic saints.

'It sometimes helps to remember, Aubrey, that this life is just a preparation for the next. Looked at in that light, it's easier to bear one's cross.'

Aubrey cast a glance at the sympathy cards (which, unfortunately, Marilyn had left unscathed). Even *they* denied death. He had snorted in derision at one of their pat rhymes:

> *Those who mean the most to us*
> *Are never really gone,*
> *But are transported to a better place*
> *Where we will follow on.*

The words were so close to Frank's, he wondered if the vicar had a sideline in penning verses – the trashy, sentimental stuff you saw in every card-shop. The fact that sympathy could be purchased made it still more spurious. Just grab a card, toss a few coins on the counter and – lo! – empty, flowery phrases could be sent to the bereaved, to save you the embarrassment of having to broach the subject personally, or think up something meaningful to say.

There was silence for a moment, filled by the steady ticking of the clock. That clock was like his wife: dependable, meticulous, never running fast or slow, but providing a consoling sense of order and regularity. He was just the opposite – or had become so since her death – unstable, unpredictable, wayward and shambolic.

The vicar cleared his throat, although the pesky man showed no sign of going. He was now leaning back in his chair, as if ensconced for the whole day. 'And we mustn't forget,' he quavered, 'to give thanks for the many happy years you and Pearl enjoyed together.'

Oh, so it was counting-blessings time now, was it? His parents had been good at that. When he broke his leg, aged ten, his mother had informed him that he was lucky to have legs at all, since he could easily be a double amputee. And earlier on, when their house was bombed in the Blitz and he was sobbing from the shock, his father had snapped, 'Shut up and stop snivelling! At least we're safe in the fucking cellar.'

'I wonder if it would help, Aubrey, if we said a prayer together?'

Aubrey moderated his spontaneous 'No fear!' into a mumble of assent. With any luck, once the prayer was over, Frank would make a move.

The fellow sat up straighter in his seat; assuming an elevated tone, to match. 'Eternal Lord, we beseech Thee to look with mercy on Thy suffering servant, Aubrey, and to grant him peace and acceptance in his …'

Aubrey's mind had strayed to M-Theory – not that he understood it, nor, for that matter, much else about theoretical physics. All he'd managed to grasp from the recent TV programme was that it was an attempt to reconcile the various superstring theories, and that there were probably eleven dimensions, instead of the more familiar three. The presenter had even suggested that there might be multiple universes – maybe an infinite number – and had dismissed our own universe as small and insignificant and something of a sideshow. Indeed, he'd said in humbling conclusion that it might actually be beyond the grasp of paltry human beings ever to fathom the true nature of reality. Yet, in face of such dizzying speculations, most God-men clearly thought that their own trifling brand of Popery or Anglicanism constituted entire and absolute Truth.

'Amen,' the reverend murmured, eyes still closed; hands still piously joined.

'Amen,' repeated Aubrey, although more to the TV presenter than to any Eternal Lord.

After a brief pause, the vicar rose to his feet. 'Well, it's been a pleasure to see you, Aubrey, despite the sadness of the occasion.'

Trying not to seem too eager, Aubrey accompanied him to the door, but, once in the hall, Frank started on a new tack, apparently still reluctant to leave.

'Have you any plans at the moment? I wondered if you intend to sell the house?'

Aubrey shook his head. It was very much Pearl's house: neat, compact and shiny-bright (at least since Marilyn's onslaught). When they'd first married and were looking for a home, they had viewed a ramshackle cottage, with peeling paint, a dodgy roof and a rampant garden overgrown with weeds. Although he'd fallen totally in love with it, he had let himself be overruled by Pearl, who wanted something bandbox-fresh and manageable, without so much as a crack in the ceiling or a daisy on the lawn. In fairness to her, she had always kept both house and garden pristine, and it would seem disloyal to sell the place that had been her home for close on half a century. Besides, if he moved to a small flat, there wouldn't be room for her china collection, and it would be tantamount to sacrilege to dispose of the host of bosom friends she had cherished for so long. Although, in truth, he could do with the cash. Ever since he'd lost his pension when the firm he'd worked for all his life went into liquidation, life had been something of a struggle. Being six months short of retirement age when the crash occurred, he hadn't received a penny in compensation. Things had deteriorated further with Pearl's cancer diagnosis, which had forced *her* into retirement, too.

'Well, if there's anything you need, Aubrey, don't hesitate to ask.'

He smiled politely, although uncomfortably aware that the things he needed were unlikely to be provided by the vicar: a chef to cook his meals, a phial of morphine to sort out his insomnia and Marilyn Monroe to remind his ageing loins of the long-lost joys of sex.

'Oh, no,' he muttered, grimacing as the doorbell rang.

The Reverend Frank must have decided to earn more Brownie points by calling in again. He was tempted not to answer – except suppose it was the postman? He was expecting his first package from Book Club Associates, who, as part of a special promotion, had offered a range of science books at amazingly low prices. The books, he hoped, would help him get to grips with M-Theory, which he'd decided to explore, if only as a distraction from his grief. The M, he'd learned already, constituted a problem in itself, since no one knew exactly what it stood for. Many suggestions had been posited, from Membrane, Mathematical and Matrix, to Mother (as in the mother of all theories) and Master (as in master theory), whilst the cynics had suggested Missing, Murky and Mystery, on account of the fact that the theory was more or less impenetrable. But, whatever the M might signify, it would be safer altogether than the double M of Marilyn Monroe. Randy old men were utterly pathetic, as he already knew to his cost.

Opening the door, half-nervous, half-expectant, he saw neither Frank nor the postie, but a middle-aged bloke he could only describe as faded spiv. The tie was vulgar, the dark suit worn and shiny, the fixed smile unctuous, the handshake smarmy.

'Vincent Grundy. I left my card yesterday.'

'Your card?'

'Yes, I put it through the letterbox. I'm interested in buying silver, gold, jewellery, china—'

'Sorry,' Aubrey said, interrupting the list. 'But I don't do business at the door.'

'I offer extremely favourable prices, sir. You won't get a better deal – that I can guarantee.'

Well, at least he was sir, and not Aubrey. And although he had no silver, gold or jewellery (Pearl's few rings and bracelets having been left to her favourite nurse), there was a hell of a lot of china going spare. Would it really hurt to sell a couple of the figurines? Who would even know?

'Come in,' he said, although grudgingly. He didn't like the man's thin lips, his sludge-brown eyes and putty-coloured skin. However, he ushered him into the sitting-room with as much grace as he could muster, and took down Ocean Beauty from the shelf, handling her with care, indeed devotion, as befitted the top favourite in Pearl's extensive tribe. 'What would you give me for this?' he asked.

Vincent peered at the figurine as if it were a piece of shit, then said, in near-derision, 'I'm sorry, sir, but there's no call for this sort of thing.'

No call? So how did Royal Doulton stay in business, or Hummel, or Boehm Porcelain, or all the other firms Pearl had patronized?

'Knick-knacks like this are completely out of fashion now.'

Really? In that case, why did the glossy catalogues still plop on to the doormat; the special offers arrive in every post? Knick-knacks indeed! Snatching back the Mermaid from the man's offensive grasp, he replaced her on the shelf.

'Hold on! Not so fast. I'll give you a fiver – although that's far more than it's worth.'

A fiver was an insult. That slinky little Mermaid had cost at least two hundred.

'Tell you what, how about fifty quid for the lot? In fact, I'll be doing you a favour, taking them off your hands. No one wants this kitsch stuff any more.'

Aubrey all but shoved the odious man across the room and into the hall. 'And don't come back!' he bawled, giving the front door a slam. Fifty quid, for Christ's sake!

Slouching back to the sitting-room, he was aware of countless pairs of eyes fixed on him in cold contempt.

'Traitor!' Thumbelina hissed.

He bristled in indignation. 'I got rid of the blighter, didn't I? Refused to take his cash.'

'If he'd offered more, you'd have taken it fast enough.'

'Fancy inviting him in, in the first place!' Esmeralda fumed, pursing her cherry lips. 'Pearl must be turning in her grave!'

'And look at the state of this room,' Autumn Splendour chided. 'Marilyn bought you all those dusters and you haven't used a single one.'

'Or washed your stinking trousers,' the Queen of the May chipped in.

'Slob!' Aurelia accused.

'Randy brute!' jeered Jasmine. 'If you spent less time lusting after Marilyn Monroe, you might find a few minutes to dust us.'

'No point,' he tried to remonstrate, despite the fact he was fatally outnumbered. 'Dusting's a total waste of effort. Do it once, and it only needs doing again.'

'If you really want to know,' the snooty Miss continued, ignoring his interruption, 'Pearl always found you rather gross. That's why she bought *us*, of course – to escape your crude demands. She felt the need to surround herself with people of distinction, people in possession of natural style and class, to compensate for her lecher of a spouse.'

'Yes, she often used to confide in us,' Ocean Beauty confirmed, now taking part in the general execration. 'Tell us what a trial you were. However high her standards, you would always drag her down.'

Suddenly, she took a step towards him, and all the other figurines began moving from their shelves, closing in, bearing down, jostling and surrounding him, until he was in danger of suffocation. And they were all shouting accusations; even the ones upstairs joining in the diatribe. 'Traitor!' 'Ruffian!' 'Monster!' 'Lout!'

China fingers were wagging, china fists raised in indignation, china faces distorted in expressions of disgust. China angels plucked their harps in discords of disdain, while china fairies used their wands to beat him round the head. Even the china bambinos let out wails of protest, and their reproachful elder siblings swelled the chorus of complaint.

All at once, he dashed into the hall, flung open the front door and, despite his age and bulk, began pounding along the street in pursuit of Vincent Grundy. The guy was still in sight, thank God, about to turn in to another house, fifty yards along the street.

'Wait!' he shouted. 'Wait! Come back! You can have them all – have everything.'

He clung on to a gatepost, feeling a sudden sense of liberation, so astounding and acute, it was like a revelation from on high. He could be freed, at last, from those foppish, phoney figurines that had held him in subjection for two tyrannical months! He had somehow reached a crisis-point; could no longer bear their sanctimonious faces, their self-important posturing, their endless castigation. And it wasn't just the figurines – the ultra-delicate bone-china cups and saucers also drove him to distraction: too small and itsy-bitsy for a bloke of six-foot-three. He needed a *pint* of tea, for pity's sake, not a derisory thimbleful. And his strong coffee stained the insides of the cups, which only reinforced his sense of being gross and yobbish. He was sick of feeling an intruder in his own prim and decorous home – a home better off without him, so all its other occupants believed.

'Do you buy fabrics, too?' he asked, in desperate hope, clutching hold of Vincent, as the man doubled back to join him.

'Depends,' the guy said, warily. 'I'd need to see the stuff.'

Aubrey all but dragged him back towards the house. Here was a chance to rid himself of the frilly bedroom curtains, the chichi satin counterpane (salmon-pink, with ruffles), the stack of silken cushions littering the bed. If he couldn't sleep, why did he need curtains? And those poncy cushions were just impedimenta, to be offloaded or sent flying every time he needed to lie down. As for the fluffy bedside rugs, all they did was clutter up the place and shed guilt-inducing, snow-white wisps on the darker, smooth-pile carpet. Every item in the preening house was too refined and smug for him; the whole place a gilded cage, tarnished by the simple fact of his living there at all. Only now had it dawned on him – and with electrifying force – that he must sell not just the contents but the namby-pamby house itself.

Vincent was discussing the recession, as the pair turned into his gate, but Aubrey barely heard. His whole attention was focused on a further wild idea, sprouting like a lush green shoot in the desert of his mind: why not find another dilapidated cottage – yes, one with peeling paint, a dodgy roof and a garden overrun with weeds? He could spend the rest of his old age there, with no one to reprove him; no conceited, nagging figurines; no ornaments at all. The only person he'd allow past his moat and drawbridge would be Marilyn

Monroe. Double M might be perilous, but now he *wanted* danger; wanted every Madcap M missing in his life to date – Marvels, Mischief, Messiness and, Most of all, Majestic Massive Mammaries. He and that Momentous Minx could revel in the squalor of their steamy little love-nest, indulge in Miraculous Mating, from Morning through to Midnight, until he pegged out from the unaccustomed exercise – or expired from simple bliss.

No, not simple bliss – Magnificent Martyrdom.

Tulips

'Quiet today,' Julia observed, pausing by the desk on her way to shelve an armful of books.

Claire looked up from the screen. 'I suppose the weather's keeping everyone indoors.'

The rain slamming at the windows served to underline her point, all but drowning her voice, as a sudden, still more frenzied blast rampaged against the glass. Hardly April showers, she thought – more a deluge or a cloudburst. She had a sudden image of the library floating down the water-logged street like a second Noah's Ark; the books lined up in twos, the staff transmuted into animals: tall, gangling Bill, a giraffe; svelte Olwen, a gazelle; Julia, a dragon (breathing fire, despite the flood), and herself – now, what would *she* be? An ocelot? A warthog? A millipede? Rhinoceros? Something singular, for certain, so she could experience a different kind of life; break out of her rut.

Just at that moment, the door was flung open by a striking-looking man – dark, dramatic, dishevelled and drenched through – who catapulted himself inside and strode up to the desk, showering raindrops in his wake.

'Listen,' he urged, in a deep yet ringing voice – a far cry from the muffled tones employed by many library-users. 'I've just had this amazing dream! I was trapped in a cage of tulips – not ordinary tulips, but exotic ones with frilly petals in a fantastic orangey-yellow colour. I was tiny, like a manikin, and they were huge, like giants, so I was totally surrounded by them. It was as if they were prison-warders, ordered to guard me, day and night, though only for my good, you understand.'

He paused for breath; rain plopping on to the desk from his

shock of wild black hair. Despite the cold outside, he was wearing neither coat nor jacket, and his saturated shirt was clinging to his chest, revealing the outline of his ribs. Claire found herself distracted by his narrow-shouldered, slender figure – almost girlish, in a sense, although contradicted by highly masculine features: the scruff of not-quite stubble on his chin, the thick, emphatic brows, the vibrant Adam's apple pulsing in his neck, as if it shared his own exuberance.

'I just knew it was the subject of a poem, maybe a whole series. But, before I write it, I need to find out about the tulips – whether the ones I dreamed actually exist. Trouble is, my damned computer's crashed, and I haven't had a minute yet to call someone in to fix it. So I wondered if *you* could help.'

'Yes, of course,' Claire said, glancing with interest at his soaked and balding cords; their unusual shade of aubergine echoing the purple of his shirt, and pleased to see that this (apparent) poet fitted the Bohemian stereotype. Besuited gents like T.S. Eliot or Philip Larkin, whose photos had graced the display-board during the library's Poetry Week, were less exciting altogether. 'You're welcome to use our computers. They're over there, at the back. Hold on a sec – let me just check the booking-screen to see which ones are free.'

'No, you don't understand. I have to leave – right now! I'm giving a reading in Bristol and I'll miss the train if I don't get off sharp.'

'Well, we're open all day tomorrow.'

'Tomorrow I teach. We poets have to earn a crust, and no one seems frightfully keen to pay us for actually writing the stuff.' He smiled disarmingly, reaching out a slender hand – effeminate again, with long, pale, tapering fingers, at variance with the dark, tangled hairs on the wrist. 'Would it be an awful cheek to ask *you* to do the work?'

Not so much a cheek as slightly tricky. People were meant to do their own research, and Julia was a stickler for the rules. Library staff could help, of course: show customers the range of stock in the catalogue, along with any relevant periodicals, or arrange computer sessions for beginners, to explain the mysteries of the Internet. It was fine to hold their hands until they'd grasped the fundamentals but, after that, they were left to their own devices.

'Never set a precedent,' Julia was always saying. 'If we start spoon-feeding one customer, we'll end up spoon-feeding the lot.'

Claire doubted it, in fact. This man was a one-off; seemed to possess the natural right to demand services and privileges denied to lesser mortals. And, frankly, she was grateful. One got bored with the usual punters: blue-rinsed matrons twittering over the latest Jilly Cooper; geeky nerds obsessing about arcane points of local history; run-of-the-mill enquirers checking holiday guides. No one had ever revealed their dreams to her before.

'And if you could dig out a few tulip books, that would be fantastic. Big glossy ones, if possible, with close-up photographs, so I can see the details of the petals and the leaves. The leaves in the dream were sharp and pointed, and really rather lethal, towering over me like huge, green, unsheathed swords, but I haven't much idea about what real tulip leaves are like. To be honest, I know zilch about flowers. But, since the dream, I feel inspired to find out everything, then weld the two together – the dream-world and the natural world, so that—'

'My name's Fergus, by the way,' he said, suddenly interrupting himself. 'Fergus Boyd Adair. Actually, you may have some of my books in stock – well, they're only pamphlets, really, so, on second thoughts, probably not.'

Definitely not, she corrected silently. Their meagre poetry section didn't stretch to pamphlets. In fact, his name meant nothing to her, but it struck her as exactly right, with its air of cheeky bravado, not only for a poet, but for this one in particular. All three names were Scottish, although he spoke with no trace of an accent. Indeed, his voice was almost plummily English – rich and deep and sensuous, as if composed in equal parts of honey, brandy and buttermilk.

'Look, give me a piece of paper and I'll draw the tulips for you, shall I? Then you'll have something to go on.'

She passed a sheet across, relieved that it was Bill's day off, and that Julia was out of sight, still busy shelving books. Her two colleagues shared the view that if you gave anyone an inch, he or she would inevitably take a mile. She saw things rather differently: give people an inch and they might transform it into a mile, through their own talents and initiative.

And this man did have talents – that was obvious from his drawing: a powerful and professional sketch, yet completed in a scant three minutes. If his poetry matched his artistic skills, he might soon be on the road to fame. After all, many poets had to struggle at the outset for any sort of recognition, let alone a living wage. Although, with a reading in Bristol, he must already have a public, so perhaps *she* was at fault for never having heard of him.

'See,' he said, leaning over the desk to point out details on his sketch, 'the petals are double and sort of ruffled at the edges, as if they've been snipped with pinking shears. Where I've shaded them is orange, and those unshaded bits are yellow. And the insides of the petals are streaked and speckled pink, which I've indicated here with little dots. Do you get the general idea?'

She nodded, still on the watch for Julia, who would want to take control, and was bound to shush his loud, insistent voice, which seemed to echo round the building; even carry to the street outside. Actually, no one in the library was either studying or browsing, so a little noise was surely not a problem. Julia, however, was such an ancient fossil, she would label it as 'racket' and 'intrusion'.

'Shit!' he said, glancing at the clock. 'I'm going to miss that train if I don't get off in two seconds flat. Look, will you be here on Friday?'

'Er, yes.'

'Great! I'll call in then, and see what you've come up with.'

'Ask for Claire – that's me.'

'OK, Claire, see you on Friday, for definite. And thanks a million. You're an angel – no, an archangel!'

As he scorched out of the building, she seemed to sprout great feathered wings and began soaring up to some vast celestial sphere, where everything was marble-white and shimmering; the air itself a lighter, purer blend. Alas, a swift descent was necessary, since Julia chose that moment to stride back to the desk.

'Who was that moron?' she asked disparagingly. 'I've never heard anyone make such an awful din! And he more or less cannoned into me in his rush to get away, and didn't have the manners to apologize.'

His mind was probably on tulips, Claire didn't say. As was her own, in fact. She was determined to track down his 'dream-flower', and unearth every book on tulips the library possessed. 'He's doing a … a research project and needs some specialist stuff. I'll just check the catalogue.'

As she'd hoped, there were several interesting items held in their Reserve Stock. She decided to go up to the stockroom and fetch them right away. She needed to be alone, in order to bottle his vital essence before it dissipated; stick in her mental scrapbook the dark disorder of his hair and blaze of his compelling, burnt-toast eyes; the saturated shirt and trousers brazenly delineating every angle of his body. In just ten minutes, she had changed from library assistant to archangel; from tame mother-of-two-teenagers to swoony adolescent, already fatally besotted.

'Mum!' Susanna shouted down the stairs. 'What have you done with my clean shirt?'

'In the drawer,' Claire shouted back. 'Where it's meant to be.'

'It's *not*. There's not one single shirt there.'

With a stab of guilt, she suddenly recalled that Susanna's shirts (not to mention Rodney's) were still piled up in the laundry basket, waiting to be ironed. The tulip research had driven all else from her mind. 'I'll bring one up, OK?'

'Well, quick – or I'll be late.'

Hastily, she set up the ironing board, wondering, as so often, why she was the one who always did the ironing. Admittedly, with three A-levels on the near-horizon, her daughter's life was pressured, but there was no excuse for Rodney. She worked as hard as he did, so he ought to help out in the house, but his mother had brought him up to believe that such division of the chores was undignified, if not emasculating.

While she waited for the iron to heat, her thoughts returned to last night's dream – a peculiar, surreal dream, in which she was being born from a tulip's cup; expelled into the world by gently pulsing, pushing, orangey-yellow petals. She knew Fergus would be fascinated; maybe even use it for one of the poems in his series, which meant she'd be immortalized.

'Something's burning,' Rodney observed, venturing into the kitchen, with his usual worried frown.

She dashed from ironing board to stove – too late. 'Your kipper!' she exclaimed, removing from the grill-pan its black disintegrating skeleton.

'I'm not bothered,' Rodney shrugged. 'To tell the truth, kippers feature on the menu rather too often for my taste.'

'They're good for you – that's why. And you refuse to take fish oil in capsule form, so I have to get it down you somehow.'

'You shouldn't believe all that rubbish you read. One minute, they're pushing fish oil as the super-food to beat all else, then they change their minds and it's pomegranates or wheat-grass, or some other damn-fool thing.'

'Shit! What a smell!' Daniel exclaimed, screwing up his nose in disgust, as he torpedoed in to join them, his hair uncombed; the laces of his trainers trailing loose.

'Daniel, don't say "shit". You know Dad doesn't like it. And why are you wearing jeans to school?'

'It's "Jeans for Genes Day". I told you twice, last night, but you weren't listening to a word I said.'

Another surge of guilt. She had been glued to the computer, totally absorbed in the long, intriguing history of the tulip.

'I don't actually agree with it,' Rodney remarked, seating himself at the table, oblivious to the fact that it hadn't yet been laid. 'Just because some businesses go in for this "Dress-down Friday" nonsense, it doesn't mean that schools should be allowed to follow suit.'

'That's different, Rodney,' Claire put in, trying to make amends to her son. '"Jeans for Genes" is a charity thing and—'

'Which reminds me, Mum,' Daniel interrupted, 'have you got a pound? We're expected to cough up, as soon as we arrive, and I'm completely stony-broke.'

'I don't know why you children are always short of money,' Rodney snapped, 'when we give you huge allowances each month.'

'They're *not* huge, and we're *not* children. I'll be leaving school in two years' time.'

'Over my dead body! You'll stay till you're eighteen.'

'Oh, don't start that again,' Claire groaned. 'I thought we'd agreed we'd wait till your next birthday before deciding anything. Daniel, get the cereals out, please, and the marmalade and stuff. I'm terribly behind today.'

'You're telling me! Where's Sue?'

'Waiting for her shirt.' Claire raced back to the ironing board, wondering what to wear herself. It might be Jeans-for-Genes day for Daniel, but certainly not for her. It was imperative that Fergus should notice her as woman, and not just as library assistant. On Tuesday, she'd been a chrysalis, clad in dreary brown, but today she was proposing to emerge as a brilliant butterfly. And if Julia's gimlet eye registered the transformation, well, she'd better pretend she was going on to a party after work and wouldn't have time to—

'*Mum!*'

'Coming!' Having handed over the still only half-ironed shirt, she deliberately refrained from nagging Susanna about the state of her room. She couldn't imagine Fergus wasting precious energy on such footling things as discarded clothes piled ankle-deep on the floor, or dressing-tables covered in spilt make-up. Odd how one brief meeting with a man still a virtual stranger should have influenced her attitudes; made her less concerned about the usual tedious daily round: had they run out of toilet rolls; did Daniel need new shoes?

'Mum, are you OK? What's wrong? Won't you be late for work?'

'Yes ... I'd better get a move on.' She stole a glance at her daughter, envying her flawless skin. It seemed unfair, if not perverse, that *she*, the forty-something mother should have broken out in spots, while eighteen-year-old Susanna had a perfect, peachy complexion. But stress always gave her flare-ups, and the last few days had been more than usually busy, as she added hours of tulip research to her already hectic schedule. There had been definite compensations, though, as the tulip slowly metamorphosed from a common-and-garden flower, to status symbol, luxury item and priceless trading product – a prima donna, in short. At the height of the tulip mania, or so she'd discovered yesterday, one single tulip bulb had sold for 6,000 Dutch florins, when the average annual income was a paltry 150.

She couldn't wait to share such facts with Fergus, and kept wondering when he'd appear today – first thing, she hoped, otherwise the sheer strain of anticipation would reduce her to a wreck.

*

'Claire, sorry to be a pain, but I've just been called away to cover for someone in Bedford. Which means you'll have to run the Reading Group, at two.'

'Oh, no!'

'What's the problem?' Bill asked, obviously surprised. As the one who'd first suggested the Reading Groups, she was viewed as their natural champion.

'It's, er, not a problem.' She could hardly explain that, having waited all morning for Fergus to breeze in, it would be intolerable to miss him should he show up in the early afternoon. 'It's just that … I looked out some books for a reader and said I'd—'

'Can't Julia take care of it?'

'Yes, I suppose so.' She could just imagine Julia's reaction if she handed over her sixty-eight-page print-out. She had prepared it with the greatest devotion, but Julia would condemn it as misspent time and a shocking waste of paper. 'We can't mollycoddle people like this, or we'll be accused of favouritism – raising expectations we can't meet for other readers'. The wretched woman was also certain to insist that Fergus paid the standard fee for photocopying, which, at 15p a sheet, would probably clean him out. Since she'd done most of the work at home, she'd intended giving it to him for free – and on the quiet.

'So is that OK, Claire?' Bill was asking.

'Yes, of course. I just wish you'd given me a bit more notice.'

'I couldn't, I'm afraid. This thing came out of the blue. Apparently, one of their staff was carted off to hospital, just half an hour ago. And since we're the nearest branch to them, I could hardly refuse to help out in a crisis.'

'All right, fair enough. What book is it they're doing?'

'*The Lovely Bones*. You know it backwards. And the room's prepared – chairs out, posters up. And, if you don't mind me saying, Claire, you do look very decorative today.'

Julia had been less flattering. Hadn't she 'rather overdone the blusher?' (Yes, an attempt to conceal the spots.) And was 'orange a wise choice of colour?' (Maybe not, but her aim was to match the tulips, even down to ruffles.)

She returned to the desk, where Julia was stamping books. Once she was free, Claire entrusted her with the first twelve pages only – of the print-out, then gestured to the stack of books, piled up on the shelf behind. 'Could you say I'd like to see him? There are certain things I need to explain, so perhaps he could hang around a while, or pop back later on.'

'Can't *I* explain them, Claire?'

'Not really. It's, er, complicated.'

She left it at that. Members of the Reading Group were beginning to arrive, which meant she should be in the upstairs room, ready to run the show. Once there, she found Thelma and Michelle already involved in heated discussion.

'I don't know how you can say it's uplifting, Thelma, when it's all about some ghastly girl who's brutally raped and murdered, and then relates her story from a realm beyond the grave. I found it unutterably bleak from start to finish.'

'Well, in that case, you read it wrong. There's a definite note of hope at the end, which changes the whole spirit of the thing.'

'Good afternoon, ladies,' Claire said brightly. 'It's great that you're already exchanging views, but shall we wait till everyone's here? Otherwise you'll have to repeat yourselves.'

Grumbles of assent. Claire braced herself for further arguments. This particular group were notorious for their conflicting views, and, on one occasion, had even come to blows. The dissension she could handle: what she couldn't face was the prospect of missing Fergus. She hadn't spent an agonizing hour dolling herself up in orange flounces for the sake of supercilious Thelma and truculent Michelle.

'You're very fidgety,' Julia observed.

'Not at all,' Claire mumbled, with yet another glance at the clock. Fifteen minutes to closing time.

'I suppose you're keen to get off to your party.'

'Party?'

'You told me you were going to a—'

'Oh, yes. Of course. It slipped my mind.' Her 'party' gear now seemed a shade ridiculous. Julia was right, in fact – orange *wasn't* a wise choice of colour. Acceptable for tulips, but not for a plumpish, blondish (and probably past it) human female, who looked better dressed in inconspicuous beige.

Between customers, she gazed out of the window at the brilliant April sunshine, which seemed to mock her sense of crushing disappointment. These last few days, the weather had been as mercurial as her moods; switching from serene to stormy and back again, with perverse and spiteful glee.

'Are you sure that man didn't come in?' she asked again, returning to the desk, after helping a reader locate the gardening section. Gardens had reminded her of tulips – not that she needed a reminder.

'Look, I've told you twice,' Julia snapped, 'he didn't. Anyway you've been here yourself all day, apart from an hour or so running the group.'

'Yes, but weren't you out at lunch then?'

'No. Do we *have* to keep going over the minutiae of where I was, and when?'

Yes, Claire murmured soundlessly, we do. She needed to be absolutely certain that Fergus hadn't come and gone without anybody noticing. Unlikely. He wasn't a shrinking violet who would shuffle in and huddle in a corner. Besides, Olwen, too, had been keeping a lookout for him, whilst setting up the display of 'Great Inventors'. Maybe the whole thing was a hoax. Fergus Boyd Adair was probably Joe Bloggs in reality – a plumber or estate agent – or certainly no more of a poet than *she* was the Queen of Hearts. But what would be the point of such deception? – it didn't make the slightest sense. And, anyway, he'd seemed completely genuine; enthusiastic, eager for her help, and envisaging a whole new poetic project.

'Hey, you at the desk, are you deaf or something?'

Claire suddenly noticed a woman standing waiting: a stiff-coiffed matron, tut-tutting in impatience.

'Did you hear what I said?' she barked aggressively.

'Er, no. I do apologize.'

The woman gave an exaggerated sigh. 'I don't know why we pay our rates, when you people are so useless.'

Claire switched on a placatory smile, although inwardly alarmed by her own peculiar mental state. Could an obsession with a poet actually make you blind and deaf? 'How can I help?' she asked, endeavouring to sound brisk and on the ball.

The woman seemed slightly mollified; her glare changing to a frown. 'I'm looking for a book, but I don't know what it's called or who wrote it.'

'Well, can you give me some idea of what it's about?'

'No, I can't. You see, I had it out before – last year – but never got round to reading it. All I can remember is that it was big and blue – I think – with a picture of a church on the front.'

Claire ran through a mental repertoire of books: church architecture, ecclesiastical history, or some novel, perhaps, set in a country parsonage. 'Was is fiction or non-fiction?'

The woman didn't appear to know the difference, which made things still more difficult, yet, a mere ten minutes later, the book had been miraculously located (on the trolley by the returns desk), and a grudging 'Thank you' had even escaped the woman's lips. Once she'd shuffled off, Claire allowed her mind to migrate back to Fergus. Perhaps he'd never returned from Bristol – been killed in a train crash or mown down as he crossed the street. Or was simply too ill to come out: laid low with flu, or stricken with consumption, like Keats or D.H. Lawrence. Writers had notoriously bad health, and poets in particular seemed alarmingly accident-prone. Shelley had drowned at thirty; Byron died of fever in some Greek campaign or other, again pitifully young. She should be wearing black, not orange, and certainly her mood was dark as she prepared to help the other staff usher out the last remaining customers and get ready to lock up. Tomorrow was her Saturday off, and the place was shut on Sundays, so the earliest she might lay eyes on Fergus was a good sixty hours away – too achingly distant to provide a shred of comfort.

Then, suddenly, the dreary, dying library exploded into life, as a tall, dark, dashing figure swooped full-pelt through the door and bounded up to the desk.

'Sorry! Terribly late! Meant to come hours ago, but words were gushing out of me and I didn't want to stop the flow.'

Everyone looked up – Bill and Olwen with interest; Julia in distaste.

'Claire, you look sensational!' Leaning right across the desk, he gazed at her with undisguised admiration. 'I adore the orange. It's exactly the same colour as the tulips in my dream. What a weird coincidence. And, talking of tulips, I don't expect you've had a minute to find out anything about them.'

'Well, actually—'

'Though I'm praying that you have, because they're coming out of my ears – or at least tulip poetry is. It's funny, you know, you can ignore a subject all your life – I mean, I hardly know a tulip from a daffodil – then, all at once, the world is full of tulips. They're the only flower in the world for me at present.'

Yes, she agreed. *And* for me.

'Well, did you find a book or two?' he asked, still scrutinizing her outfit. 'Listen, forgive me being personal, but I can't believe how you've changed. You should always wear bright colours, you know. They make your eyes look bluer and—'

'We're about to close,' Julia put in; her voice as strident as a piece of chalk rasping on a blackboard.

'Yes, I'm keeping you all. Most inconsiderate. But I'll be gone in a sec – I promise. Just tell me, Claire, did you find some books?'

'I found twenty-two, in fact. Not all of them exclusively about tulips, but including books on art and nature, a few useful ones on Holland and the bulb-fields, lots of gardening books, of course, and even—'

'He can't take out more than eight at a time,' Julia interrupted. 'If he wants the others, he'll have to bring the first ones back.'

No problem. The more often he came in, the more delighted she would be. But what about her research? It would take ages to explain all the different sources she'd consulted, and the tulip's use in medicine and cooking, as well as in trade and garden-design, and a host of other areas. She was also dying to convey to him how, although she'd once viewed tulips as comparatively low in the hierarchy of flowers (neither romantic like red roses, nor exotic like camellias; not highly scented like freesias, or even endearingly bizarre like red-hot pokers), that had changed entirely now. Indeed, she could almost understand the crazy sums paid at the height of tulipomania. The flower had come to be regarded, then, rather like a work of art: a thing of such rare beauty it was, in essence, priceless. Yet how could she discuss such matters in any sort of depth, when Julia was already glaring at the clock? Besides, they were sitting within a few feet of each other, so her colleague was bound to eavesdrop on any personal chat. And undoubtedly remind her (should she herself 'forget') that readers had to pay for printed matter, extorting every last penny of the cost.

Fortunately, just at that moment, one of the last stragglers suddenly rushed up to the desk with three DVDs to rent, and, while Julia was ringing them up on the till, she quickly took her chance, lowering her voice to a whisper.

'I do have more information, Fergus – print-outs from a whole variety of sources. The problem is—'

'It's lock-up time.' He completed the sentence for her, now speaking equally softly; his usual trumpet blare muted to a lyre. 'Don't worry, I understand. Tell you what – why don't I walk you home?'

Walk her home? Impossible! She might run into Susanna, coming back from netball practice, or her evil neighbour, Ruby, might be snooping, as so often. Given her predilection for mischief-making, Ruby could easily inflate a simple tête-à-tête into an adulterous affair, then regale the entire street with tales of her debauchery.

'Yes, good idea,' she said, with studied nonchalance. Any risk, however ill-advised, simply had to be discounted for the thrill of this man's company.

'Who in God's name's that?' Rodney groped out a hand for the alarm clock, peering at its illuminated figures.

'I'll get it,' Claire said sleepily, rolling out of bed. 'Maybe it's the milkman.' She had an uneasy feeling she hadn't paid his bill for several weeks, so he was probably on the warpath.

'Well, tell him not to wake us up so early – especially not on Saturday.'

She grabbed her dressing-gown and tiptoed down the stairs, hoping the shrill peal of the doorbell hadn't woken the kids.

Her 'pacify-the-milkman' smile changed into an expression of astonishment as she came face to face with an enormous bunch of flowers: orangey-yellow tulips, with ruffled, frilly petals, and pink streaks in the insides. The man holding them was a total stranger – not that much of him was visible, half-concealed as it was by his booty.

'Are you Claire Henderson?' he asked.

'Er, yes.'

'Good! I was instructed to give you these in person.'

Barely had he handed them over, when he turned tail and sprinted down the path, then continued along the street, as if on fire.

'Wait!' she called, but he was already out of sight, and she could hardly hurtle after him in bare feet and a dressing-gown.

The flowers felt heavy in her arms, and weren't wrapped in any sort of paper. Water was dripping from their stems, making damp spots on her night-clothes. Stumbling into the kitchen, she laid them on the table, torn between elation and anxiety. It was obvious who they were from, but how could she explain to her family so extravagant a gift? Tied to one of the tulip stems was a small white envelope. Scarcely able to contain herself, she tore it open and read the note inside.

How can I ever thank you for all that work you did on my behalf? And, better still, for giving me a new, exciting project: to ravish you among the tulips. Ring me – now! Fergus.

'*Ravish*' her! Blood rushed to her cheeks as she read the words again. Things were going far too fast – her own stupid fault for leading him on. Deliberately, she hadn't told him she was married. Why bore him with tedious tales of married life, when it seemed imperative to charm him, impress him with her research skills, play the role of poet's Muse? Three glasses of wine had clearly turned her head, and the exhilaration of being with so beguiling a man – not to mention a much younger one: a zingy twenty-nine to her own fading forty-four.

So what did she do now? Phone him, as he had ordered so peremptorily? Out of the question. Never, in twenty years of marriage, had she cheated on her husband, and didn't intend to start. Or should she simply chuck the tulips in the dustbin and pretend they'd never arrived?

Equally impossible. It would be sacrilege to destroy such expensive and unusual flowers – the exact tulips of his dream. How on earth could he have afforded them? The pittance he earned from teaching would hardly fund such largesse. Even more inexplicable, how had he managed to track them down, when she herself had failed, despite checking literally hundreds of varieties in books and specialist catalogues, and on every site online? The sheer range of different species was astounding, and she could barely spell their complicated names: *tulipa kaufmanniana, tulipa taihangshanica, tulipa grengiolensis.* Some of the English names, in contrast, had fired her imagination, expressing, as they did, her own churning sense of danger and excitement: Eros, Bacchus, Queen of Sheba, Virtuoso, Brilliant Fire.

And these particular tulips – not just pictures on a page or screen, but vibrantly substantial – made her feel a further bond with Fergus, as if she were living through another of his dreams. Uncatalogued, unclassified, they seemed to hail from some unfathomable realm beyond the scope of flower-shops or the reach of normal suppliers. And that enigmatic stranger entrusted to deliver them, was he a mystic messenger or just a casual errand boy? All she had really registered was that he was short and plain and pale – hardly any match for the spectacular bouquet. Typical of Fergus, of course, to do things to excess. Even in the bar, he'd wolfed half-a-dozen packets of cheese-and-onion crisps, one after the other, scarcely bothering to chew.

'I haven't eaten for *days*, Claire. When I'm writing well, that takes precedence, and everything else – food, drink, sleep, fresh air – is more or less irrelevant.'

Her own regime of regular, well-balanced meals seemed dull in the extreme, and she longed to share his all-consuming passion for an art. In fact, sitting with him in that dim and intimate corner of the bar, she had lost all track of time, and hadn't even cared that her family at home were still waiting for their supper (and doubtless wondering where the hell she was). Had it been a mere eight days ago? Centuries seemed to have passed – not days – and, in fact, she'd become increasingly depressed, assuming he must have forgotten all about her. Yet how magical to think that he had spent that time ferreting out so incredible a present.

Suddenly, she heard footsteps on the stairs. Rodney, or the kids! She dived towards the table to gather up the tulips and hide them somewhere safe. Too late.

'Good Lord!' her husband exclaimed, shambling into the kitchen in his old-fashioned stripy pyjamas. 'How the hell did *those* get here?'

She stared at them, unspeaking, racking her brains for a reply. 'That … that woman sent them.'

'Which woman?'

'You know – the one I've been helping, who's doing a book on tulips.'

'She must be made of money. That's a heck of a lot of flowers!'

'She … she just wanted to say thank you for all the time I spent.'

'Well, I wish she'd waited till a bit later in the day. It's a bit of a cheek, isn't it, waking us at this ungodly hour? *And* at the weekend.'

'Oh, she didn't come herself.'

'Who did, then?'

Again, she cast around for inspiration. 'Er, Interflora.'

'In that case, I'm getting on the phone to them immediately. They've no right to make deliveries so early.'

She tried to calm him down. He was never good in the mornings and, deprived of his Saturday lie-in, became tetchy in the extreme. 'It's not worth it, Rodney, honestly. If you work yourself into a state, you'll never get back to sleep, and we're out late tonight, remember.'

'I was out late *last* night, Claire, which is why I object to—'

'Mum!' Susanna shouted from the landing. 'What's going on? Do you *have* to wake the whole house?'

'Sorry, darling,' she muttered, as Susanna came pounding down the stairs, wearing nothing but a frown and an elongated T-shirt. 'Someone sent some flowers and—'

'Flowers? Fantastic! That must be Joe. We had this massive argument last Sunday, so he must have decided to make up.'

'You didn't *say* you'd had a row. I'm sorry, love. I know how much he—'

'Mum, you've been in your own world these last few days. None of us could get through to you. If I told you I'd won two million on the lottery, I doubt that you'd have heard.'

Claire sank into a chair, the mass of flowers reproaching her. She'd not only neglected her daughter, she'd also betrayed her husband – in thought, if not in deed.

'They're not yours, Susanna,' Rodney told her peevishly. 'They're Mum's. Sent by some crazy woman who doesn't realize that working people try to catch up on their sleep at the weekends. So I suggest we all go back to bed before Daniel wakes and—'

'I *am* awake,' called a truculent voice from just outside the door. 'And it's all your fault for shouting.'

Claire glanced from the tulips to the faces of her family: all resentful and annoyed. Yet, however guilty she might feel, that dangerous, wicked, titillating phrase, 'ravish you among the tulips', was exploding through her body like a firework, and she was whooshing up to the stratosphere in great rocket-showers of orangey-yellow flame.

'Those flowers were duds,' Susanna said disparagingly, gesturing to the vase in the centre of the supper-table. 'Look at them, Mum, drooping after just four days. I bet that woman got them on the cheap.'

Claire said nothing. In contrast to her daughter, she was intrigued by the way the tulips had changed from prim, upstanding Puritans to abandoned, sexy sluts. Their formerly rigid stalks were now lithe and wild and supple; bending in all directions, reaching out, as if desperate to be touched. The petals, too, had opened up, revealing their most private parts: pistils, stamens, intimate pink streaks, while even the leaves seemed lasciviously moist and fleshy.

'Mind if I get on with my coursework now?' Susanna asked, finishing her last spoonful of dessert. 'Miss Barrett said I should have added a bibliography and several more quotations, to back up what I've said.'

'No, go ahead. I'll wash up and Daniel can wipe.'

'That's not fair! Why is it always me?'

'Because you haven't got exams,' his sister retorted, pushing back her chair and flouncing out of the room.

'I've got coursework, though, just the same as her. Mum, let me off tonight – go on!'

'All right.'

'Want *me* to help?' asked Rodney, unconvincingly. He, too, had left the table, but was already headed for the sofa, with his wine-glass and *The Times*.

Claire shook her head, relieved to be alone, in fact, so that she could fix her mind on Fergus. She'd been hoping – indeed praying, despite her lack of any fixed belief – that he'd show up at the library again, but his continued absence posed a real dilemma. If she phoned him, as he'd asked, she might give the impression of being ready (indeed eager) to be 'ravished', yet if she didn't ring, he might well feel rejected, or offended by her rudeness in failing to thank him for the flowers. And those flowers were omnipresent. They had filled four separate vases, so she seemed to be confronted by him everywhere she went. Even in the kitchen, their once tight-furled leaves leaned eagerly towards her, as she began the washing-up, as if to say, 'Take a risk. Take a chance. What have you to lose?'

Her family, for one thing. If she involved herself with Fergus, the affair was bound to be discovered, and she might land up in the divorce court, branded an unfit wife and mother. Yet, if she held back for the children's sake, those children would soon fly the nest – Susanna to university; Daniel to some job or other. No one left but her and Rodney, repeating the same tired platitudes in a now half-empty house.

All at once, she strode back to the living-room, dish-mop still in hand. Rodney was lying on the sofa, his paunch all too apparent as he sprawled against the cushions. Only since meeting Fergus, had she noticed just how old he seemed – indeed, older than his fifty-five years. The frown lines on his forehead appeared to have bred and multiplied in just the last few days, and his once robust hair was now thinning so pathetically, patches of his freckled scalp were visible beneath.

'Rodney,' she said, 'let's go out.'

'Go out?' he repeated, turning round to stare at her. 'What now, you mean?'

'Yes, why not? We never do anything spontaneous. The kids are old enough to manage on their own, yet we're always stuck indoors, glued to some stupid soap.'

'We went out on Saturday.'

'Only to that ghastly do. Where's the fun in sitting still for hours, listening to dreary speeches?'

'Claire, you know perfectly well we have to support Drugscope, if only out of duty. It may mean a few dull evenings, but that's a small price to pay for the marvellous work they do.'

'But they're all such stuffed shirts – worthy and po-faced. I almost died of boredom.'

'What's got into you, for heaven's sake? Those people are really decent – unselfish and committed and—'

'OK, keep your hair on! But, reverting to this evening, why don't we go dancing? It's ages since we—'

'Because I'm shattered, Claire – that's why. I couldn't dance if you paid me.'

Fergus could dance. She could see him in her mind, frisking among the tulips; dancing with *her* – all day and all night, without flagging – leaping and cavorting until they collapsed, not from exhaustion but because they were desperate to make love. Instinctively, she knew it would be special (passionate and fierce, as if they were running on adrenaline), and that he'd use his range of poetic skills – imagination, inspiration, creative ingenuity – to try out wild positions and do astounding things. Rodney had a dodgy back and had to move with caution, for fear of further damage. And he'd become nervous, of late, about getting an erection, so the whole bedroom thing was increasingly fraught. How could she relax, when he was either wincing in pain, or casting anxious glances at his equipment, as if he feared it might let him down – again?

Having slouched back to the sink, she took out her annoyance on a grease-encrusted pan, only to be interrupted by Daniel, who came to find her in the kitchen, maths book in his hand.

'Mum, I need some help. I just don't get this algebra.'

'OK,' she said, rinsing the last few plates. 'Sit there at the table and I'll be with you in a tick.'

No problem with maths. She was in remarkably good practice now, from constantly adding up the minutes since she had last laid eyes on Fergus, and – far more enthralling – totting up the countless times he would ravish her and ravish her among those rapturous tulips.

Claire switched off *Gone With The Wind*. She had no desire to watch a rampant Rhett Butler making love to Scarlett O'Hara,

when everything inside her was screaming to join in. Yet the
silence seemed oppressive once the screen had gone dead and
there were no more gasps of passion. Mooching into the hall, she
removed Susanna's scarf from the banisters and idly straightened
a picture. Without her usual chores – cooking supper, washing-up,
helping out with homework, chauffeuring Daniel back and forth
to football training or five-a-side or swimming club – a surge of
unused energy was throbbing through her body, with no outlet, no
fulfilment. It was rare for all the family to be out on the same
evening, but Rodney had gone to Rotary, Daniel was staying over
with a school-friend, and Susanna was at a play rehearsal. She
ought to use the time to catch up with the ironing, or make a cake
for Drugscope's Easter fête, yet her thoughts were very far
removed from any aspect of good works. She was preoccupied by
one thing only: the fact that Fergus hadn't made any further
move. Could she really blame him, though? By totally ignoring his
note, turning down his challenge, she must have hurt his pride.
Poets were highly sensitive, so, for all she knew, he could feel
deeply wounded.

It had even struck her yesterday that he might have actually
stolen the tulips and was now banged up in gaol. How else could
he have acquired them, when he was struggling to make ends
meet? Yet stealing them made no more sense than buying them. As
far as she could ascertain, this particular variety, with its colour,
markings and petal-shape, simply didn't exist. Which only
increased her obsession. Weren't inexplicable dream-flowers pecu-
liarly precious? And wasn't it vital to see him again, if only to
discover where he'd found them?

In fact, she went to sit at the dining-table, just to gaze at them
again, as she'd been doing the whole week. Their colour had deep-
ened to a blatant, blowsy orange, as if they'd come on heat and
were smouldering with desire. Yet they also looked unkempt and
almost slatternly, flinging themselves all over the place, clearly
frantic to escape the vase and break loose in rebellion. Even when
delivered, they had been free of any ties or wrappings; anarchic
from the start. The last bouquet she'd received (from her mother
on her birthday) had been double-wrapped, first in shrouding
cellophane, then in stiff, confining paper; the stalks fastened with

tight rubber-bands, as well as restrictive string. It had taken her a good ten minutes to remove their fetters and let them breathe. But these tulips were true mavericks and, as each day passed, became more and more unbridled; now splaying out their petals in the most licentious manner; pushing their brazen faces almost into hers. Scentless when they first arrived, they had even developed a smell: a musky odour – rank and frank and sexual, as if they were using every wile to get themselves – well, ravished.

She glanced from their orange tumult to the photos on the sideboard: her family reproving her; reminding her that, as wife and mother, it was utterly reprehensible to be thinking of another man. Deliberately, she went over there, fixing her attention on the photos, as if, that way, she could ground herself in duty and fidelity. But her eye was caught not by pictures of her own kids, but by a snapshot of herself as a child, neatly dressed in school dress and clean white socks, and demurely holding both her parents' hands. In fact, she had been a wild child, unruly and obstreperous, but that side of her had been ruthlessly suppressed by a disciplinarian father and strict, God-fearing mother. Yet some tiny but determined part of that pulped and trampled tomboy seemed to be alive still, clamouring and fizzing just below the surface.

Well, she must murder it again – cold-bloodedly, remorselessly – to save herself from danger. And there was another, equal danger that she might be making a total fool of herself. Suppose Fergus had simply penned his note as a crazy bit of poet-speak – something he'd regretted ever since? After all, why should he want to bed a woman fifteen years his senior?

Except she was no longer forty-four, but going on fourteen. Everything inside her was in ferment, like the tulips; begging to be noticed, begging to be touched. And, soon, it would be too late – this one chance lost for ever. In just a few more days, these flowers would fade and shrivel, sag and wilt, close up; fit only for the dump. And she herself would slowly limp towards stagnation and sterility.

All at once, the phone rang. Fergus, she thought, darting over to pick it up. Tired of waiting for her call, he'd decided to ring *her*. The prospect was so overwhelming, she could barely find her voice to say hello.

'Claire, it's Jenny Kirkland. Sorry to bother you again, but I was wondering if I could rope you in to help with—'

Immediately, she put the phone down, hoping Jenny would assume they'd been cut off. She *wouldn't* help. Not with any more good causes or tedious, worthy charities. Not with charity fêtes or school bazaars. Not with Rotary or Mencap or Age Concern or Drugscope. And, suddenly, impulsively, she dialled a number herself, to prevent Jenny ringing back – a number she had no right to dial; a number she was mad to dial; wicked and immoral to dial; an action she would most definitely regret.

'Hi, Fergus here. Who's that?'

'It's Claire,' she said, in a voice she didn't recognize – the brazen voice of the tulips, flaunting and flirtatious and refusing to be gagged. 'I just thought I'd let you know that …' For one split second, she lost her nerve; had to hold her breath in an agonizing pause, but, screwing up her courage, she pictured Fergus naked in a flushed and frenzied fanfare of ardent orange flowers, and continued in a rush, 'I'm ready to be ravished any time you care to choose.'

Repair

'Washing-machine repair, ma'am.'

Angela stared in disbelief at the tall, gangling man standing on the doorstep. Slowly she registered each detail: the thick, unruly hair, the colour of ripe straw; the wary, long-lashed eyes, somewhere between grey and blue; the angular figure with the slight stoop to the shoulders, the high cheekbones, narrow face. The resemblance was uncanny. Of course, the clothes were totally different. Simon's usual attire was a sweater and blue jeans, whereas this man was wearing a uniform: a navy polo-shirt with HOOVER embroidered on the pocket, smart, black, working trousers and a navy anorak. His hands were different, too: broad and tanned, with bitten nails, rather than Simon's pale, slim, freckled ones. Even so, it—

'Have I got the right address? You *are* Miss Blake? 16 Lonsdale Road?'

Shaken still, she nodded. 'Yes … sorry. Do come in.'

'So what seems to be the trouble?' he asked, stepping into the hall and wiping his feet on the non-existent doormat

Where did she begin? Even now, days later, she couldn't quite believe that Simon had walked out. They had been together two whole years; even talked of marriage, for God's sake. Yet that callous way he'd left, with no warning or discussion, just a cruel, curt note.

'According to my work-sheet, you've had a few problems before.'

None at all. Since the day they'd met, she and Simon had never had the slightest tiff, let alone a serious quarrel.

'A broken fan-belt, back in March.'

She tried to concentrate on broken machines rather than on

broken hearts. 'Yes. And the pump went, in July. The other man said—'

'Larry?' he interrupted. 'He's no longer with us. He left the company and went to live up North. I've taken over his area.'

She could barely remember Larry – just a blur, a cipher, not this living embodiment of Simon.

The guy pointed to his name-badge. 'Jack,' he said, putting down his tool-box and unfolding a sheet of paper.

She was almost disappointed that he didn't share Simon's name, along with his appearance. Even the way his hair grew was identical to Simon's; springing up in an exuberant, self-willed fashion, as if refusing to obey a barber or a comb.

'Well, if you could show me the machine, ma'am....'

She ushered him into the kitchen – a dark and poky room, but with wild magenta walls. Although handy with a paintbrush, Simon refused to stick to conventional colours, like magnolia, or wishy-washy white. Their bedroom was electric-blue; their bathroom marigold.

She watched Jack manoeuvre the machine out from the wall, noting the ease with which he did so – a strong, capable type, like Simon. Then having unscrewed the top, he lifted it off, exposing an array of pipes and wires. She was in his way – she knew that. The kitchen was too cramped for them both, especially once he'd spread out his tools on a dustsheet on the floor. Yet she couldn't bring herself to leave. She had only to half-close her eyes to turn him into Simon – Simon here again, back again, life returned to normal.

'Cup of tea?' she asked. If she spun out the tea-making process, she would have a perfect pretext to observe him.

'No, ta.'

'Coffee?'

'No.'

'Or I've got some fruit juice in the fridge.'

He shook his head; his concentration already focused on the task in hand. Well, she'd better ask about the machine; gain his attention that way. She just had to see his eyes again; that blue-steel gaze she knew so well. So far, he'd avoided eye-contact, whereas Simon always looked at people with direct and fierce intensity, as if he could read the inner secrets of their mind.

'Have you any idea *why* it keeps breaking down?'

'Could be anything.'

'What sort of thing?' she persisted.

Still he didn't look up, just gave an impatient shrug. 'Maybe a faulty thermostat. Or the outlet-pipe might be blocked with gunge. Or ...'

His voice tailed off. He was here to do a practical job, not indulge in a theoretical discussion. She leaned against the sink, trying to work out whether he was older than Simon, or younger. Maybe the exact same age: two weeks short of thirty-four.

'When's your birthday?' she asked suddenly.

He turned round to stare, wiping a smear of oil from his face. 'What?'

'I'm ... interested in star-signs. Oh, I know people rubbish astrology, dismiss it as a con, but actually I'm not so sure. Loads of different societies believed in it for centuries, so maybe they were on to something. As for me, I get these strong gut-feelings about people and their birthdays. I can't explain it really – I've just always been that way. *You*, for instance, are almost certainly a Capricorn.'

'Yeah,' he said, with a startled look. 'Dead right. I'll be thirty-four in a fortnight – December 29.'

She shivered, half in fear. December 29 was Simon's birthday, too. The coincidence was just too great. Spooky and unsettling.

Silence again, apart from the squeal of the screwdriver and the intrusive ticking of the kitchen clock. Since Simon's departure, it had begun ticking more emphatically, as if counting out each second of his absence. And the days seemed twice as long. She had called in sick at work, and time now dragged and dawdled, with no 9 to 5, no structure, to pull it into shape. And nights alone in the double bed stretched to infinity and back, especially at this time of year, when it was dark from four in the afternoon to eight o'clock in the morning. Just a week to the winter solstice: the lowest, darkest, saddest day, and officially the shortest – although this year it would feel like the longest. Would it be dark and sad for Simon, or had he shacked up with someone new; some woman he'd been keeping secret but seeing on the sly? There was no proof, of course, but why else would he have left? In fact, at this very moment, he might be with the hateful, scheming creature, running his hands down her naked, nubile body....

She blundered out of the room; found refuge in the lounge, although there was no escaping Simon. His photos hung on every wall – studies of London low-life: a homeless man stretched full-length on a bench, wearing mismatched socks; a night-cleaner in a deserted office block, pausing in her dusting to stare out at the moon. Photographers were renowned for their sensitivity, so how could he have acted in such a brutal way?

She paced round and round the small, cluttered room, avoiding piles of books, lengths of wood, and Simon's half-built bookshelves. He'd been trying to finish the job since they'd moved here, back in March, but never seemed to find the time to do much more than tinker. Strange he hadn't taken his books with him, or his precious record collection – only his laptop and his Blackberry, his shaving gear and watch.

Having edged towards the door, she hovered just outside it, listening for sounds from the kitchen. She wanted to breathe Jack in; soak up his presence; put the smallest possible distance between them. If he was Simon's double, then it was vital she stay close.

Inexorably drawn back to him, she pretended she needed a glass of water, and stood running the kitchen tap, watching as he worked. As a child, she'd had a dog called Jack – a small, wire-haired, manic mongrel who'd slept on her bed at night, shared her weekly Mars Bars. She remembered crying into his fur the day her father left. Did *all* men leave, eventually? Perhaps it was built into their genes; part of the y-chromosome.

Jack was kneeling on the floor now, prising off the back of the machine. As he bent forward, a gap of naked flesh appeared between his trousers and his top. She gazed in fascination at the tiny golden hairs on his skin, which were glinting in the light; almost asking to be touched. Sultry-dark herself, she had always loved Simon's English fairness: the freckles on his arms; the way his hair turned lighter in the sun. Not that they'd seen the sun since the beginning of November. The weather had been continually overcast – moody, brooding, turned in on itself, as if going through a depressive phase, with no therapist to help.

Was Jack aware of the silence, she wondered? Unlikely. For him, she barely existed – just another job on his work-sheet; another anonymous client, forgotten by the evening. Her presence in the kitchen was of little more importance to him than the presence of the cooker or the sink. Yet, for her this was a godsend, and maybe in the literal sense. Some unknown power must have dispatched him here for a reason – as a sign of hope, perhaps. If she ignored his hands, his uniform, it was *Simon* who was kneeling at her feet.

'Have you found the problem?' she asked, at length, longing to commune with him.

'Yeah. Fan's gone again.'

'But we only had a new one in the spring. And a complete over-haul, as well....' If necessary, she would discuss the machine's whole history – anything to keep him talking.

He shrugged. 'Sometimes these things happen.'

'But why?' She wanted answers – answers from Simon, some sort of explanation. A scribbled note was actually insulting, and had said nothing anyway.

'Could be a defect in the belt. Or the drum may be overloaded. Are you putting too much in?'

Not now, she thought. This week's wash had looked pathetically small without Simon's shirts and socks, his pyjamas, gym-clothes, muddy walking gear.

'I'll need to phone for a new one, OK?'

'OK.' She hardly cared. It was other things that needed mending; more precious things, by far.

He snapped his mobile open, started spelling out her details to somebody the other end – name, house-number, street-name, post-code. 'Nope,' he said, running a hand through his hair. 'There seems to be a problem with the housing. The fan keeps sticking. Do you have a replacement?'

She envied him his work – practical and physical – manual work, not head-work. His mind was on pumps and fan-belts, not on absence, darkness, loss.

Shutting off the mobile, he sat back on his heels. She was aware of the black trousers straining over his thighs. Strong, skinny thighs, like Simon's. She imagined them now, straddling her body, or drawn up around her waist; the feel of his hot, sweaty skin as he thrust and threshed against her. Simon made love in vivid, flaunting colour: marigold, electric-blue. Was *that* why he had gone – because she couldn't match his passion; was a 'magnolia' kind of lover: tepid, safe and boring? Maybe he'd met a girl who rivalled him in sheer brilliance and flamboyance; a truly scarlet woman, torrid in the sack.

'There isn't one in stock, so they'll have to ring around – see if they can get it somewhere else. They'll phone back in fifteen minutes.'

'Oh … good. Look, let me make you a coffee now.'

He might want to wait outside in his van, snatch fifteen minutes' shut-eye, or sneak a cigarette, rather than share a cup of coffee with her. The thought induced a surge of panic, so she went to stand in the doorway, blocking his escape; talking really fast, to prevent him saying no again. 'Actually, I could do with one myself. I'll make proper coffee for us both. How many sugars do you take? And do you prefer hot milk to cold? And if you fancy a biscuit, I bought a load last week....'

Simon had bought them, in fact – Christmas biscuits in a big, round, glossy tin, with a picture of the Horse Guards on the lid. He always picked out the chocolate ones, whilst she preferred the plain. 'We're so compatible,' they used to laugh, in the early days, 'even down to biscuits.' Perhaps the new female would also want the chocolate ones, and resent him pigging the lot. Tiny things like that could undermine relationships; destroy them in the end. And, with any luck, the bitch would get annoyed about his tardiness in doing household jobs; insist he got a move on, nag him till he snapped.

Reaching up for the tin, she prised off the lid and removed the padded gold-foil roundel lying on the top. How snug the biscuits looked, nestling close together in their matching gold-foil bed. She and Simon had been like that, snuggling up to one another beneath their padded duvet. Now she was a broken biscuit, a mass of useless crumbs.

'Take several,' she urged, proffering Jack the tin.

'Mind if I hog the chocolate ones? I'm mad for chocolate – any kind.'

Of course. She already knew that. 'Well, have them all. Go down to the second layer.'

'Are you trying to fatten me up?'

He sounded suspicious rather than amused. Perhaps he feared she was chatting him up, and might actually pounce, given any encouragement. She was tempted, in fact, just to pay Simon back. Instead, she edged away a little, busied herself with the coffee pot. When it came to coffee, Simon was a connoisseur; insisted that they buy it from the Italian delicatessen, whose proudly plump proprietor ground the beans to order. As she unscrewed the jar, the rich, deep-roasted, mocha smell brought memories of Sunday mornings: coffee in bed; papers jumbled on the floor; his kisses hot and pungent, tasting of Continental Blend.

She jumped as Jack's mobile rang. He answered through a mouthful of biscuit. 'You got one? Great! I'll call by this evening and fetch it.'

As the kettle erupted in a shuddering boil, she experienced the same turmoil in her chest. So he'd be here again, this evening. Maybe spending hours with her, if the part proved hard to fit. She could make him supper – knew the kind of food he'd like: a choco-late pudding, obviously, with something male and meaty first: *carbonnade* of beef, perhaps, or steak in ale, or oxtail. Simon detested salads; jibbed even at a piece of fish, unless it was fried in batter.

Her hand was shaking as she poured the boiling water into the pot. 'That's fine,' she said, once he'd rung off. 'I'm not going out or anything.'

'What?'

'I mean, if you're coming back this evening, no problem – I'll be here.'

'Oh, it won't be this evening. I'm up to my ears till God knows when tonight. *And* the next few days. With it being so close to Christmas, everybody's on my tail. And some of them calls are urgent – women with half-a-dozen kids and loads of nappies to wash.'

Simon hadn't wanted children. She'd hoped he might come round to it, eventually, although she had never forced the issue; remained content with what they had: fantastic sex; shared tastes in books and music; the same sense of humour, political beliefs.

She tried to control the tremor in her voice; adopt a businesslike tone. 'Look, nappies or no nappies, this job is just as urgent as theirs. I *need* you to come back, OK? I'm the client, so I call the tune.'

With a gesture of annoyance, he reached for his phone again. 'I'll give the office a bell, see if another engineer is free to—'

'No,' she interrupted. 'It must be you. Someone new to the job will only mess things up.'

'We all have the same training,' he explained, a note of irritation in his voice. 'Everyone in the company knows these machines like the back of their hand.'

'Maybe so, but *you* took on the job, so I expect *you* to finish it.'

'I'm sorry, ma'am, that's impossible.'

'Don't call me ma'am, OK? I'm not ma'am, I'm Angela.'

He stared at her a moment, then spoke in almost a pitying tone, still avoiding the use of her name. 'I'm going to put in a request for Gordon to come out. He's had thirty years' experience, and he's totally reliable.'

An image of her dog suddenly intruded into her mind. Jack had been put to sleep by the vet at the age of only four, with inoperable cancer of the pancreas. Four, for dogs, was equivalent to twenty-eight for humans – her own age, in point of fact. She still remembered every detail: the injection into his flank, the dreadful silence while they waited for the drug to take effect, Jack's final piteous shudder, followed by the vet's soft, solemn voice, 'He's gone now.'

'Please,' she begged, switching from insistence to entreaty. 'Do come. I'll pay anything you like. And I don't mind what time it is. Make it as late as you like. Just suit yourself, but *come*.'

He said nothing whatsoever, just reached out for another biscuit, as if to play for time. The crunching noise sounded louder than the tick-tick of the clock. Her life seemed poised on a knife-edge. Depending on his answer, she might tip over into panic – demeaning, frightening breakdown – or limp and hobble forward in some damaged but not hopeless shape.

'Please,' she repeated, her voice shaky from the force of her desire. 'It means so much, means *everything*.'

In the ensuing hush, she fixed her whole attention on his tools: a set of seven screwdrivers, lined up according to size; red-handled, battered pliers; shiny silver spanners; rolls of electrical tape, and a few spiky, sharp-toothed implements, with vicious, snapping jaws.

When he finally spoke, his voice was quite emotionless. 'Excuse me a minute, will you, ma'am?'

Pushing past her, he strode into the hall. She gripped the worktop for support. Was he walking out? And without a single word? He'd left his tools behind, but that didn't mean a thing. Perhaps he was scribbling her a note, an insulting, cowardly note. She strained her ears for the scratching of a pen; heard nothing but the slam of the front door.

He'd gone. Like that. Cruelly. Unforgivably. Hadn't told her why. Hadn't asked her what she felt. Or discussed the situation. Hadn't even thought to ask if she could pay the rent without him. Who cared about the rent? It was *him* she craved – as an addict craved a drug – his mind, his soul, his skills, his wit, his cock.

Shutting her eyes, she took a sip of coffee; tried desperately to change the date – turn this barren Wednesday into the Sunday before last: blissed-out with him in bed; hands cupped round her coffee-mug; piles of Sunday papers jumbled on the duvet. She could feel his open, sensuous lips nuzzling along her neck; the shockwaves lower down, as his fingers traced—

Useless. She was bundled up in sweaters and standing in the kitchen, not lolling naked in a dishevelled double bed. Even the coffee was insipid; nothing like their usual brew. Despite the sludge of bitter grounds muddying the cup, she hadn't made it strong enough – a tepid sort of dishwater, with no kick to it, no flavour. No wonder he was shagging someone else. His new lover would be brimming over with caffeine and adrenaline; a full-bodied double espresso, potent, scorching-hot.

She sank down on to the floor; knelt where he had knelt, hiding her face in her hands. A long time seemed to pass – hours, perhaps, or days; maybe a full week. They must have reached the solstice now: the shortest, saddest, darkest, longest day.

She started as the doorbell rang; struggled to her feet. The postman bringing Christmas cards. Friends wishing them a happy Christmas, unaware that Simon's name could no longer be conjoined with hers on any card or envelope. Those friends would probably disappear, as well. People found it hard to cope if a couple went their separate ways, and often avoided *both* partners, to save themselves embarrassment.

She limped to the front door, rubbed her eyes in shock. Could it be an illusion – this change of mind, reprieve? Slowly, she registered each detail, to ensure she wasn't dreaming: thick, unruly hair, the colour of ripe straw; wary, long-lashed eyes, somewhere between grey and blue; angular figure with a slight stoop to the shoulders, high cheekbones, narrow face. Yes, all real, all tangible.

'It's OK,' he said, 'I'll come back.'

'You'll come back?' she repeated, not daring to believe the fact until she heard it from his lips once more.

'Yeah. I'll come back.'

Wonderingly, she let him in, scared by the elation tingling through her chest; the uproar in her body, ferment in her head.

'I've managed to swap things round, postponed another job. So if you're in at six this evening, I'll pop straight round from my last call and …'

The words she barely heard, too shaken by the fact that he had met her eyes, at last, and his fierce, intense, blue-smouldering stare was piercing to her innermost core, repairing every damaged part – yes, even her broken heart.

'Thank you, she whispered, '*Simon.*'

Margarine

CLAREMONT GRANGE
CENTENARY CELEBRATION

You are cordially invited ...

Margery ripped the invitation in half and tossed it into the bin. Never would she set foot in that loathsome place again. The envelope contained a letter – in addition to the gold-bordered card – which she gave a cursory glance. An appeal for a donation, no doubt. No, it merely gave further details of the celebration itself: a picnic lunch, followed by a performance of *The Pirates of Penzance*, enacted by the current pupils, and then a formal evening dinner, with speeches by the Head and various distinguished alumnae. Hardly an enticing prospect – an amateur production of Gilbert and Sullivan, and endless dreary trumpetings about the school's superior position in the league tables. About to crumple up the sheet, she suddenly noticed the name at the bottom, typed beneath a bold but illegible signature: Clarissa Scott, née Talbot-Young.

She stood motionless, heart pounding, all her childhood passion reigniting in a rush, at the sight of that alluring name. She was a child again, a willing slave to the most talented and beauteous creature in the whole of Claremont Grange – a much older girl, completely out of reach, with long golden hair and violet eyes, and a range of different skills: school prefect, hockey captain, editor of the school magazine. If Clarissa Talbot-Young was organizing this event, then she, the once ardent admirer, simply must be there, despite the fact she had deliberately avoided all previous reunions.

This was a challenge impossible to ignore; a chance for the lowly servant to wreak her revenge, at last.

Throughout her years in that hated institution, Clarissa had used her and abused her; accepting every menial service as her natural right and privilege, whilst taunting her unmercifully. Yet, she'd continued to worship her tormentor as a goddess and a queen, glorying in each mortification, as preferable to being ignored. When Queen Clarissa finally left school, aglow with an Oxford scholarship, her plain and podgy skivvy had been inconsolable, actually missing all the drudgery and donkeywork, the constant errands and thankless tasks, performed for that enthralling tyrant.

She strode into the bedroom, startled by her sudden sense of outrage. For over thirty years, she had banned the school from both memory and thought, yet now it seemed imperative to confront Clarissa in person; tell her loud and clear what a bully and a brute she'd been.

She began riffling through her wardrobe, intent on finding an outfit for the occasion that would stir no shameful memory of the dumpy, unprepossessing child Clarissa would remember, with her ill-filling uniform (bought always second-hand), and the braces on her teeth. Of course, the goddess would have changed as well: the long golden hair probably short and grey these days; the slender figure thickening round the waist. In fact, the five-year age-difference would actually work in her own favour now, since Clarissa would be coming up to sixty, due for her pension and her bus-pass, while she herself, by some strange stroke of luck, was still pre-menopausal.

Her reflection in the mirror provided a certain reassurance: her hair was largely its natural tawny brown; her figure in good shape, with no trace of the former puppy-fat; no grotesque and greasy pigtails just asking to be tugged. But she was determined to leave nothing to chance. In fact, why settle for some existing garment and run the risk of looking out-of-fashion, when she could invest in a brand new outfit, head to toe? She would also book a session at the hairdresser, for a decent cut and re-style. Such matters, in her normal life, were of very minor concern, but this, she knew instinctively, was a crisis situation. As a child, she'd been an outcast through no fault of her own: the only one in a roll-call of 300 girls who lived with a single mother, shamefully divorced – and lived not in grace and style, but in a cramped two-up, two-down. It might be rather late in the day to make the point that base-born Margery Tomkins could now hold her own in the world, but that was exactly what she intended – and to hell with the consequences.

As she nosed into a parking space between a BMW coupé and a silver-grey Mercedes, she cursed herself for not having come by train. Not only was her own car the smallest, lowest-status one in sight, but she had got completely lost *en route* and was now humiliatingly late. Before getting out, however, she just had to repair her face, even if it made her later still. The make-up she'd applied this morning with such determined care was already beginning to smudge and melt in the fierce heat of the car. BMW drivers would have built-in air-conditioning, but her third-hand Nissan Micra didn't boast such luxury. Quickly, she retouched her lipstick and powdered over the shine; noticing with alarm that her hands were not quite steady.

Incredible that just the sight of Claremont Grange could produce such fierce reactions. The gracious, indeed splendid house – a former Rothschild mansion – appeared to her like a Borstal or a boot camp, with lowering prison-walls and no windows except grudging slits. And the extensive grounds, with rolling parkland stretching lush beyond, seemed to have shrunk to the odd stunted tree, naked of any leaf or flower, even in mid-June. The weather was, in fact, idyllic, with a beneficent sun and baby-blue sky, but for her it was September, grey and overcast. She was five years old again; being dumped here by her grandparents, whom she could barely even see, half-blinded as she was by tears, and by an overlarge school hat.

'You're an extremely lucky little girl,' they told her, 'to be getting such a first-rate education. And you've *us* to thank for it.'

And then they drove away, Grandma quite forgetting to turn round and wave goodbye. She stood watching, sobbing, until the car was just a speck, and she was dragged off to her dormitory by somebody called Matron, who was tall and thin and crackled when she walked.

It was years before she realized that by paying her fees at boarding-school, her grandparents were actually solving the problem of their errant son – her father – who had left the marriage, left her mother penniless, and gone to live in Hawaii with a Polynesian beauty-queen. Not only did it salve their conscience, it also saved her father from having to involve himself in her upbringing – or even, for that matter, having ever to see her again. If she were at school all during term-time and with her mother in the holidays, there was no reason for him to squander time and money travelling thousands of miles to visit. She had long ago accepted the situation, refusing to indulge in anger or resentment, however much she had detested Claremont Grange. Yet her sortie here today had revived her sense of being lonely and uprooted, and completely out of place; a common weed in a stylish flowerbed, which might be chucked on the rubbish-heap, should her Grandpa's cash run out.

Determined to suppress such thoughts, she rammed on her new hat and made her way past the side of the house to the expanse of lawn behind. The hum and buzz of voices crescendoed as she walked towards the mass of languid females, sprawled on picnic rugs and groundsheets on the grass. Fighting a strong instinct to turn tail and bolt for home, she forced herself to weave her way between the various groups; eyes peeled for Clarissa. However changed the Queen might be, she knew she'd recognize her instantly, if only by the churning in her guts.

'Margery!' a voice called. 'Fancy seeing *you* here! You haven't been back for years.'

Never, in fact, she didn't say, recognizing a former classmate, Stephanie; still ginger-haired and freckled, although now distinctly overweight. The woman was scrambling up to greet her, and at least half-a-dozen others from her year began smiling, waving and introducing themselves. Not that she had a problem remembering their names, which were tripping off her tongue as easily as if she were back in class: Philipppa, Elizabeth, Felicity, Lucinda, and the twins, Elspeth and Virginia. No one had a 'common' name like Margery, of course – another badge of inferiority, she had soon learned to her shame. On one hideous occasion, they'd heard her mother call her Marge, and immediately given her the nickname 'Margarine' – a name she'd loathed, but which had stuck till she left school.

At least they appeared to have forgotten it, thank Christ, and all trace of condescension had completely disappeared, as they made room for her on the tartan rug; even admired her hat.

'Perfect timing, Margery!' Lucinda said, with a smile. 'We were just about to make a start on the nosh. And what would you like to drink? I'm afraid we've finished all the champers, but there's enough wine here to get us all well and truly plastered!'

Only then did she notice the ice-buckets and wicker picnic hampers; the pretty patterned china and hallmarked knives and forks. In her particular circle, a picnic involved eating with one's fingers from, at best, a paper plate – and eating something basic like a sandwich or pork pie. But here, spread out in banquet mode, was a whole poached salmon resplendent on a silver platter; an exotic layered terrine; what looked like a roast pheasant, and a huge cache of caviar. There were also mounds of fresh hulled strawberries, topped with clotted cream, and a variety of elaborate desserts, in pretty cut-glass bowls. They had been instructed to bring picnic food to share, so she had bought a pasta salad on her way home from work last night. In fact, she had totally forgotten it, in her distress about arriving late, and left it curdling and sweating in the car, together with a bottle of undistinguished wine. Now she blessed her oversight, since she realized with embarrassment that she should have brought *home-made* food, served in ritzy style; not an uncouth plastic tub, grabbed in haste from Asda.

As she continued to survey the feast, she noticed there were even damask napkins, and a bone-china dish containing exquisite little pats of butter – which immediately set her reflecting on her nickname. Butter was traditional and naturally superior, pure and undefiled, whereas margarine, in contrast, was an upstart: synthetic and adulterated, a garish-coloured mongrel, with no breeding or finesse – and very like her mum, in that respect. Clarissa and her cronies had once dismissed her mother as a 'pleb', and though she hadn't understood the word, she had felt the deep contempt in it. The other girls had entirely different mothers: delicate, well-spoken women, with soft, white, work-shy hands, who wore floaty floral dresses and high heels, instead of her mum's miniskirts and dirty, battered plimsolls. And they all had proper fathers who lived with them at home, and not in Honolulu with a bimbo. And they owned dogs and horses and villas in Provence, and went on skiing trips in winter, and employed live-in cooks and nannies. Even her rich grandmother did all the cooking herself (as well as piles of housework), and she and Grandpa never went away, except once, to some small guesthouse in Southend. In any case, their money was despised at school, as not being 'the right sort', although she had never really understood why any kind of money could ever be judged 'wrong'.

'So, Margery, how *are* you?' Lucinda asked, offering her a platter of asparagus.

'Er, fine,' she said, deliberately refusing any food. She could hardly gobble theirs, having contributed nothing herself.

'It must be – let's see – thirty years since we last laid eyes on you.'

'It's actually thirty-six.'

'Well, tell us what's been happening all that time?'

'Oh … this and that.' It felt wrong to be the centre of attention; every eye now turned on her with interest. At school, she had learned her place, as someone best ignored.

'Do you work at all?' asked Stephanie.

'Oh, yes.'

'And what line of work would that be?'

'I run a charity called Kids-in-Crisis, which I set up in the eighties. It helps disadvantaged children who—'

'Brilliant! Good for you.'

Stephanie had not only interrupted, she had sounded rather patronizing. OK, Margery thought, if you don't care about abused and battered kids, let's change the subject, shall we? 'And how about you, Stephanie? I remember you were a whiz at maths. Did you follow that up and become a big noise in the City?'

'Far from it!' Stephanie laughed. 'I've never really done a thing – except bring up my three sons, of course.'

Margery stiffened at the mention of children; knew she'd be judged inadequate on the grounds of having none, and not even having married. Her mother's own experience had put her off matrimony for life. Fortunately, she was saved an inquisition by the appearance of Miss O'Sullivan, their former English teacher; now stooped and grey and fading, but instantly recognizable by her hook nose and fierce black eyes.

'Lucinda! How lovely! And Elspeth and Virginia, still inseparable, I see. And that's Stephanie Simmonds, isn't it? Yes, the same red hair. Wonderful to see you all!'

Extraordinary, thought Margery, that this figure of authority – indeed, a martinet – should be embracing her former pupils, even insisting they call her 'Mavis'.

'Ah, Felicity, *you* I'll never forget! You were always trouble, weren't you, and trouble with a capital T! I remember you asking me once why we had to study Wordsworth's shitty daffodils!'

In the ensuing burst of laughter, Margery realized that Miss O'Sullivan had failed to acknowledge her at all. Hardly any wonder, when she had invariably tried to hide at school and make herself invisible. Well-bred girls like Felicity, overflowing with confidence, could afford to be 'always trouble', but not her, the parvenu. She sat in silence, listening to the jokes and banter, until Miss O'Sullivan ('Mavis' was a step too far) eventually moved away to liaise with another group.

'She's not still teaching, is she?' asked Lucinda, gazing after the tall, bent figure, with its shock of coarse, grey hair.

'Good God, no! She must be nearly eighty.'

'Actually, I met the present English mistress when I first arrived,' Virginia remarked. 'And *she* looked about sixteen!'

More laughter. Once it had abated, Margery asked, with studied nonchalance, 'I presume Clarissa's here?'

'Yes, she's over there by the cedar tree,' Elizabeth replied, 'with quite a few of the others from her form. It's priceless, isn't it, the way we've formed ourselves into little tribal groups, according to which year we were.'

'It's not surprising, really, though,' Felicity put in. 'I mean, the higher forms seemed so old and scary, and we're probably still reflecting that. I remember being quite in awe of Clarissa.'

With little cause, Margery thought, glancing at the woman's chic designer suit. As the daughter of a judge who drove a vintage Daimler, Felicity had been smugly safe from any bullying attacks.

'Apparently, she's something of a star now,' Philippa observed, spreading caviar on *ciabatta*.

'Yes, marrying Lord Pemberton is certainly a feather in her cap, not to mention her own CBE.'

'And both her daughters are high fliers, don't forget. In fact, didn't Annabel get hitched to some famous film producer?'

Margery took refuge in her wine, beginning to feel distinctly out of her depth. She wasn't in the habit of hobnobbing with film producers, nor was she on first-name terms with any peer of the realm. In fact, she appeared to be reverting to her former lowly status, as she remembered, with a squirm of shame, how mortified she used to feel when her school-mates called her 'Margarine'. Imaginative to a fault, she had pictured herself as a tub of cheap, disgusting stuff, maltreated by Clarissa, who would stick a dirty knife in her, tainting her with toast-crumbs and globules of boiled egg. Or she'd be snatched from the fridge and left out in the broiling sun, which reduced her to a rancid, oily mass. Or the queen would even spit into the carton, sweep it from the table with a derisive curl of the lip, then chuck it in the rubbish-bin.

Often, she'd felt close to panic, experiencing the actual sense of being coffined in a bin; fighting for each laboured breath as she was crushed against other dregs and dross: potato peelings, jagged cans, clammy tea leaves, chicken bones. And, cowering amidst that toxic waste, she'd imagined how repulsive she must smell – the sickening stench of failure.

Such bitter recollections made her even more determined to take a stand, for once; challenge her oppressor and settle these old scores. 'I think I'll go and say hello to Clarissa,' she said, speaking with feigned casualness, as if she intended to indulge in a little idle chatter, rather than a tongue-lashing. 'I remember her so well.'

'But, Margery, you haven't eaten a thing.'

'And barely touched your wine.'

'Don't worry, I won't be long. Back here in a tick.'

Advancing towards the cedar tree, she was aware of her stomach turning nauseous somersaults, but she made herself walk on, resolving to pursue her quarry, whatever it might cost. However, she noticed with alarm that even pronouncing Clarissa's name caused her voice to gag and grate.

'My ... my friends said she was over here, but I ... I can't see her anywhere.'

'No, she's just gone inside to spend a penny,' some Sloaney type replied: 'You've only missed her by a couple of minutes.

Disconcerted, she turned on her heel, only to realize this was a blessing in disguise. She could hardly shout abuse in public, whereas a private confrontation would leave her free to be as vicious and as vengeful as she chose.

Crossing the expanse of lawn, she headed for the house, making for the downstairs cloakroom she remembered from the sixties. The whole layout of the school might have changed since then, of course, but, no, the cloakroom was still there, although totally deserted. Clarissa must have nipped upstairs to the much grander bathrooms adjacent to the dormitories. Before going up to join her, she took a quick peek in the school-hall, concealing herself in the doorway. How free and relaxed the pupils seemed, compared with her own stiff and scared obedience. The intimidated child she'd been would never have dared to sprawl or slouch in such a slipshod fashion, let alone shriek with raucous laughter. (In fact, she couldn't remember laughing even once at school – not in thirteen years.) And the uniform was also much more casual – no longer a severe grey tunic, prim white blouse, and black, frumpy, lace-up shoes, but T-shirts, for heaven's sake, worn atop jaunty pleated skirts, and a wild assortment of free-and-easy footwear: trainers, sling-backs, ballet-pumps, in cheerful fruit-drop colours.

Mindful of her mission, she tore herself away and began climbing the flight of handsome wooden stairs, although assailed by painful memories even there. Clarissa had once ordered her to go upstairs on her hands and knees and lick each step in the process. She had slavishly obeyed, of course, tasting grime and dust on her tongue, but willing to be chastened because the Queen was taking notice of her.

Fired by new indignation, she tried the first large bathroom on the left, but found that empty, too. She stood a moment, however, marvelling at its sumptuousness. Claremont Grange was a listed building, so any modernization must be subject to strict rules, and certainly here, at least, there was no sign of even minor change: the same toilet 'thrones', with their polished mahogany seats; the same huge bath, with lions' paws as its feet, carved in elaborate detail; the same ornamental tiling, bright with birds and flowers.

Mechanically, she found herself walking further on, making for the dormitory she had slept in when she first arrived. In contrast to the bathroom, the place was completely transformed. Gone were the stark white counterpanes, the high, white-curtained beds, each a private 'cell', cut off from the others, to discourage dangerous intimacy. The new divans were companionably close, topped with coloured duvets and strewn with cuddly toys. She recalled her sleepless nights here (all such toys forbidden); the longing for her mother so intense it was a pain; the yearning for a goodnight kiss or consoling bedtime story, instead of only silence and severity.

Drifting on to the infirmary, she remembered daily cod-liver-oil and occasional syrup-of-figs (one disgusting, one delicious), and her long spells in the sick-bay, with cystitis, tonsillitis, bronchitis, laryngitis. Whatever 'itises' might be, she had hated them for confining her with Matron; keeping her a prisoner in that bleak and pallid room. Naturally, she had failed to understand back then that physical illness could be caused by mental pain.

'For God's sake!' she muttered to herself. 'Don't be such a misery.'

She should be counting her blessings, not indulging in self-pity. In point of fact, she'd been extremely fortunate to inhabit such magnificent surroundings, when she might have been at a sink-school, with no ornate ceilings, spacious rooms or acres of extensive grounds. And she could have landed up with rotten teachers, poorly trained and incapable of discipline, instead of the likes of Miss O'Sullivan, with her Double First from Cambridge. In any case, why linger in the past when she had now achieved success, with a satisfying job and good friends who shared her values? She felt not the slightest envy of her classmates' hedonistic lives; their snazzy cars, or social whirl of Henley, Ascot, Glyndebourne. Nor, strange as it might seem, was she jealous of their children. Kids-in-Crisis had become her cherished child; one she'd nurtured lovingly from its frail and feeble babyhood.

Indeed, she was beginning to see that the very idea of a showdown with Clarissa was both pointless and demeaning. They were both grown women now, and what had happened in their school-days was of very little consequence. She must return to the picnic and do her best to enjoy it; make the day a genuine celebration, not an exercise in reprisals and revenge. She could celebrate her own good luck in having soaked up poise and polish here, which had given her the confidence to mix with any level of society – a crucial aspect of her job when it came to raising funds. Besides, there was little point in searching any longer for Clarissa, when she must have long since left the house and be back outside, chatting with her friends.

As she ran downstairs and along the panelled corridor, she suddenly blundered to a halt; overcome with a heady mix of panic and sheer awe. *Could* that be Clarissa, standing by the window, or just a dream, a mirage?

No. The Queen was there – a real, concrete, breathing presence. And not fat or grey at all, but still divinely elegant; her gleaming golden hair now swept up in a chignon; the violet eyes as lustrous and long-lashed as ever. Her overwhelming instinct was to prostate herself and lick the woman's feet; beg to be allowed to do any menial service for her: carry bags, wash dirty clothes, clean mud-encrusted hockey boots.

Had she gone insane? She was no longer an inferior child, but an adult and an equal, and, if she had any sense at all, would enlist this wealthy woman's support for her ever-needy kids-in-crisis. Clarissa's glitzy circle might well donate substantial amounts, if she could only get her act together and explain the crying need.

Impossible. She was incapable of any rational action; incapable of thinking straight. She was in the grip of passion – a passion even more intense than it had been in her schooldays. It was not enough to kiss Clarissa's feet; she craved to kiss her on the lips; touch her breasts; slip a hand inside her blouse; feel the warmth and texture of her skin. Something must be *wrong* with her, she realized with a surge of guilt. Was that why she had never married – not because her mother's divorce had put her off the prospect, but because no man could ever rival her intense love for a female?

Her heart was pounding so wildly, with bewilderment and shock, she had to cling to the wall for support.

'Hey, are you OK?' Clarissa asked, striding over with the same regal bearing she'd possessed as a young girl.

Margery nodded mutely. The woman's sheer physical proximity had left her dumb, and reeling.

'My name's Clarissa Scott. I don't think I know you, do I?'

The lack of recognition was a slap across the face. Margery felt its force and fury spread throughout her body; scorching every limb and cell, leaving deep, red marks.

'I helped to organize this jolly little junket, so I want to check who's actually turned up. Could you give me your name and—'

'Actually, I thought you might remember me,' Margery suddenly blurted out, in a shrill, unsteady voice. 'Margery Tomkins. We were ... thrown together quite a lot at school.'

'Oh, *Margarine*!' Clarissa cried. 'Of course!'

The nickname felled her. Instantly. She was dwindling at a stroke; becoming synthetic and adulterated, common and inferior, with no breeding, no finesse. Dirty knives were being stuck in her, until she was disgustingly polluted with gritty little toast-crumbs and snail-trails of boiled egg. She was contaminated, tainted; a green fur of mould giving off a nauseating smell.

'Fancy seeing dear old Margarine,' the queen continued, with a mocking laugh. 'Well this *is* a surprise, I must say. So, are you coming outside, to join us; provide us with a spot of diversion? You were always rather priceless, I recall – I mean, the way you never seemed quite to get the point. And what happened to your peculiar little mother? Is she still—?'

Margery closed her ears, unable to endure another word. And, with one last look at her despised, desired tormentor, the mongrel and the upstart slunk away, making for the rubbish-bin, where trash like her belonged.

Charmayne

'Look, buzz off! I'm in a rush.' Adam snapped his fingers at the small, white, curly creature that had been following him since he left the Rose and Crown, despite his constant attempts to shake it off. But the dog merely seemed to smile, as if enjoying a good joke.

'Scat, I said! Go back where you belong.'

The owner would be distraught, no doubt, but he just didn't have the time to go wandering round the area with a bundle of damp fur in his arms, shouting 'Have you lost a dog?' to everyone in sight. Besides, it was freezing cold: April on the calendar, but not in terms of temperature.

'Listen, pooch,' he said, squatting down at pavement level to try to impress upon the animal that he wanted to be left in peace, 'you've chosen the wrong chap. I'm not the sort who's into throwing balls or sticks, or going walkies in the park.'

Useless. The creature continued trotting at his heels, meticulously keeping pace with him; slowing when he slowed, and breaking into a bouncy sort of lollop if he strode ahead in an attempt to give it the slip. To tell the truth, he felt a tad ridiculous to be accompanied by such an effeminate breed. If he had to have canine company, then a boxer or Alsatian would definitely be preferable to this soppy ball of fluff. And its Hollywood-style collar was a further source of embarrassment: flamboyant scarlet leather, studded with rows of heart-shaped rhinestones, drawing glittery attention to themselves. He had assumed in his ignorance that the main point of a dog-collar was to identify its wearer's name and address, but this particular one was patently for show.

Once he reached his office block, he stood with his back to the door, determined to leave his pursuer firmly on the other side. 'This is the parting of the ways, my girl. Entry *verboten*, OK?'

But as he nipped inside, the dog somehow sidled in behind him, resisting his attempt to shut the door in its face. Then, having shadowed him up the stairs, it waited, expectant, outside Webster Web-Design, as if it had been accepted on to the payroll and was ready to start work.

'Go *home!*' he ordered, adopting a much sterner tone and stampeding down the stairs again, in the natural expectation that the hanger-on would follow suit. Perversely, though, it refused to budge, and remained sitting on the landing, with what he could have sworn was a look of mocking triumph on its face.

'OK,' he muttered, 'you win.' And, stomping back upstairs, he opened the door to the office and the dog went bounding through – the keenest employee in the annals of the firm.

'Where the hell did *you* come from?' Matthew asked, starting in surprise as the dog rushed over to lick his hand, as if greeting an old friend.

'I can't get rid of the bloody thing. It followed me back from the pub.'

'Well, shouldn't you return it? Someone there will be doing their nut.'

'I tried to, for heaven's sake, but not a soul in either of the bars knew anything about it.'

'That's an expensive piece of dog-flesh,' Phil observed, joining in the conversation now that he'd finished on the phone. 'My Aunt Fran used to breed them.'

'What is it, then? I know nothing about dogs. I can just about tell a poodle from a Rottweiler, but that's as far as it goes.'

'A bichon frise.'

'A what?'

'Bichon frise.'

'Never heard of it. Sounds like the French for beef and chips!'

'Yeah,' jeered Matthew. 'Why not skin it and serve it up for lunch! Or, better still—'

'How d'you spell it?' Adam interrupted, keen to categorize the creature, which had now darted over from Matthew to Phil and was displaying ecstatic pleasure at having discovered yet another chum.

'I'm not sure, to tell the truth. All I know is they can change hands for up to a grand.'

'You're joking!'

'No, I'm not. They're known as yuppie puppies – all the rage with celebrities and film stars and what-have-you. Lola Loveday used to own one, and, when she won her Oscar, the dog was all dolled up in some ritzy gown, the same style as hers, and made by the same designer.'

'Yuk!' said Matthew, grimacing.

'It's a friendly little bugger, though,' Adam mused, as he stroked the curly head.

'Yeah, they're very sociable. Great with kids, so Aunt Fran used to say.'

'Look, *we're* not kids,' Howard said, suddenly appearing from his private office. 'Though it sounds as if it's playtime here. That's quite enough about dogs, OK? And, anyway, it can't stay here. We're busy – or we should be.'

As if to plead its case, the dog jumped up against Howard's leg, scrabbling its dusty paws against his dove-grey trousers, only to be instantly repulsed. 'You'd better ring the police,' he said to Adam. 'Report the dog as lost and let *them* sort it out.'

'But suppose they make me go down to the station? It'll waste a hell of a lot of time, filling in those sodding forms. As if I didn't have enough to do.'

'So why go out for lunch if you're so busy? Some of us make do with a sandwich at our desk.'

'Hardly lunch,' Adam retorted. 'A packet of crisps and a pint. Anyway, I needed a break.'

'We *all* need a break.'

'Look, returning to the dog,' said Matthew. 'It better be gone by three. Frank Foster's coming then, and it's not exactly conducive to our image. I mean, it looks like a bloody powder-puff, and we're meant to be a young, thrusting business at the forefront of technology, not a beauty parlour.'

'Well, what do you suggest? Chucking it out of the window? If it breaks its leg, the owner's bound to sue. Anyway, it's pissing down with rain.'

'What, again?' asked Adam, peering disconsolately through the smeary glass. It seemed to have been raining every day since he split up with Lynette. Not that he missed her – really. Well, apart from the sex, of course.

'And suppose it starts peeing all over the place?' Matthew persisted. 'Or crapping?'

'It won't,' said Adam, with more conviction than he felt. 'It's not a puppy, so presumably it's house-trained.'

'Well, it's bound to yap, and we don't want a hell of a racket when we're trying to talk design.'

'They don't yap, they bark,' Phil informed them, getting up a moment to fetch paper for his printer.

'Worse still.'

'We'll gag it.'

'Throttle it, more like.'

'Look, do be fair,' said Adam, downloading a client's website, yet aware that his attention was still focused on the dog. It had now returned to sit by his computer, and was wagging its plumed tail, as if acknowledging him as its official rescuer. To tell the truth, he liked the sense of being regarded with affection, not to mention trust – rare these days in his personal life. 'It hasn't made the slightest sound so far. In fact, it appears to feel totally at home here.'

'Yeah, that's the trouble. We'll probably be stuck with it for ever.'

''Course we won't! Some frantic owner will move heaven and earth to get it back.' Phil was still struggling with his printer, now sorting out a paper-jam. 'And they're bound to offer a reward. What say we share it, Adam?'

'Bloody cheek! It's me that found it, so it's me that gets the cash. Tell you what, though, I'll treat you all to a pint.'

'Big deal!' said Matthew sardonically. 'But listen, Adam, I've just thought of something else. It's obviously a woman's dog. No male would be seen dead with a poncy thing like that, let alone that god-awful collar – fake diamonds or whatever. Now, you're in need of a new girlfriend, since you gave Lynette the push, and if dogs are meant to resemble their owners, this particular owner's just got to be a bubbly little blonde. Imagine the scenario – gorgeous blonde is heartbroken at loss of precious dog. You return it safely, she becomes your willing slave and—'

'Cut it out! Knowing my luck, the owner will be ancient, hideous and married.'

'Well, grab the reward and run, then. Either way, you can't lose.'

'*We're* losing, though,' Howard remarked, raising his voice in irritation, as he strode out again to intervene. 'Time, as well as business. Let's forget about blondes and concentrate on deadlines, shall we? Adam, ring the police right now and get that thing ejected before it buggers up our deal with Frank.'

'Will do,' Adam muttered, picking up the phone. Having wanted to be rid of the dog, he now felt a certain bond with it, if only because it riled his hated boss.

'Well, I have to say, you're quite a girl.' Settling back in his armchair, Adam stroked the soft white bundle on his lap, and was immediately rewarded with a teasing little tongue-kiss on his nose.

Having never owned a dog, he'd been surprised, indeed relieved, at how docile this one was – no fuss, no wiles, no anguished yelps. It appeared to have accepted him as master, and clearly approved his stylish flat as a damned-near-perfect home. Nor had it complained about the menu, but devoured half a canful of Gourmet Game with gratifying relish. And now it seemed as riveted as *he* was by the European Cup semi-final between Liverpool and Chelsea; its dark eyes fixated on the screen with genuine curiosity. If Lynette had been as accommodating, they might never have had to part. But she hated sport – and football in particular – and, far from eating with zest, merely toyed with her food in a maddening sort of fashion (semi-anorexic, he suspected). Worst of all, she invariably messed the place up with her clutter, refusing categorically to put anything away. Nor was she blonde, petite and cute, but rather on the lanky side, with hair best described as beige.

'So why did you live with her?' the dog appeared to ask, as if tuning in to his every thought.

'Because she was bloody good in bed, mate! Which makes up for a hell of a lot. But if there's too much aggro *out* of bed, a bloke begins to wonder if it's worth it, in the end.'

As he spoke, the dog gazed at him with undisguised devotion:

74

exactly what he wanted from a woman – wanted, but never seemed to find, alas. He needed to be master, in any form of relationship, although you couldn't say so nowadays, of course. With Pooch, he called the tune and she obeyed. He had told her when and what to eat; made it clear that his bed was out of bounds, and that jumping up on his new black leather sofa was also overstepping the mark. And, far from making any protest, she had simply acquiesced in sweet submission. Not only that, he had company, at last, to compensate for the previous lonely weeks, yet was spared the irritation of mindless female chatter. Admittedly, the lack of sex was still a major problem, but he was coming round to Matthew's view that a romantic outcome might just be on the cards. If Matt was right about dogs resembling their owners, then there was a sporting chance he'd meet his ideal woman: combining the darkest possible eyes with the fairest possible hair, as well as being demure and dainty and, best of all, amenable. Only once in his life had he known one – when he was an acne-ridden stripling of fifteen. Charmayne had been a fellow pupil at Thames Valley Comprehensive, although completely unobtainable; not only two years older but so ravishingly beautiful and exceptionally sweet-natured, she would never have involved herself with a plain and spotty schoolboy, in trouble as a bully.

She had remained his model of feminine perfection throughout the years that followed, but never again had he encountered the reality, despite the fact he had changed from uncouth bully to law-abiding bloke. Blondes were two-a-penny, but they invariably had blue eyes and/or stubborn temperaments, always arguing the toss on matters big and small. Yet maybe his luck had changed, at last, and Pooch's owner would have bewitching jet-black eyes, a mass of ash-blonde curls and – almost unbelievable – would allow *him* to rule the roost.

The relief would be enormous. He was pissed off with Internet dating; had met more than enough 'stunning', 'caring' women, all with a 'GSOH' – which, in fact, none of them possessed. And blind dates were equally hopeless. The last two in particular had put him off for life: one a dotty vegan into star signs; the other a near-harridan, who'd spent the evening putting him right when she wasn't putting him down. This time, he knew exactly what he wanted: a submissive, docile meat-eater, who would look at him with total adoration, as Pooch was doing now. He stroked her in sheer gratitude – picturing her owner lying naked in his bed: begging for it, wild for it, agreeing with alacrity to anything he asked, however abandoned or way-out.

Once the match was over (a knuckle-clenching game, resulting in a draw), he gave a gigantic yawn, only now aware how long the day had been. First, the rigmarole with PC Pegg, who'd urged him to phone the RSPCA, as well as Battersea Dogs' Home, and also suggested taking the dog to a vet, in case it had been chipped. Up till then, the word 'chip' had applied to paintwork, potatoes, casinos and golf, but not, repeat not, to dogs. However, 'chipping' turned out to be an identification process, in which a microchip (the size of a grain of rice and containing a special code) was inserted under the skin, thus logging the dog into a central database. Apparently, vets and rescue centres could read the code with a scanner, and so reunite lost pets with their owners. He'd had to wait an age, though, surrounded by a whining, growling bestiary, only to be told that Pooch *hadn't*, in fact, been chipped.

'Why not, my girl?' he asked her now, but her ardent reply – a whole series of fluttery kisses – failed to clarify the matter. Maybe the owner was so sensitive and kind, she couldn't bear her beloved pet to suffer even a second's pain from the needle inserting the chip. Or perhaps she'd assumed in her innocence that the pair of them would never lose each other. He could imagine her delight at being reunited with the dog – although it wouldn't end there, of course. The three of them would stay together; become an instant family. He had never wanted children (another bone of contention with Lynette). Kids were ruinously expensive, not to mention messy and disruptive. But two gorgeous, placid females, with him as C.E.O., would constitute the perfect threesome.

'Hey, listen,' he said. 'Let's go for a stroll to the pub. A bit of fresh air might wake me up, and, anyway, I think we ought to celebrate.'

Pooch didn't need a second invitation, but sprang off his lap with touching eagerness and rushed over to the door; her whole small body quivering with excitement. Lynette would have complained about his 'drinking problem', or said she couldn't be fagged, or insisted they went not to the George and Dragon (where all his mates hung out), but to some pricey, rackety club.

Before leaving, he took off her collar and changed it for the one he'd bought: real leather, but low-key – the plainest in the shop, in fact. He also switched on the answer-phone and double-checked it was working. He couldn't afford to take the slightest chance. Having given his number to the vet, the police, the Dogs' Home and the RSPCA, it would be downright irresponsible to miss the owner's call, when that very call might be the start of a whole new glorious chapter in his life.

'Listen, Howard, I'm sorry to bring her in again, but I just can't leave her shut up in the flat. It's cruelty to animals.'

'And what about cruelty to people, inflicting that thing on the rest of us?'

'Come off it, Howard, the others aren't that bothered. Ask Phil. He actually likes her.'

'Well, I can't say she's any trouble,' Phil conceded, as the dog rushed over to say hello, how are you?

'And what do *you* think, Matthew?'

'Well, I was dead against it at first, but I have to admit, when Angie came in yesterday, she seemed completely smitten with the creature. In fact, I doubt if we'd have persuaded her to sign up with us at all, if Pooch here hadn't charmed her.'

'See, Howard?' Adam crowed. 'Three against one.'

'OK, OK, I'll put up with it the rest of this week, but if the bloody owner hasn't claimed her property by then, it'll have to go to a dog-pound.'

'I'd nick her, if I was you,' said Matthew, 'and sell her for a fortune. They say it's a growth industry, stealing pedigree dogs. I mean, who's to know if you just forget about the owner and make a nice fat profit?'

'*I'd* know,' said Howard acidly. 'And for God's sake, no more dog-talk! I'm off to see Megatron and I expect the rest of you to get on with some work. As for *you*, Pooch, sit down and shut up!'

'You can't really call her Pooch,' said Phil, once Howard was safely out of earshot. 'It's not right for a pedigree. And bichons have real class, you know. Aunt Fran was always telling me how they go back bloody centuries – well, to the 1100s, at least. She said sailors used to barter them, as they moved from place to place, so eventually they were taken all over the world. And later, so she told me, they became all the rage in Renaissance France, a sort of fashion accessory – I suppose what we'd call a must-have for the courtiers. Apparently, one of the French kings used to carry his wherever he went, in a specially made basket, tied with fancy ribbons round his neck.'

'For Christ's sake, don't give Adam ideas! That's all we need to put our clients off – one of our top designers with a bloody berib-boned basket round his neck!'

'Shut up, Matthew! I'm loving this. I mean, it could have been a mutt that followed me out of the pub, and instead I find it's a royal favourite.'

'The Italian nobles doted on them, too,' Phil remarked, strolling to the water-cooler. And they were painted by famous artists like Goya and—'

'So what do we call her?' Matthew interrupted. 'Francesca de Rimini?'

'How about Queenie,' Phil suggested, sipping his water as he ambled back to his desk.

'A bit plebby, don't you think?' Adam settled the dog snugly beside his chair before switching on his computer.

'Princess, then.'

'Not easy to say when you're calling her to heel.'

'Snowball?'

'Twee. And far too obvious.'

'Fang,' said Matthew, grinning.

'Get lost!'

'Well, Fluffy, then.'

'Demeaning. Phil's just told us she's a classy little bitch, so I don't want names like Trixie, Flossy, Lucky and all that sort of thing.'

'Well, give her a proper woman's name – something upper-crust like Olivia or Chloe.'

'Why not Lady Muck, and be done with it.' Matthew slurped his coffee with a complete lack of finesse.

'I know!' said Adam suddenly.

'What?' the others asked, all looking up from their screens.

'Charmayne.'

'That's just as plebeian as Queenie. Who ever heard of a royal called Charmayne?'

'*And* difficult to call.'

'And doesn't suit her any better than Pooch.'

'Yes, it does,' said Adam, smiling to himself. 'It's actually the perfect name.' He gave the dog a congratulatory pat, murmuring to her *sotto voce*, 'I hereby christen you Charmayne. And when your owner comes to fetch you, let's hope she'll be a clone of the first sensational Charmayne!'

'Shit! Who's that?' Adam muttered to himself, jumping as the door-bell pealed. No one called this early on a Saturday, unless – God forbid – Lynette had come storming round to collect her bloody lamp, as she'd been threatening for some time. It was *his* lamp, in point of fact, and he had no intention of handing it over without a showdown, if not fisticuffs.

He strode to the door in annoyance (first turning down the gas beneath his still raw scrambled eggs), flung it open, and was thrown to see a stranger on the step: a small, slack-jawed man, with piggy eyes, pouty lips and bleached-blond hair curling in a halo round his head. The guy's clothes were emphatically camp: blinding-white trousers; flamboyant shirt the colour of crushed strawberries, and a soft white leather jacket, studded along each sleeve with a row of glittery hearts. Oh, my God! he thought.

'So *very* sorry to turn up unannounced.' The voice was breath-less, girly. 'But I dared not waste a second trying to reach you on the phone. The minute I heard you had my dog, I just had to race right round here to make sure that it was true. Please say it is. Oh, please!'

The man's words barely registered. Adam was otherwise engaged – recalling Matthew's contention that dogs resembled their owners. Yes, absolutely right. Here, standing just outside his flat was a curly blond, short in stature, small in size, whose eyes, though barely visible, were undeniably dark. He held on to the door-frame for support, as his new gorgeous, docile female, his new loving, doting family, crumbled into dust.

'Where *is* she? Can you fetch her?' The guy clutched his arm with plump, perspiring fingers, his voice rising higher still.

Adam's own voice seemed hoarse and croaky, as if it had rusted up. He cleared his throat; paused for what seemed aeons, before finally blurting out, 'She ran away.'

'Oh, no!' The cry was so anguished, so close to black despair, Adam all but relented – almost, but not quite.

'Yeah. Last night. She vanished – just like that. I searched the whole damned area, stayed out for hours, got soaked to the skin, in fact. But not a sign of her.'

The man drew himself up to his full height – a pathetic five-foot-four. 'How could you be so careless? That's criminal neglect! You must have left the door ajar, or a window open somewhere, or—'

'For fuck's sake!' Adam shouted. 'I've put up with her for two sodding weeks, fed her on the fat of the land, taken her for endless walks, practically killed myself looking after her, and then you have the nerve to …' He broke off with a twinge of guilt. The only walks Charmayne had had were from the bus-stop to the office, and to and fro to the pub. And her diet never varied now from basic beef or rabbit chunks (half the price of the Gourmet range). Too bad. This man still had a bloody cheek to start accusing him.

'*You're* the one who's careless,' he yelled, returning to the fray, 'for having lost her in the first place. Why the hell did you let her out of your sight? And why leave it almost a fortnight before trying to get her back? That's asking for trouble, isn't it? My place obviously seemed strange to her, so she was bound to escape and try to find her real home.'

The man appeared to collapse, his voice chastened now and whispery. 'Yes, you're right – I'm sorry. She ran away from my mother's house for just that very reason – must have felt unsettled there and become desperate to track me down. But I've been in Tenerife – a little break from this dismal English weather, although now I curse the day I ever went. My silly cow of a mother didn't dare to tell me that Frou-Frou had sneaked off. She knew I'd go berserk, you see, and probably take it out on her. But if only I'd known, I'd have flown back straight away, of course.' Strangling a sob, he continued in a wail, 'When I think that I've been lying on a beach, sunning my stupid self, while my darling dog was wandering the streets.'

Adam opened his mouth to object, when suddenly the fellow seemed to totter on the step.

'Oh, Lord!' he whimpered. 'I'm feeling awfully faint. It's the shock, I'm sure – first the huge relief, then this crushing blow. May I come in a moment? My heart's not all that brilliant and I think I'm—'

Adam pulled him hastily inside, closed the door and steered him towards the nearest seat. He didn't want the blame for a cardiac arrest, on top of all his other problems.

'My name's Tyrone,' the fellow said, appearing to recover suspiciously fast, once he was ensconced in an armchair, sipping a cup of coffee and munching a ginger-nut.

'I'm Adam.'

'Pleased to meet you, Adam. I just wish we could have met in less tragic circumstances. But, look, I want to hear every single detail of how you found my Frou-Frou – where she was, what state she was in, how long it took before—'

'Sorry,' Adam said, 'but we can't waste time on that. What you need to do – and do this very instant – is get down to the police station and tell them she's gone missing again.'

'You mean, you haven't told them yourself? But that's completely irresponsible! Where's your conscience, your basic sense of duty?' Tyrone sprang to his feet, knocking over his cup of coffee, which spread in a dark stain across the immaculate cream carpet.

'Fucking hell!' Adam ran to fetch a cloth and began scrubbing at the stain with the same anger as he berated his accuser. 'For Christ's sake, stop insulting me! I was out all hours last night, looking for your bloody dog, and as for this morning, I haven't had a minute to myself.'

Too true. He'd been up since the bloody crack of dawn, for his 8 a.m. appointment at the poodle-parlour. OK, *he* was to blame for not having groomed the dog. Its complicated double-coat needed daily brushing and, if neglected, became matted and unkempt. Phil had examined all the knots with obvious disapproval; finally advising him to seek help from the professionals.

'Look, I'm sorry about the coffee,' Tyrone had the grace to say, although the concession was short-lived, since in seconds he was back on the offensive. 'But I still think you've been extraordinarily selfish, not to mention heartless. In fact, I don't know how you slept a wink last night, knowing—'

'Get out of my flat – this minute!' Adam interrupted, raising a clenched fist. It had the desired effect, since the lily-livered fellow rocketed out of his chair and charged headlong through the door. Adam watched from the window, as he went panting down the street to his monstrosity of a car: a long, low, vulgar limo, the exact colour of his shirt.

Once he'd scorched away, Adam stormed back to the sitting-room and gave the carpet a second vigorous drubbing, before dumping his ruined breakfast in the bin. His mind was churning with a nauseous mixture of anger, guilt, self-doubt and indecision. Why, in God's name, had he told that string of lies, instead of simply returning the dog? Tyrone must be loaded, judging by his car, and would have shelled out a fat reward – maybe even doubled it when he heard his precious animal was being pampered at Posh Pets. Did he really want to keep her, now that all hope of a romance with an entrancing female owner had blown up in his face? Besides, the creature had outstayed her welcome. There were claw-marks on his best new leather sofa, scratches on the paint-work, muddy footprints right here on the kitchen floor. OK, he enjoyed her company, but was she worth the mess she caused, not to mention the increasing cost? Just today's session at Posh Pets would set him back a cool £50.

In fact, it was almost time to fetch her. They'd given him the earliest slot – the only one available – which meant he'd had to sacrifice his usual Saturday lie-in. Not that weekend lie-ins were likely when you were saddled with a dog – another reason he should have told Tyrone exactly where she was, and let *him* collect her and pay the bloody bill. Maybe he could hare down to the police station, nab the bloke before he left, and report the news that Frou-Frou had returned. It would mean another lie, of course: she'd come back in such a bedraggled state, his only option had been to take her to a dog-groomer.

Would Tyrone believe it? He didn't really care. What bothered him far more was the thought of actually parting with Charmayne. Whatever the hassle and the aggro, they had in truth developed a close bond; spent almost every minute together; working as a duo in the office; watching sport in the evenings, before trotting down to the pub for a pint and a game of darts, then back to the pub at weekends. Indeed, the dog was quite a star among his drinking pals, and he'd noticed several dishy women observing him with interest (which they'd never done before), simply because he owned a cutesy dog.

So what now? Did he fetch Charmayne himself, or go straight to the police station in the hope he'd catch Tyrone? Even if he arrived too late, they'd have the fellow's details on computer, so he could simply phone or email, and arrange to reunite him with his pet. Then, free again, unburdened, he could return to his simple, pre-dog life.

Simple, maybe, but lonely. He reached for the packet of bran-flakes, shook some into a bowl, and tried to force himself to come to some decision – not easy, when such contradictory feelings were clashing in his mind. On the one hand, there was no denying that Charmayne was more difficult to handle than when she first showed up; on the other hand, she worshipped him – the only person who ever had in his thirty years to date. There was also the moral issue of depriving Tyrone of his rightful property, not to mention breaking the poor guy's heart – a heart already dodgy, judging by the recent little episode. And supposing he popped round again, to check if the dog had come back? He might *see* her this time and bust a gut in fury. Should he dye the creature black? Go into hiding? Leave the country? Top himself?

All at once, he tipped the branflakes down the sink, grabbed his wallet, coat and door-keys and swept out of the flat. He *wasn't* collecting Charmayne. Posh Pets would have to keep her longer – all day, if necessary. He was catching a train to Reading, to watch them play Tottenham Hotspur, and refused to spend another minute even *thinking* about dogs.

'So where's your pal?' asked Phil, as Adam slouched into the office, on his own, for once.

'In disgrace.'

'Why, what's the little bugger done?'

'Don't ask.' He threw himself into his chair and stared moodily at the blank computer screen. Bloody females! They always messed things up. In fact, the more he thought about it, the more he realized that Charmayne and Lynette had certain things in common; both bossy and demanding, untidy and unreasonable. And both had started out as paragons, impossible to fault, but gradually deteriorated until they were more or less insufferable. Phil had told him it was *his* fault for failing to exercise the dog or look after it responsibly. But who was bloody Phil to take that sanctimonious tone, just because his aunt knew a bit about the breed? Besides, even Phil would take his side when he heard about last night. The little bitch had actually jumped up on to the table, grabbed the pizza off his plate, dashed into the bedroom with it and dropped it upside-down on the counterpane, where it left a big, red, greasy stain from the tomato and the cheese. And when he shouted at her, she simply barked in defiance, and continued barking frantically all evening, until he'd had furious complaints from both his neighbours.

'No Charmayne?' said Matthew, sauntering in with mug of tea in one hand and a doughnut in the other.

He shook his head.

'You haven't lost her, I hope?'

'No such luck.'

'Why, what's up?'

'Nothing.'

'Listen, mate,' Phil remarked, interfering, as usual, 'you can't leave her in the flat all day. Bichons need a lot of toilet-breaks.'

'You're telling me!'

'Small bladders, I suppose. So what do you plan to do? If you go back every couple of hours, Howard will do his nut!'

'I don't want to talk about it.'

'OK, OK, keep your hair on! You're very grouchy these days, you know.'

Adam said nothing. Of *course* he was grouchy. It was only natural, now he'd come to see that there was no such thing as love. It was always cupboard love, he'd realized, and thus a total con. Charmayne only loved him for the perks he provided: a knob of his breakfast sausage, a bite of doughnut in the office, a saucerful of lager in the pub. And Lynette had been the same. In fact, she had moved in with him originally because his snazzy flat was a definite advance on her own grotty basement bed-sit. And since he earned far more than she did, he was the one who paid for dinners out or trips abroad. Neither she nor Charmayne really gave a shit. And they had both destroyed his property, with no trace of shame or guilt. Lynette had broken his iPod and smashed half his best Heal's china, while Charmayne had chewed two cushions into shreds.

Even now, he was risking the sack. If he went home before the lunch-hour, to let the creature out, Howard might explode. His boss was increasingly miffed about the dog, so would welcome an excuse to rid himself of the pair of them. At present, he was out, thank Christ, seeing a client in Kilburn, but if he returned at noon and found him gone, all hell was bound to break loose.

Well, he wasn't going anywhere. Charmayne would have to wait. His salary, his job, his workmates, meant infinitely more than some unruly, boisterous dog.

'Fucking bloody hell!' Adam barged from room to room, horrified at the sights that met his eyes: a pile of stinking dog-shit on the carpet; a puddle of piss in the kitchen; the new bedspread ripped to pieces; his rubber plant a shattered wreck, knocked over on its side, the ceramic pot broken into shards and earth spilling every-where. And the cause of this destruction was actually rushing up to greet him with effusion, tail wagging in delight.

He beat the dog. Without the slightest compunction. In fact, it was lucky to escape with its life. And, the minute he'd cleared the carnage, he intended to take the brute straight to Battersea Dog's Home. *They* could find bloody Tyrone and restore his precious dog to him. He'd had more than he could take. Besides, if that mincing queen started accusing him again, he couldn't trust himself not to overreact.

For now, he shut the dog in a cupboard and ignored its piteous howls while he got to work with detergent, disinfectant and half-a-dozen cleaning cloths. However, even after his labours, the carpet was still stained, the bedspread quite beyond repair, and the rubber plant fit only for the dump. And a smell of disinfectant and dog-poo still lingered in the air, mingled in one stomach-curdling reek.

He sank on to the sofa, although when he closed his eyes to shut out all the chaos, an image of his seventh birthday party suddenly swooped into his mind, for no reason he could fathom. Yet, there he was, an only child and self-sufficient little lad who preferred his own company to that of other boys, trying to tell his bossy mother that he didn't *want* a party. His mother overruled him, of course, laying down the law in her usual dictatorial fashion, despite the fact he was right, as it turned out. The party guests had broken his best toys; opened presents meant for him (and even nicked a few); grabbed the nicest sandwiches, and gobbled so much birthday cake, he'd been left with only crumbs.

He had realized, at that early stage, that other people invariably spelled trouble, and now, as he sat contemplating, it dawned on him with startling force that it was best to be an only child for ever. If you had to share your space or your possessions, disaster would ensue. He'd seen it with his contemporaries: their elegant houses cluttered up with baby paraphernalia; their once tranquil lives ruined by the demands of wilful kids and nagging wives; their futures compromised by acrimonious *ex*-wives, dunning them for every cent they earned. And he himself had blithely risked the same appalling fate by trying to find a partner. He had always told his girlfriends that children weren't an option, made that clear at the start of all relationships, but it had still been quite a gamble, it struck him only now. A condom might have broken, or some crafty little female pretended she was on the Pill, then presented him with a pregnancy and asked *him* to foot the bills. He'd avoided that, thank God, but he was now stuck with worse than a baby – a dog without a nappy.

He jumped to his feet, determined not to waste a second more. Once he'd delivered Charmayne to the Dogs' Home, he'd come straight back here and revel in his solitude, his privacy and peace. It was Saturday tomorrow, so he'd go out and replace the bedspread; buy another plant; even look at carpet shops and decide if such a major expense was feasible or not.

Such a decision was trifling compared with the all-important one he was making at this instant – the most significant decision of his life: from this day forward he would settle for lifelong bachelorhood; remain single till he died. Never again would he let woman, child or animal come so perilously and shatteringly close.

Christmas Stocking

'So what are you doing for Christmas?' Brigit had to raise her voice above the insistent music throbbing through the pub, and the guffaws of the group at the next table.

Hannah played for time. The question was like 'How are you?' in that, unless you were in radiant health, no one wanted an honest answer. 'I'm … still making up my mind,' she said, faking a casual smile, yet uneasily aware that the correct response should be something more conventional and cosy: 'I'll be with all the family in the country,' or 'at home with the kids, of course.'

'Well, if you fancy joining us at *Chez Antoine*, you're welcome. We booked the table ages ago, but I'm sure they can squeeze one more in. We're quite a crowd already, but – hell, the more the merrier.'

'Thanks, Brigit, it sounds great. But, actually, I'm … thinking of going abroad – you know, for a bit of winter sun, or—'

'Haven't you left it rather late to book?' Karen interrupted.

'Yes, deliberately,' she lied. 'More chance of bargains then. And what about you?' she asked Karen, keen to shift the emphasis from her own Christmas plans – or lack of them.

'Oh, I'm going to my sister's, although I can't say I'm looking forward to it. You see, I'm allergic to my brother-in-law. He invariably gets pissed at Christmas and starts some frightful row.'

'*We'll* get pissed,' said Brigit, taking a swig of her spritzer, as if to undermine the point. 'You can bet your life on it.'

'Yeah, but only nicely pissed. You won't shout abuse, or throw up over the Brussels sprouts. One year, dear precious Philip even wrecked the bloody Christmas cake.'

'You're joking!'

'I'm not. He smashed a bottle down on top of it and reduced it to a mass of crumbs.'

'Shit! What a brute. Why doesn't your sister leave him, for God's sake?'

'Not easy with four kids. Anyway, she says he's great in bed, and I suppose that compensates.'

'It wouldn't for me,' Ruth shuddered. 'Anyway, talking of getting pissed, let's have another round. Hannah, same for you again?'

'No, better not. I'm driving. In fact, I ought to get off pretty sharp, so, if you'll all excuse me—'

'Where you going?' Brigit asked, always the nosy-parker.

'Just ... visiting relatives.' That was true in one sense – dead relatives, at least.

'Well, Happy Christmas, whatever you decide to do!'

'Yes, Happy Christmas!' the others chorused. 'See you on the 2nd.'

'Don't remind me!' Hannah grimaced, although, in truth, she was already counting the days until she was safely back at work. By January 2, the twin obstacles of Christmas and New Year would be over and done with, thank God.

Having collected up her coat and bag, she picked her way between the crowded tables; one group sporting paper hats; another, rather the worse for wear, singing along to the music. 'Jingle Bells', 'Rudolf, the Red-Nosed Reindeer' – the old favourites had been playing in succession. And no corner of the pub was free of its Christmas overlay: garlands, decorations, fairy-lights, holly wreaths, menus boasting turkey dinners, bar staff wearing Santa caps....

She paused at the door to button up her coat, glancing back at her workmates. They'd probably stay here the whole afternoon, getting happily plastered, and normally she, too, would stay – if only not to seem a spoilsport. But for the last two months, she had felt distanced from them all, as if inhabiting a different world – a funereal and grey world, totally out of tune with this gold-and-scarlet junketing. Admittedly, they were all younger than her – mostly in their twenties still, while *she* had reached that stage when hours of drunken partying seemed hardly worth the hangover – but it wasn't just a matter of age. There seemed to be a high brick wall between her and other people, cutting her off in a dark, solitary cell.

It was barely half-past-three as she drove away, yet the street-lamps were already on, and the natural light was waning to a leaden, murky blur. It had been overcast all day, as if the sun had felt too weary to drag itself out of bed, or make the slightest effort to show its face and shine. She nosed along the High Street, turning on the radio, to try to lift her mood, only to switch it off again in the middle of 'White Christmas'. Never before had Christmas seemed so … so relentless. Every bar and shop and restaurant, every radio and TV programme, newspaper and maga-zine, was celebrating the Holy Day of Hype. Which, in the circumstances, seemed almost an affront.

She turned left at the Crown and Anchor (festooned with a couple of reindeer pulling a silver sleigh), then drove the now familiar route: past the common, past the school, then five miles tedious motorway, until the turn-off for the cemetery. Having parked outside the sombre wrought-iron gates, she picked up the bouquet from the back seat of the car, and, cradling it like a baby, trudged along the path towards the grave. She had chosen flowers in preference to a wreath, and tulips rather than lilies, since wreaths and lilies were symbolical of death, whereas tulips suggested spring, new life. She was kidding herself, of course. Her parents were hardly likely to thrust up out of the earth again, like a couple of hardy perennials. The cruellest thing had been losing them both within six months of each other. Yet typical of her mother to follow her husband's lead, as she had done in all their sixty years of marriage. Or perhaps she had simply died of grief, unable to cope without him.

She laid the flowers down on the uneven grassy knoll. The absence of the tombstone made the grave look achingly forlorn, as if it were just some makeshift thing, lacking in formality. The stone had barely had time to settle after her father's death in April, before it was yanked up in October, to allow her mother access. Now, it was at the stonemason's, awaiting its second inscription; delayed, they said, by a glut of winter deaths. The word 'glut' had stung, as if her parents were just part of a production line – or a destruction line, more like.

As she squatted down on her haunches to remove an insolent weed, she seemed to hear her mother ask: 'So what are you doing for Christmas?' – that dreaded question she had fended off at least a dozen times already – in fact, been fending off, in some ways, all her life. She had never told a soul that she had spent every single Christmas cocooned and safe in her parents' house – yes, even as an adult – since it made her sound wimpish and pathetic. Usually, she muttered something about being 'with the family', hoping the phrase implied a whole huge tribe. Her family, in point of fact, were extremely thin on the ground: no siblings – and thus no nieces and nephews – no uncles, aunts or cousins, and no grand-parents on either side – or none that she had ever seen except in photographs.

Not that she'd been lonely, with just her parents for company. And a threesome, for them, had been something of a miracle, since they'd long given up all hope of a child when her mother conceived at the age of forty-five. And, once they had a daughter to spoil, after twenty childless years, they had invariably gone overboard at Christmas, to make up for lost time: storms of cooking, yards of tinsel, miles of paper chains, whole shrubberies of holly and ivy, and enough presents to make Santa jealous. Her mother had even made a brand-new outfit for the Christmas fairy every year, happily sewing tiny taffeta dresses, organza underskirts and stiff-ened, gauzy wings, while her patient dad glued sequins on to wands.

She freed the flowers from their confining sheath of cellophane. It seemed important they should breathe and blossom, not lie coffined in a shroud. 'Well, Mum,' she whispered, 'whatever I do for Christmas, it won't be a patch on yours.'

She picked her way towards the ramshackle structure where garden tools were kept: spades and forks and rakes and suchlike, along with old tin buckets and various odds and ends. Having eventually succeeded in tracking down a vase, she filled it from the watering-can. The cobwebbed corners and musty smell reminded her of her father's garden shed, which, as a child, she had trans-formed into a wigwam, or an igloo, a castle, or a palace, even Noah's Ark. She had probably never been that happy since, she realized, with a pang.

The whole graveyard seemed deserted – no sign of even the surly guy who normally appeared about this time, to round up any stragglers and herd them towards the exit, so that he could lock up and go home. There *were* no stragglers today; no visitors save her; only the shadowy presences of rows and rows of tombstones. Most people, presumably, would either be at work, or struggling to finish their Christmas shopping before tomorrow's general exodus. She envied all those lucky enough soon to be *en route* to some planned and solid Christmas destination. Only failures were alone at Christmas; people on the shelf, like her. She had friends, of course, but most of them were busy with their own families and plans, and although Judith had invited her for both Christmas Day and Boxing Day, she had turned the offer down, suspecting it might have been prompted by an element of pity.

Self-pity was still worse, though, and, as she carried back the vase, she made a conscious effort to reflect on her good fortune, compared with the suffering world. She wouldn't be sleeping rough on Christmas Day, or battling cancer, or being tortured in some foreign gaol, or trying to beg a crust – or even stuck, like Karen's sister, with some violent pig of a husband. In fact, instead of feeling sorry for herself, she ought to volunteer to man a helpline over Christmas, or serve turkey to the down-and-outs. The only problem was, if she broke down and cried in the middle of a call, or the middle of the lunch, it wouldn't be much actual help. Next year, perhaps, when – if – she felt less raw.

Having arranged the flowers as best she could, she stood a moment by the grave, saying a silent farewell to her parents. Thank God there was no one around to see her tears, which continued in the car, making dark stains on her shirt, as she drove back up the hill, then manoeuvred her way through the jammed and busy town, before heading out to Westfield, to deliver Judith's presents. Some of her fellow motorists were visibly frustrated by the traffic jams, blaring their horns, or cutting in on each other, or even winding down their windows and yelling foul abuse. But aggression was just part of Christmas – as was loneliness.

Judith's house blazed with light, outside as well as in. Strings of fairy lights were looped around the doors and windows, and a brilliantly lit Christmas tree stood inside the porch. She glanced up at the sky, so dark and drear in contrast; no stars, no glint of moon-light; only a thick bank of lowering cloud. She shivered suddenly, imagining the zillions of galaxies that dwarfed their own Milky Way to puny insignificance. And those baffling things she'd read about, like Dark Matter and Dark Energy, which not even cosmol-ogists appeared to understand. In fact, as far as she could gather, the greater part of the universe was unseeable, unknowable, immeasurable and inexplicable, so was it any wonder she some-times felt like an ant confronting Everest?

The chimes of the doorbell brought her back to earth, followed by the sound of footsteps pounding down the hall, as Judith's eldest, Patrick, raced to let her in. 'We're just decorating the tree,' he announced, in a tone of breathless self-importance.

'It looks as if it's done already.' She gestured to the shimmering tree, resplendent in the porch.

'No, that one only has lights on. The *second* tree has loads of things. Want to come and see?'

'Just give me a minute to say hello to your mum.' She stepped into the warm, cluttered hall; found Judith at the kitchen table, feeding Alexander.

'Sorry, almost finished. Great to see you – take a pew. Patrick, can you get our guest some fruit juice from the fridge.'

'She's not a guest; she's Hannah.'

'Well, all the more reason to make a fuss of her.' Judith switched the baby to her other breast, mopping up a drool of milk. 'When Ben gets in,' she added, 'we'll have something a bit stronger.'

'Thanks,' said Hannah, as Patrick passed her a stained plastic beaker full of lurid scarlet liquid.

'Patrick, grown-ups get proper glasses – I've told you that already – and give Hannah decent juice, not that ghastly pop stuff.'

'It's not ghastly – it's my favourite.'

'Don't worry, it'll do fine.' Hannah's smile felt forced and false. Watching Judith breastfeed was always an ordeal – the sheer longing for a baby of her own, followed by the surge of panic that it would probably never happen. Her mother had achieved it very late, of course, but her mother had been married then for more than twenty years, whereas *she* had yet to find her man – or at least one who wanted children. Her first boyfriend, Geoff, adored kids, but he'd gone off to be a monk, of all things. And Mark's own unhappy childhood had made him wary of fatherhood, while Andrew had a problem with commitment. And that had been the sum total of her love-life, apart from a few sporadic flings.

'Want to help with the tree?' Patrick asked, jigging up and down impatiently. 'I'm in charge, but I'll let you put a *few* things on.'

'Yes, love to. In a minute, though.'

'Grown-ups always say "in a minute". But it never *is* a minute, more like half-an-hour.'

'Right, ten minutes, I promise – not a second longer.'

'OK,' he agreed grudgingly, before rushing off at his usual frenzied pace. Patrick seemed to explode with energy; even spoke like a radio commercial, trying to pack a spate of words into a quick-fire thirty seconds.

'Where are the girls?' she asked, once he'd thundered along the passage into the lounge.

'Oh, driving Patrick mad, and breaking half the ornaments, no doubt. I know I should be supervising, but it's been a total madhouse here today. My parents came round earlier and stayed the entire morning, then Ben's sister popped in, and—'

'Gosh, d'you want me to shove off? It sounds as if you could do with a bit of peace.'

'Don't you dare go! Friends are different. I just hope you'll excuse the mess. I haven't had a moment to clear up.'

Hannah glanced around at the so-called mess – a source of envy, actually: kids' drawings pinned up on the wall; abandoned toys littered underfoot; children's gloves and woolly hats flung down on the dresser, and a pile of home-made Christmas stockings sharing the table with lengths of felt, pots of glitter and fuzzy stick-on letters. 'Who made these?' she asked.

'Oh, they're all Tara's handiwork. She's made one for each of the family, and an extra one for you.'

'For me?'

'Mm. With your name on. But I mustn't spoil the surprise. She'll give it to you herself, once I can drag her away from the tree.' Judith put the baby over her shoulder and gently rubbed his back. 'So, Hannah,' she asked, looking her friend directly in the eye, 'have you decided yet what you're going to do for Christmas?'

The pause seemed endless; finally broken by a loud burp from Alexander.

Judith laughed. 'That's his way of saying "please come here". We'd love to have you – I've told you enough times. And you can stay as long as you like – right on to New Year, if you want.'

'It's sweet of you, but—' She broke off in mid-sentence, unable to explain her deep unease about carrying off the role of Auntie Hannah, when she wasn't a genuine aunt, in fact, and didn't really belong. Judith always had a crowd for Christmas, all bona-fide relatives, and most of them in couples. She knew she'd feel an interloper, with all that reminiscing about treasured family memories; all those family traditions she wouldn't understand; all those little in-jokes baffling to outsiders, and – hardest to endure – all that kissing under the mistletoe. Even the word 'Mum' could bring a pang of grief, now she had no mother herself, nor child to say it to *her*. She cleared her throat; sat stroking one of the red-felt Christmas stockings. 'Maybe next year, Judith, but this year I'm going abroad.'

It wasn't a lie. She *was* going; had made the decision just now. And she would opt for a destination where Christmas wasn't celebrated in any shape or form, and ensure it was a holiday for singles, so she would be spared the sight of happy, cosy families, at least in the hotel. In fact, once she had done her bit here – helped Patrick decorate the tree, read *Milly-Molly-Mandy* to the girls, said a quick hello to Ben – she would go straight home and make a packing-list, and be waiting outside the travel agent's the minute it opened in the morning.

She shifted from foot to foot as the woman in front of her – a tall, supercilious blonde, too thin for her own good – changed her mind for at least the seventh time.

'No, hold on – I'm not sure I like the sound of that hotel. I do particularly want a sea view, and you told me they'd all gone at the *Vittoria*. In fact, I'm going off the whole idea of Sorrento. Would there be a sea view somewhere else – say, Amalfi or Capri?'

The poor chap behind the desk clearly possessed heroic fortitude. Having duly found a sea view in both Amalfi and Capri, the wretched woman suddenly took agin Italy in general (having already turned down Portugal and Spain), and now switched her attention to Greece.

Hannah listened with increasing impatience as every suggestion made – Santorini, Ithaca, Athens, Skyros, Crete – was tetchily dismissed.

'The problem is,' the clerk explained, 'if you opt for a singles holiday, you're much more limited for choice, especially in the age-band thirty-five to forty-five. They're the most popular, you see, and get booked up months in advance.'

Oh my God, thought Hannah, ears twitching at the phrases 'Singles ... thirty-five to forty-five'. This spoilt, skinny bitch might be just the sort of person she'd find herself beside on a coach tour or excursion; even forced to bunk up with, if all the single rooms had gone. And there might be other people every bit as odious: unhappy spinsters bewailing their lack of partners or their benighted, lonely futures; self-righteous divorcees bitter about their ex's, comparing bloody battles over custody or maintenance, even damning the entire male sex. *She* had never been bitter about any of her men – still loved Geoff, the monk; respected Mark for his honesty, at least, and harboured cherished memories of Andrew, despite his lack of commitment. Did she really want to spend her time with a bunch of miseries, especially when she felt so low herself?

Edging out of the queue, on the pretext of needing more brochures, she picked up 'SINGULAR' from the rack again, and re-read the fulsome promises inside: *Seek adventures in paradise with a group of like-minded singles, who'll soon become firm friends ... Although travelling on your own, never, with us, will you feel alone, or lonely, but move effortlessly beyond yourself into a new, exciting world ... We strive to treat each individual guest as a member of our own family....*

Unlikely. In fact, no more realistic than the improbably blue skies and impossibly blue sea preening in the photographs. Far from a family atmosphere, the reality would be moaners and complainers, like that blonde grouch at the desk, still bleating to the clerk about how she couldn't abide the 'Welcome Parties', laid on as part of the trip. Whatever it was – Welcome Parties, meals or staff, rooms or even sea views – would all be judged sub-standard;

indeed the very *air* would fail to come up to scratch. Better by far to stay at home than be stuck with such companions. Her wisest course would be to treat Christmas like an ordinary day; a chance to catch up on the list of chores she had been postponing since October. No need for elaborate cooking – a sandwich would do her fine – and, once she'd finished her work, she'd spend the evening watching strictly non-festive television.

'Thank you, Blondie,' she whispered, *sotto voce*, to the woman, as she rammed the brochure back into the rack. 'You've just saved me a mint of money, not to mention four wasted days.'

She glanced around the neat and shining flat with a certain sense of achievement. Christmas Eve had proved as good a time as any to tackle the spring cleaning, and at least she'd cleared the decks for tomorrow's marathon, when she intended to update her software, sort out her database, send a shoal of emails, and generally bring order out of chaos.

Part of the plan was early bed tonight, if only to stop herself from dwelling on *last* year's Christmas Eve: her mother decorating the Christmas cake; her father, in a frilly pinny, making his mulled punch (with no hint of the pneumonia that was to kill him four months later). And she, the forty-year-old child, continually offering to help, but being instructed to 'recover' after what they called her 'stressful' job, and just let herself be pampered.

'That's finished,' she hissed. 'Over and done with. You've enjoyed all that indulgence for forty feather-bedded years. Now it's time to move on.'

The flat was mercifully quiet, so at least she wouldn't be disturbed by next-door's music pulsing through the walls, or the usual footsteps clack-clacking back and forth across the wooden floor above. Both those sets of neighbours were away, and the old codger in the flat below never made a sound, so she could catch up on her sleep, as well as with the jobs.

Having undressed and cleaned her teeth, she wished herself goodnight, and pulled the duvet right up to her chin. Outside was frost and snow – traditional Christmas weather. Except for her it *wasn't* Christmas, so, as she settled down and closed her eyes, she forbade her mind to wander along beguiling Christmas byways, but kept it strictly counting sheep (and Muslim sheep, at that).

Five-thousand sheep later, she was still maddeningly awake, so she dragged herself out of bed again to make a milky drink. In the kitchen, she caught sight of the home-made Christmas stocking, which she had deliberately left lying on the table. But perhaps it was unfair to Tara not to hang it up, when the child had taken such pains with it; gluing contrasting strips of felt around the top, and attaching a coloured bead to each wonky, lurching letter of the HANNAH.

In the end, she took it back to bed with her, and sat sipping her drink, while gazing at it hanging from the footboard. The only trouble was, it brought such floods of memories: the pre-dawn excitement as she reached out in the dark, and found the empty stocking transformed with bulging booty. She was allowed to unpack it while waiting for her parents to wake up. (Proper presents came later, and were opened around the Christmas tree, after a breakfast of stewed figs and coddled eggs.) First, she'd tip out all the contents, so she could reach the tangerine nestling in the toe. She could smell the zingy citrus tang as she dug her thumbnail into the peel; felt a spurt of juice on her face; heard the crunching of a pip she'd somehow swallowed in her haste.

Next came the chocolate coins, each encased in gold foil; the foil embossed with magical things like prancing lions and dragons, and the Three Kings, in fancy crowns. Chocolate tasted weird combined with tangerine; the one bland and smooth and velvety, the other sharp and fresh. But both tastes were soon deliciously swamped by the chalky crunch of sweet cigarettes, which came in a proper grown-up packet, with WOODBINES stamped across it. Having wolfed a couple (teeth aching from the sweetness), she would smoke a few more, at leisure; inhaling like her Dad did, tapping imaginary ash into the non-existent ashtray, and blowing pretend smoke-rings at the ceiling. And, once she'd extinguished the butts, it was time to unwrap the tiny gifts, feeling them first through the paper, trying to guess their contents from the shape. Sometimes, it was bath salts, the gritty sort, in psychedelic colours like puce-pink or peacock-blue, which never quite dissolved in the bath, so she'd find herself sitting on a little pile of gravel. Or there might be a new hair slide she could wear for Christmas lunch: a red plastic flower or turquoise butterfly. And always a glass animal; triple-wrapped in tissue, so its frail legs wouldn't break. And, usually, a diary – one year a Barbie Diary, the next a Hungry Caterpillar, or maybe Raold Dahl, or Tolkien, or the Nature-Lovers' Companion. And, her favourite of all, when she was eleven-and-a-half, a leather-covered beauty in a padded pink-plush box, with its own tiny lock and key.

But whatever diary it might be, she always did the self-same thing: flicked swiftly through the pages, almost to the end, until she reached Christmas Day the *following* year, and wrote HAPPY CHRISTMAS HANNAH!, in big capitals across the page. She wasn't sure exactly why – perhaps to remind herself that, once this current Christmas was over (indeed fading to a blur), another one was waiting to explode in all its glory, with pantomimes and carols, new toys and games and books, huge crackling, golden turkeys, squidgy-sweet mince pies.

It was only as she drained her milk she realized that she'd been awash in forbidden Christmas thoughts – in fact, so lost in child-hood memories, she had forgotten bleak reality. With a sigh, she switched off the lamp, so she could no longer see the stocking, and, having settled down to sleep again, forced herself to resume her task of sheep-counting.

However, by the time another hour had passed, her antipathy to sheep had increased to such proportions, she would have happily asphyxiated every ewe and ram in the known world and beyond. Wearily, she got up once more, to find a magazine. Reading an undemanding piece about fashion or celebrities might help her to relax.

In the lounge, she stopped to look at her parents' photograph, taken just a year ago. How spry they still looked, despite their total age of 176 years! They had never become doddery, or vacant and confused, but remained vigorous and sharp until a few months before their deaths. Pressing her lips to each face in turn, she gave each a tender kiss; relieved that none of her friends were there to see. She was already considered peculiar for having loved them so immoderately, when it was more fashionable these days to accuse parents of abuse, or at least of negligence. She gazed at her mother's mild blue eyes; the gnarled, veiny hands folded on her lap; the hair arranged in soft, white, Mr-Whippy waves, and freshly permed for the occasion of the photograph. Next, she studied her father: his shy, unassuming expression, as if overwhelmed by the honour of a professional photographer actually coming to their home, with a camera on a tripod, and special lights and filters. *She* was the one who'd organized the session, as a present to herself; wanted her parents immortalized on a scale beyond the casual photos taken on her mobile.

She tucked the gilt frame under her arm, then, having fetched some magazines, stood it on the dressing-table, where she could see it from her bed. Her parents could keep guard while she read her *Cosmopolitan*. Soon, she was deep in an article on fashion, although increasingly annoyed by the stress on 'must-have' items – 'must-have' knee-high boots, 'must-have' beaded evening-bag. She glanced at the Christmas stocking: flat and empty still. It was way past midnight, yet Santa hadn't come. And he *wouldn't* come; had completely failed to grasp her own personal list of 'must-haves': a decent man, and marriage, a brood of lovely children, commitment, lifelong love.

Flinging the magazine on the floor, she stumbled out to the bathroom to find the sleeping pills. Her GP had prescribed them after the two bereavements. But she hadn't wanted her grief dulled; felt it only fitting that she should lie inconsolably awake after such a loss. She took a couple now, though. They would make her pretty dopey in the morning, but she no longer even cared. She had nothing to get up for – no one to get up for – and the jobs she'd planned would simply have to wait.

As she returned to her room, she almost ripped the Christmas stocking from the bed. All it did was emphasize her empty, fruitless life; nothing of any value in it; not even sweet frivolities.

'Thanks for nothing, Santa,' she muttered, pulling the duvet right over her head and praying for total oblivion.

Her mind felt slack and soupy as she opened her eyes to darkness. She sat up in a daze, and suddenly glimpsed the Christmas stocking hanging at the end of the bed – a *bulging* Christmas stocking.

She rubbed her eyes in disbelief. It must be some trick of the light – except there wasn't any light; just the gleam of a tangerine, winking at her from the bottom of the stocking.

Her hand groped out towards the bedside lamp, only to pause as it found the switch. OK, she might be mistaken. The sleeping pills could well have blurred her faculties, especially as she had taken them so late. But that first miraculous glance had showed the stocking full to overflowing, just as in her childhood, so why check on its reality, try to prove it an illusion?

She lay back, closed her eyes, began the wondrous process of unpacking all the treasures. First, the tangerine, tingly in her mouth, than the overlay of chocolate, velvety and smooth, followed by the sugary crunch of the WOODBINES. Next, the bath salts – gritty and puce-pink; then the hair slide: black and white, in the shape of a cat, with twinkly emerald eyes. Then the tiny glass giraffe, triple-wrapped in tissue, so its long neck wouldn't break. And the most perfect diary in the world, a big, important, scarlet one, its pages edged in gold, like a Bible or a Prayer Book, and with a matching gold-and-scarlet pen attached.

Having uncapped the pen, she flicked swiftly through the pages, almost to the end, until she reached Christmas Day next year. Then she wrote in big, bold capitals, HAPPY CHRISTMAS, HANNAH!, right across the page.

And, suddenly her grown-up self knew, beyond all doubt, that next Christmas *would* be happy. Impossible to explain. In fact, in the absence of her parents, she would surely still feel aching loss. Yet, that inner voice continued to assure her that, despite the grief, despite the loss, things would be transformed.

She lay mystified, head muzzy from the pills. None the less, she couldn't help but entertain the faintest gleam of hope – like the orange gleam of the tangerine she thought she might have seen.

Had she seen it? Truly? It was just possible, perhaps. As was the hope of happiness.

Just possibly.

Perhaps.

Turning Point

'Do you *have* to go, my love?'

She nodded, already sitting up and throwing off the duvet. But he caught her by the waist and drew her down again, pressing his hot, damp body into hers.

'The time always goes too quickly,' he whispered, twisting his fingers through a strand of her hair, as if to hold her captive.

Not for me, she thought, hating her own edginess. Couldn't she enjoy a few brief hours of pleasure without the continual worry that clamped her in its jaws these days? Her body might be here, with Rory, but her mind was still at home. She kissed him, in compensation – a long, tender, lingering kiss.

'Please stay a wee bit longer.'

'I'm sorry, Rory darling, but I can't.' Determinedly, she slipped from his embrace. 'I'll shower first, OK?'

'OK.'

The shower seemed a vital part of the affair: washing off not just his sweat and smell, but her anxiety and guilt. She ran the water as hot as she could bear, then used the balding nail-brush to scrub his traces down the sluice. Returning to the bedroom (the skimpy towel covering only her bottom half), she found Rory still sprawled full-length on the bed, clearly intent on luring her back.

'Just one more kiss before you go.'

She shook her head. Wonderful to be adored, but he didn't understand her situation. 'Shower's all yours. I've left you the decent towel.'

'I'm sorry things are so basic here.'

'Don't worry, I don't mind.' It amused her, actually, that they should meet in this bare, shabby room above a charity shop. It seemed fitting, in a way, that below them should be stacks of stuff – faded, old and second-hand – when they, too, were past their prime. And at least they were safe from discovery, since the flat was vacant at present, and Rory had an arrangement with the owner – an ancient, unsuspecting guy, who asked no awkward questions. And, as the shop was a good twenty miles from both their respective homes, there was little danger of running into anyone who might gossip or tell tales.

As she towelled her hair, she peered down at the street: people bustling along the pavement with shopping bags or pushchairs; couples taking tea in the café opposite; a group of children wobbling past on bikes. This small, pretty town didn't seem quite real; merely the backdrop to their monthly meetings, and comprised of just one room; its other streets and whole civic life mysterious and closed to her. Rory, too, was something of a mystery, since he had told her almost nothing about his job or wife or home. She knew only part of him – the lover, not the husband; the playmate, not the boss. Having never had an affair before in thirty years of marriage, she'd had to learn the rules: don't discuss your spouse; leave your problems and your guilt behind.

Easier said than done.

She squinted in her powder-compact to re-apply her lipstick and comb her tousled hair. There was no mirror in the room, let alone a dressing-table, so she did her toilette sitting on the bed. Then she smoothed the sheets and duvet, plumped the one thin pillow and tidied their few things away: wine bottle and glasses, half-eaten chocolate bars, two empty Durex wrappers. She it was who insisted on the condoms, fearing pregnancy as much as infection, despite being fifty-one. Four children were enough, and, as yet, there hadn't been the slightest sign of the menopause. Perhaps she was a freak of nature and would avoid it altogether, while her less fortunate contemporaries burned and drowned in hot flushes and night sweats.

'Delia, are you sure I can't drive you home?' Rory reappeared, damp-haired from the shower, the large, purple towel looped around his neck.

'Positive.' His body still intrigued her. Naked male bodies had featured very rarely in her life – other than her husband's, of course. Indeed, she hadn't even realized that penises could vary quite so much. Morris's was thin and long and now retired from active service, whereas Rory's was short and squat and super-charged. The two men were different in other basic ways: Morris tall and skinny, his pale, myopic eyes half-hidden behind specta-cles; his soft, white, straggly hair thinning with each passing year, whilst stocky, thickset Rory had emphatically dark hair (barely tinged with grey, as yet), which grew exuberantly thick and strong, and required constant taming and trimming by the barber. He was combing it now, the small, brown, plastic pocket-comb no match for its unruly strands.

'I hate to think of you struggling on the bus.'

'I don't struggle – I just sit and read. When you've never learned to drive, Rory, you get used to public transport.' In truth, Morris had been her transport all these years, and the fact he could no longer drive had been something of a shock – one of many, recently.

Rory came up behind her, ran his fingers sensuously along the nape of her neck. 'They forecast heavy rain for later on, and I don't want you getting wet. I know you always worry about people seeing us together, but I could drop you half a mile away – that should be safe enough.'

'No, it's still a risk.' She couldn't really tell him that she preferred to travel back alone; needed time to change from the role of mistress to that of wife and carer. 'And I'm well prepared, in any case, with an umbrella and a mac. In fact, I'd better get off right away. It's already clouding over.'

They always left separately, in case anyone was watching. Unlikely, in a strange town, but she was determined to be ultra-careful.

'OK, but I insist on a nice kiss goodbye.'

Rory held her both too fiercely and too long. Occasionally it irked her to be needed quite so desperately by yet another person in her life. 'Must go,' she repeated, squirming to extricate herself.

'Promise one day we'll have longer together, so we can try out lots of wild, exciting things. I'd like you to get here first thing in the morning and stay all afternoon. Go on – say you will.'

'I will,' she mumbled anxiously, wondering *how*, for heaven's sake.

*

'Morris!' she called, preparing her lies, as she let herself into the house. Not that lies were really necessary. He would have long ago forgotten where she'd pretended to be going. Indeed, even were she to admit straight out that she'd been in bed with a lover, that, too, was bound to slip his mind, given half an hour. Yet shame and apprehension were fluttering through her stomach – inevitable when she returned from these assignations.

She shook out her umbrella and removed her dripping mac, hoping Morris hadn't opened any windows. The forecast had been right; the late-September sunshine giving way to blustery wind and rain, as if even the weather was mourning the fact that she and Rory were now parted for four weeks.

'Morris!' she called again, surprised to hear no answering shout. He wasn't in his usual chair in the sitting-room, nor in the kitchen, or the room they still called his office, nor upstairs in the bedroom. She checked the bathroom and the lavatory, beginning to feel seriously alarmed. Surely he wouldn't be outside in such a deluge, although she tried the garden anyway, getting drenched in the process. She even peered into the potting shed – despite the fact his gardening days were over – found nothing but a spider and the remains of a dead bird. He must have left the house, but that, too, was inexplicable, since he never went anywhere without her. Having lost his confidence together with his memory, he now relied on her as chaperon and nanny, and always waited till she was back before venturing out, even just down the road. Could he have popped next door, perhaps, tired of his own company?

'Sorry to bother you, Peggy, but I wondered if you'd seen Morris?'

'No, but I've only just got in. Why? What's wrong?'

'Nothing – don't worry.' Hastily she backed away; hated the neighbours' pity. Dementia was shaming, especially in a man of only sixty-five. The fourteen-year age-gap between them had never mattered before. Up till just nine months ago, Morris had been his usual self: lively, energetic, keen on new experiences, young in heart and spirit.

Embarrassed by her predicament, she tried the other houses in the street, only to draw a blank each time. Rain and wind notwithstanding, she would have to go out and search for him; scour the shops, the church, the library and the park – all the places she took him in the course of a normal week. And this must be a warning to her. Never again could she leave him alone. When she next arranged to meet Rory, she must book a sitter, or at least ask one of her daughters to come over. But how could she lie to her daughters? If she fabricated some excuse, she was bound to blush or stammer or tie herself in knots, and they would never, ever forgive her if they discovered her infidelity. They were avowed 'Daddy's girls', all four.

However, there wasn't time to speculate, now that Morris had gone missing. For all she knew, he might have wandered off without his coat – or even shoes. It was her own stupid fault for not having locked the doors, but she couldn't bear the thought of treating the man she'd married like a prisoner in detention. Well, this was her due punishment for having risked her husband's life and health in order to shag a virtual stranger.

'Stop here, Tom! I think I saw someone sheltering under those bushes.'

As her son-in-law pulled up the car with a jerk, Delia scrambled out, feeling close to panic. If she herself was hungry, wet and tired, then Morris, who'd been lost for hours, would be exhausted, famished and soaked to the skin. And maybe dangerously disoriented, on top of everything else. And suppose they didn't find him? He could have died of exposure; been hit by a car as he blundered across the road.

'Wait, Mum!' her daughter shouted. 'You'll trip and fall if you don't watch out.' Nicolette caught up with her as she ran towards the bushes, stumbling in the dark. 'Slow down, for goodness' sake!'

Delia took no notice; went racing on towards the shadowy figure now looming into focus. 'Morris, it *is* you! Thank Christ! Are you all right?'

He didn't answer, just stared at her in confusion, as if he no longer recognized his wife of thirty years. And, yes, he was coatless, hatless; his best shoes caked in mud; his hair plastered to his head in dripping strands.

'Morris, speak to me. Tell me you're OK.'

'Don't press him, Mum. He's in a state of shock.'

Delia took off her coat and draped it round his shoulders, then she and Nicolette led him to the car – a slow and halting process.

'Why on earth did you go all this way?' she asked, once she was sitting in the back with him, his cold hand clasped in hers.

'Mum, he doesn't want to talk, Just leave him be until he's got his bearings.'

Did her daughter have to interfere? She *needed* to know what had happened; otherwise her own life would be thrown into chaos, just as much as his. Never before had he strayed so far from home; never acted unpredictably, or been completely lost for words like this. True he'd suffered memory problems, a loss of interest in the outside world, and some measure of confusion, but nothing on this scale. He seemed to have aged a decade since this morning, and to be deteriorating before her very eyes.

They drove back through torrential rain; the headlamps lighting up great swathes of water on either side of the road. Tom said very little, maybe secretly resentful at having been dragged out on a rescue mission when he'd planned on playing squash. Nicolette, however, kept plaguing her with questions.

'So where were you, Mum, all afternoon?'

'Just … shopping.'

'But couldn't you have taken Dad with you?'

'It, er, wasn't convenient.'

Silence. The word 'convenient' hung in the air, sounding callous, even cruel.

'I mean, the whole point of giving up your job was so you actually be *there*.'

'I *am* there, mostly, Nicolette, but just occasionally I need a break.' She had no desire to discuss Morris with her daughter, as if he were a mental case, and with no idea of what was going on in *his* mind.

'Ask *me*. I'll come and help.'

'You can't, with a full-time job.'

'Look, my boss is pretty decent. And he knows the situation. In fact, if you'd like me and Tom to stay over tonight—'

'No,' she said, too quickly. 'We're fine now, aren't we, Morris?' She squeezed his hand, but felt no answering pressure from the stiff and chilly fingers. It was as if part of him had died. 'How about a nice warm bath as soon as we get in?'

He didn't appear to have heard; was clearly inhabiting some nightmare world, closed to other people. She continued talking to him, however, if only to stop her daughter butting in. 'I'll make you a hot drink, and how about some scrambled eggs, or a cheese and mushroom omelette? Then we'll have an early night and—'

Hardly early. It was already after nine. She had searched alone, on foot, at first, and only in increasing desperation had she phoned all four of her daughters, in case by any chance they'd heard from him or seen him. Which meant they were bound to keep checking on him in future; pestering her with phone-calls to find out how he was. Of course, she shouldn't be ungrateful – she was extremely lucky to have their help at all – but none of them could understand how hard it was to be a full-time carer. *They* still had their precious independence, and jobs with intelligent colleagues, that included meaningful discussions of art or sport or politics. They could even go on holiday – see the world, spread their wings. Her own life, in contrast, had shrunk, and her main tasks at present were taking Morris to appointments with the psychologist or geri-atrician, and keeping him 'mentally stimulated' (as the doctors recommended) with simple little word-games and childish puzzles and quizzes. Was it any wonder that she had responded to Rory's overtures; jumped at the chance of reinstating some small part of a satisfying adult life?

Yet, looking at her shivering wreck of a husband, with his vacant stare, his expression of bewilderment, she felt the deepest pity, overlaid with fierce remorse. There was nothing for it – Rory would have to go. Immediately. With no reprieve.

'Delia, it's Rory. Can you talk?'

'Er, sort of.' Guiltily she glanced around, but Morris was upstairs, asleep. For some unfathomable reason, he'd begun dozing all day and lying awake all night – expecting *her* to engage in conversation throughout the wee small hours.

'Know what day it is the Thursday after next?'

Yes, she thought, Tom's birthday. She had already bought him a sweater and a box of champagne truffles.

'St Valentine's! Which means we have to meet.'

'But it's only a week since the last time.'

'I know, but this is special. Surely you can get away?'

'There's no "surely" about it, Rory.'

'Won't your daughters help?'

'Jodie can't – she's ill. And Nicolette's away. And Nell has both her children down with measles. In fact, she's going spare as it is, because her ogre of a boss has no sympathy at all for working mothers.'

'Well, what about Amanda?'

'I don't like to ask her again so soon. She'll think it weird that I have to keep going out. And, anyway, she'd need to take time off work. If only you could make an evening, it wouldn't be so difficult.'

'Darling, evenings are impossible. You know that.'

Yes, she did know, but he had never told her why, in fact. Was his own wife ill, or scared of being burgled if he left her alone in the house at night? Or did he have some sort of evening job, or charity commitment? His life was a closed book. That was one of the rules, but it was beginning to annoy her. It seemed unnatural, if not insulting, that he should shut her out so completely from all aspects of his existence beyond the lecherous.

'Look, we could make it just a quickie on the Thursday.'

Forty miles return, on a slow and bumpy bus, for the sake of 'just a quickie'?

'And I could come and pick you up, if that would help.'

'*No!* Leave it with me, OK? I'll sort something out and ring you back tomorrow.'

Once she'd put the phone down, she paced up and down the sitting-room, staring out at the spindly, naked trees, and wondering what to do. The last two meetings with Rory had lacked their usual magic. She couldn't quite explain it. He was still ardent and adoring; still a generous, imaginative lover. And it wasn't simply guilt. True she'd defaulted on her promise not to see him any more, but she'd managed to persuade herself that this breach of faith was justified. In the four-and-a-half months since Morris had gone missing, her life at home had deteriorated so much, she felt she was entitled to a monthly 'reward', in return for giving up her sleep – and sometimes, it seemed, her sanity. On top of losing her job, she had lost her entire social life. Most people kept away now, unable to cope with Morris's aggression. Once the gentlest of men, he'd actually physically attacked two of her close friends, then on Christmas Day, of all days, he'd overturned the tea-table in a fit of silent rage, breaking her precious china in the process.

She didn't blame him, in fact. Changes in personality were simply part of his condition, and the doctor had explained that some patients' violent outbursts were due to their frustration at not having any words to express deep-seated feelings. However, it didn't make life easy, especially as his conversation was either maddeningly repetitive or frighteningly irrelevant. He even forgot her name on some occasions, and neglected to wash himself or dress himself, or even reach the toilet in time, without her constant supervision.

Which surely meant she needed Rory as antidote and compensation. Yet she was increasingly distressed by the fact that, despite their sexual bond, they were so far apart emotionally and mentally. She couldn't live her life in such separate compartments, closing the door on Morris once she opened the door of the charity shop, yet Rory seemed oblivious of the stress and strain it caused. Just because it suited *him* to keep his domestic situation a matter of strict secrecy, it didn't mean she felt the same. It would actually help enormously if he let her talk things over before they got down to the sex, then she would gradually relax and be able to respond. Instead, she was expected to switch instantly from exhausted carer to avid, red-hot lover, without any chance to unwind or get things off her chest.

Perhaps exhaustion was the key, though, and she was simply overtired and judging everything in light of that fatigue. It would be crazy to give him up – a man fifteen years younger than Morris, who worshipped her body, made her feel desirable. And even more ridiculous to spend Valentine's Day coaxing her husband to finish up his broccoli, or explaining for the umpteenth time that the right shoe went on his right foot rather than the left, when she could be being pleasured by her lover.

Sidling into Gloria's Gifts, she gave a quick glance behind her, feeling her usual guilt at being here in Berkshire again, especially when was meant to be in Winchester, visiting an imaginary friend with cancer. Still, it was extremely unlikely that anyone would see her and, anyway, she had time to kill. Her bus had got in early, whereas Rory was caught in traffic and had rung her on the mobile just ten minutes ago. Besides, she hadn't had a chance so far to buy him anything, and he was bound to bring her flowers, or chocolates – maybe even both.

She began searching through the Valentine cards, trying to find a suitable one. All the words seemed wrong: 'Valentine, you're truly mine'. Hardly, when he was married to someone else and their meetings were so restricted in terms of time and place. 'You're everything I dreamed of, the answer to my prayer.' Again, a little far-fetched. 'My heart belongs to you for ever.' She was, in fact, Morris's for ever, so perhaps she should be buying *him* a Valentine. Yet it had been difficult enough this year for him to grasp the concept of Christmas. Valentine's Day would be totally beyond him.

She found herself distracted by the Valentines for pets. Perhaps easier to choose one for a beloved cat or dog than for a husband with dementia, or a lover whose sole concern was focused on her genitals. 'I love you more than words can say.' No – avowals of love were somehow inappropriate. Rory had never said he loved her, and the word seemed almost a mockery when he refused to take the slightest interest in her private life or circumstances. How could he love a woman he didn't even know?

Abandoning the cards, she wandered round the rest of the shop, beginning soon to overdose on hearts: heart-shaped candles, cushions, sunglasses and soaps; heart-shaped tins of sweets and biscuits; heart-shaped lockets, pendants, key-rings, even a heart-shaped coin-holder. Actually, it was pretty futile to buy a gift at all, since Rory wouldn't be able to take it home. And if *he* had spent a fortune on some elaborate bouquet or sexy piece of lingerie, that, too, would have to be ditched. It would look extremely suspicious if she arrived home from a cancer ward with a dozen red roses or a tarty scarlet thong. She just hoped he'd opted for chocolates, although even those posed problems. They could hardly pig a whole lavish box in less than a couple of hours, especially when he'd want to commandeer her mouth for more important things.

She checked her watch. He had explained he wouldn't ring again, but just see her in the flat at 2.15. It was now five past, so she returned to the cards and chose a large, expensive one that said 'You light my fire'. That *had* been true – save for the last two disappointing occasions – and, with any luck, the spark would reignite this afternoon.

As she approached the charity shop, she was concerned – indeed alarmed – to see a group of people crowding round the entrance. Her first thought was for Rory. Had something happened to him: a heart attack or stroke, as he climbed the narrow stairs? Only as she edged a little closer did she realize what was going on. The front window of the shop had been shattered by a brick or stone; the glass dangerously splintered, and surrounding a large hole. One policeman stood examining the damage, while another two were remonstrating with a gang of teenage boys, while the elderly ladies who ran the shop huddled in the doorway, looking shocked and tearful.

Hastily she backed away, her natural instinct to avoid the law, as if she herself were guilty of some crime. Ducking down a side-street, she tried to work out what to do. If Rory was already upstairs in the flat, he might not dare to phone her, for fear of being overheard. Annoyingly, he had never got to grips with texting and, despite the fact she'd pointed out that it was hardly rocket science and that kids of six could text, he still insisted there wasn't any need. Well, now there *was* a need: to convey information silently, when police investigations were in progress. He would certainly want to avoid the spotlight, just as much as she did. Yet how could they communicate, meet up?

'Calm down!' she told herself. The whole thing would be over if she waited a short while. The crowd would disperse, the police would march the boys away or let them off with a caution, and the street would return to its normal quiet placidity. All she had to do was make herself scarce for ten minutes or so, then creep back surreptitiously. At least the weather was good – a perfect day, in fact, with skies the colour of a duck-egg.

Venturing round the corner, she walked down another narrow lane and suddenly came out by the canal. Despite her several visits here, she had never so much as glimpsed it before, having always gone directly home, in order not to be seen. Yet the stretch of tranquil water looked idyllic: overhung by willows, with even a few daffodils in bloom along the bank. Almost without thinking, she began to pick her way along the muddy towpath, grateful for the silence and the peace. It was so long since she'd been out on her own; away from problems and dilemmas; away from a husband who clung to her like a confused and frightened child. A pair of coots were building their nest; the male bird bringing twigs in its beak, which the female inspected carefully, even rejecting a few as duds. She laughed at the bird's sheer bossiness and fussiness; the sound surprising her. Laughter was a luxury these days.

Elated, she walked on, noticing the yellow glaze on the willows, and the green thrust of nettles sprouting in the hedge. Even one brave butterfly had dared to emerge and was trying out its wings. Recently, she'd become blind and deaf to the seasons (except as they affected Morris), but here spring seemed almost tangible. She could smell it, taste it, touch it, feel it warm and refreshing on her face. And her ears, long attuned to Morris's cries of distress, now registered the birds, chirruping and twittering around her. She could make out a blackbird's song, and the beep-beep-beep of a great tit, followed by the sharp squawking of a moorhen, then the blackbird started up again, with its melodious refrain. All at once, she, too, began to sing. Why not, when there was nobody to hear? She ran through her small repertoire of love songs, noting how much anguish they contained: lovers racked by jealousy or loss; maddened by rejection, nursing broken hearts. Safer to be a daffodil, visited by the occasional bee, than a human being entangled in some difficult relationship.

Ahead of her she could see a barge tethered to the bank. She ran up to examine it, admiring its green-and-scarlet livery and the garland of pink cabbage-roses painted on the prow. It brought back forgotten memories of the one canal-boat holiday she'd been on as a child: the excitement of sleeping in a tiny cabin and waking up to wood-smoke as her mother stoked the stove; the gentle rocking motion as she lay on her bunk at night, and the whole wonderful palaver of the locks. Her father would leap out of the boat, heave both lock-gates shut, then run to the other end of the lock and open the sluice-gates, with the aid of an ancient crank-handle. A rush of water would churn into the lock with a thrilling sort of roar, and her tummy would churn, too, as if it were full of floaty bubbles. Then, after a tense wait, she'd feel the boat rise magically, like something in a fairy-tale, and the trees and fields that had disappeared while they were coffined in the lock would suddenly be there again, as they glided out and on.

The irony of childhood was that you didn't realize at the time how fortunate you were to be free of responsibilities, of worries, duties, ties; free of all the complications of sex and marriage and motherhood; free of the obligation to be a responsive, passionate lover. It struck her with a jolt that she'd been happier these last few minutes than at any time throughout the last grim year, including her times with Rory.

God, she thought, I'm meant to be with Rory *now*! She had totally forgotten him, yet he would be waiting for her, worrying, maybe searching for her in the street, and increasingly concerned. She turned on her heel and began racing back the way she'd come, then stopped, unsure, wondering why he hadn't phoned. Perhaps he'd got caught up in the whole drama of the broken window; even been detained as a witness. For all she knew, the police might still be there, taking a statement not just from him but from the two twittery old ladies who ran the charity shop. Or maybe they had rung the owner and were refusing to let anyone leave the scene of the crime until the old boy turned up. Perhaps she and Rory *couldn't* meet today; would simply miss each other altogether, on account of this random incident.

Somehow she didn't want to speculate about it, or spend any more time fretting over Rory – *or* about St Valentine's, with all its commercial hype and tawdry promises. Her overriding urge was to stay beside this serene and sparkling water, where everything in sight was renewed and reinvigorated, part of a spring explosion; a bounteous release from the drag and dirge of winter. Impulsively, she switched off her phone and continued on along the towpath, away from Rory and the town. This particular canal, she knew, went all the way to Bristol – a good eighty miles, she'd guess. The way she felt at present, she could walk that eighty miles. Extraordinary though it sounded, her former tiredness had entirely disappeared, together with her sense of long stagnation.

In fact, she began to increase her pace, until she was swinging along with a jaunty, rhythmic stride, and imagining the barge-horses clip-clopping along this very path, two centuries back, or more. She could see the clouds reflected in the water and longed to be a cloud herself, floating free and weightless. Passing another longboat, she gave a cheery wave to the owner, who was lounging on deck, with a book and a bottle of beer. The man waved back and, as she returned his smile, she was aware of her stiff face-muscles actually daring to relax. Smiling, like laughing, was a skill she had all but lost.

'Turning Point, 200 yards,' announced a notice on the bank, and, yes, ahead she could see a widening of the canal, one of many, constructed long ago when the waterways were built, to allow barges to turn round. As she walked towards it, she watched a drake come coasting down to the water, with a flash of its green head and a high-pitched 'quork, quork, quork'. It went skittering along the surface, landing with a splash, feet-first like a glider, then shook itself with a self-satisfied air, before paddling away on some important mission. Perhaps she'd be a bird, in preference to a cloud: a creature that acted on instinct; that didn't own a watch (or phone); that relished the simple magic of the moment, instead of dreading the future or regretting the past.

A woman was approaching; a small black mongrel gambolling at her heels. 'Glorious weather, isn't it?' she said, stopping to throw a stick for the dog.

'Yes, lovely.'

Lovely, too, to encounter people who didn't ask how Morris was, or shake their heads in gloom about the 'dreadful situation'. Morris, of course, would be expecting her back – or at least Amanda would. *He*'d have totally forgotten where she was and why.

Well, Amanda would have to wait. Because she was suddenly aware that she, too, had reached a turning point: her life would have to widen, change direction, expand beyond its confines. The details were still vague, but her present plan was just to keep on walking, to follow the canal until she had worked out some sort of compromise between her duties as a carer and her longing to escape. She had no food, no drink, no luggage – no shelter for the night, should she be away that long. But the whole joy of this mad escapade was to be unburdened, for once, with nothing weighing her down; nothing to do except let her mind roam free until it hit on a solution. Rory, of course was part of the imbroglio, but one of the changes she envisaged for the future was an end to all the lies. She hated the deceit she'd been enmeshed in for so long; hated her own hypocrisy, when she had always taught her daughters the value of the truth. And on this occasion, she'd tell Amanda the plain, unvarnished facts: she'd been out on an extended walk, along the Kennet and Avon Canal. Her daughters would be worried; maybe suspect she was losing her marbles, but they were used to that, with Morris, and would simply have to face the prospect of *two* demented parents.

Laughing at the thought, she jumped aside as an old man on a bike wobbled perilously towards her.

'Good day,' he mumbled, in danger of overbalancing as he tried to doff his hat to her whilst steering a straight course.

'It's more than just a good day,' she said, clearly and out loud, not caring who might hear. 'It's a crucially important one, for me.'

Thinking Without Thinking

'*Ring*, damn you, ring!'

Could you hate a mobile – a harmless piece of plastic in shades of mauve and pink? Yes. Because, despite carrying it around with her since the first moment she got up, it had remained obstinately silent the whole morning, and that alone made her want to slap its dumb, pink face. He'd promised to ring – today – and surely, even on a Saturday, he wouldn't sleep past lunchtime. Admittedly, he would have got in very late last night, and hadn't actually specified what time he would make the call, but there had been a definite understanding that they would see each other this evening. In fact, she had barely slept at all, reliving their first encounter: two strangers meeting casually, yet knowing in an instant that their fates would be entwined.

Oh my God, it was ringing! At last! Thank Christ! Snatching it up, she stuttered a 'Hello'.

'Avril, hi! It's Pam.'

Four short words, yet they possessed the power to pitch her from the highest Himalayan peak to the darkest, deepest hole.

'Avril, are you OK? Why aren't you saying anything?'

'Could I … ring you later, Pam?'

'Actually I was going to ask if you fancied coming shopping. I thought we might—'

'Sorry, I'm busy today.' No way could she risk missing this all-important call. And if he rang while she was in Debenhams or Topshop, it would be terribly inhibiting to have to speak intimately in front of Pam – or anyone.

'You sound a bit peculiar. Have I interrupted something?'

'My, er, sister's here.'

'OK, I'll give you a bell tomorrow, and maybe we can do something then.'

Tomorrow she might be with him still. Please God. 'I'm afraid my sister's … staying over.'

'Oh, right. I see. Well, have a good day.'

It would only be a good day if he rang. Fantastic if they fixed a time and place. All her adult life she had been waiting for a man like Todd. OK, she didn't really know him – yet – but gut instincts were invariably correct. There had been a television programme called 'Thinking Without Thinking', which explained how snap judgements could be more truthful and effective than decisions worked out rationally through a laborious, conscious process of cognition. To gain access to the wisdom of the heart – so a professor on the programme said – you needed to bypass certain aspects of the brain. And, certainly, when her eyes met Todd's, her heart had known, at some profound instinctive level, that this was something special and momentous. And to think it might never have happened! Normally, she hated parties and had only let herself be dragged along to Brenda's fortieth birthday bash to avoid being thought a spoilsport by her workmates.

Extraordinary how different she felt since that magical encounter. She was no longer odd man out; the only one without a husband or partner – which meant she was pitied as a loser, sometimes even shunned. And the whole weekend had been transformed, as well. Most weekends were so much empty time. The odd shopping-trip or lunch with some acquaintance couldn't really disguise the fact that she was basically alone. But now she was a woman with a diary; someone fanciable, desirable; at this very moment awaiting her lover's call.

He *would* call, and they *would* be lovers – all it needed was patience. There were a dozen different places a bloke might be on Saturday: the football field, the squash court, the pub, the gym, the launderette. Once he got back, he'd phone. And at least she had used the morning to good purpose. Her toenails and her fingernails were painted an alluring red; her legs were waxed; her whole body buffed and polished and anointed with a frangipani lotion that smelled wonderfully exotic, and she'd tried on all the knickers she possessed, before opting for the sexiest. Her outer clothes she'd left undecided as yet. No point getting out her party gear again if he suggested a session at the ice-rink before they went to bed.

Bed! They might come back here, to *her* bed, and she hadn't spared a single thought for the condition of the flat. Whilst primping and preening herself, she had left the place in a complete and utter mess. Worse, her sheets were in need of a wash, and there was nothing to drink beyond a bottle of cheap Chardonnay and some stalish mineral water. Last night, he'd been drinking beer. Should she go out and buy a six-pack? No. The flat must come first.

She dashed into the bedroom to inspect the duvet and the pillows. Both looked distinctly grubby, but as she ripped off the two pillowcases, her mobile shrilled again. Despite the pounding of her heart, she paused a moment, to rehearse her tone of voice. It was essential to sound sexy and flirtatious, so as not to disappoint him.

'Hello –o,' she said in a husky purr. 'Avril here.'

'It's Mum, dear. I wondered if you could come over right away? I need a hand with the shopping. My leg's giving me gyp and I can't seem to get my balance.'

She closed her eyes, as if that way she could block out her mother – her mother's leg, her mother's endless ailments.

'I hope it won't be any trouble. I know you said you were at a bit of a loose end today.'

'Er, things have changed. I'm ... going out.'

'What, now?'

'Well, soon-ish.'

'Be an angel and pop over first. You know what a wreck I am, once my leg swells up like this.'

'Mum, I don't think I can make it in time. I'm sorry, honestly How about Marguerite? Can't she lend a hand?'

'She's taken the children to the cinema.'

'Well, Carmen, then?'

'No, she and Guy are away for the weekend.'

Avril cursed her sisters. Not only were they married, their lives were so enviably full, they had every excuse not to help out in a crisis. *She* was the one always landed with her mother. 'Why not ask that nice kind soul at number 23?'

'Eliza? Oh, I couldn't bother *her* – not at the weekend. She works so hard all week, it's the only time she sees Michael and the kids.'

Lucky Eliza. Lucky elder sisters. 'Look, I'll try and rearrange things, Mum. I'll ring you back in a sec, OK?'

She *ought* to help. Life was pretty dismal for her mother, who had fallen prey to a whole host of minor health problems, since being widowed eighteen months ago. If she tidied up the flat first, so that everything was ready for an evening with her lover, there would still be time to do her mother's shopping. In fact, while she was out, she could buy some beer and snacks for Todd, and perhaps some candles and a bunch of flowers to make the place look more romantic. And, actually, if she answered the phone while she was out and about on errands, it would give a better impression. She would seem busy, in demand, racing from one engagement to the next, rather than staying in the whole damned day, counting every second till his call. And at least it was good weather: neither clammy-hot nor shivery-cold, and with no April showers to muss her hair, which she'd spent an age washing, then de-frizzing, then moisturizing and volumizing, and finally straightening with her special heated tongs.

Having found some off-white nylon sheets, she quickly changed the bed, wishing they were silk and slinky black. But she must concentrate on *him* tonight, so that he wouldn't notice the bed linen or the cramped and shabby bedroom; drive him to such heights of passion, all else would fade and blur. The problem was, she was completely out of practice, as well as unspeakably nervous, so she was bound to make a hash of things.

No, she mustn't be so negative. Wasn't it a feather in her cap that he'd insisted on taking her phone number? Blokes only did that if they had serious intentions. True, she didn't have *his* number, but only because he'd dashed off from the party to some other ritzy dive. Which made him more of a catch, in actual fact. This guy had friends, a pulsing social life, yet it was her he'd chosen from all the scores of people he might meet. Even his name was special. She had never known anyone called Todd. Was it just a nickname, or short for something exotic? And was it spelled with two d's or just one? Two were better – gave him extra weight. She had no idea of his surname, but that was a mere detail. In time, she would know everything about him.

The phone! Again! Every time it rang, she seemed to suffer a minor heart attack; became tingly, shaky, weak, as if all her bones had turned to bendy straws. She let it ring three times, for luck, before she picked it up, then gave a terse 'Hello', refusing to waste more sexy purrs on her mother or a friend.

'Is that Miss Avril Burrows?'

'Yes,' she said nervously, failing to recognize the voice. A deep, attractive male voice – a friend of Todd's perhaps, phoning with a message for her.

'As one of our valued customers, you have been selected to receive a special free—'

'Look, sorry, I can't talk now.'

'I'd be grateful for a minute of your time, madam. This is an offer you won't want to refuse.'

'What is it?' she asked, intrigued despite herself. Free offers were always tempting. It might be a CD of Songs for Lovers, or a jar of miracle face-cream, or cut-price calls at the weekends – all extremely useful if she and Todd became an item.

The man spoke in a breathless tone, as if announcing Oscar winners. 'As a member of the Erotica Book Club, you are entitled to a copy of *Sex and Sensuality* – the ultimate lovers' guide. The retail price is £18.99, but this will cost you nothing.'

Her cheeks were flaming with embarrassment. 'I'm *not* a member. I cancelled six months ago.' She had joined last year, after meeting Mike at her 'Brush up Your German' evening class. Once she realized sex was on the cards, she had immediately started panicking about being out of practice, but knew full well she just didn't have the nerve to pick out blatant sex-books in a shop. She'd be watched by sneery sales people who would consider her too dull and plain to be mugging up on advanced erotic techniques. In fact, she had never got beyond the basics with short-sighted, skinny Mike. After the first dizzy week, the whole relationship had collapsed, and he had even stopped attending the classes, as if determined to avoid her at all costs. Which made it still more crucial that things worked out with Todd, who was muscular, with perfect sight, and very nearly dishy. Perhaps she ought to accept the free offer. An ultimate lovers' guide would come in very handy. The previous sex-books she had purchased from the club had all emphasized the point that the best way to a man's heart was through his rampant cock.

'It doesn't matter, madam,' the man was saying, 'whether you're a member or not. You have privileged-customer status, which means the offer is still valid.'

'Great! I'll have it, then.'

'Hold on a second. I need to take some details.'

'But, if you're ringing me, you must have my details already.'

'Not all of them. This is a different division of the Club. Now if you'll bear with me a minute—'

She 'bore with him' for twenty; only losing patience when she cottoned on to the fact that the book wasn't free at all, but just a lure to persuade her to rejoin. She cursed the wasted time, although in one way she felt sorry for the chap. Making cold calls to ex-customers couldn't be the best-paid of jobs, nor the most rewarding. Like her, he was at the bottom of the heap, and she felt a sudden urge to leap the miles between them and put her arms around him; reassure him that better things were on the way – with luck. The problem was, an impatient, busy Todd might well be trying to reach her, so she couldn't really extend the conversation. The minute she rang off, she checked for missed calls (none), then for texts (only an annoying one from Carmen, sending sisterly greetings from some posh hotel in Scarborough).

None the less, she was determined to be well-prepared, so she raced around the flat, cleaning, clearing, tidying – and trying not to blame herself for the cold-caller's loss of commission. Between her mopping and dusting, she kept darting back to the kitchen to add things to the shopping list: black fishnet tights, new pillow-cases, lavender-scented room-spray, bacon and eggs, in case he stayed for breakfast – her Special K wouldn't suit a bloke. Then, having rung her mother, to get *her* shopping list, she finally dashed towards the High Street, feeling a curdled, clotted mixture of elation and sheer terror.

*

Two hours later, she was back, weighed down with heavy shopping and with a sense of increasing dread. Still he hadn't phoned or texted, and it was getting on for five now. How could they meet this evening, when he didn't even know if she was free? She tried to recall his exact words when they'd parted. Had he spelled it out in black and white that they were meeting tonight, for definite? Yes. Well, more or less. Perhaps he was a casual type, the sort who'd dispense with the phone-call and just turn up on her doorstep, expecting her to *be* there.

Which meant she must look her best, so as to give a good impression the instant she let him in. The room-spray and the pillowcases could wait. She was the one in need of further transformation.

She stood in front of the dressing-table mirror, wishing she could swap bodies with Marguerite or Carmen. Her sisters were attractive, *she* the ugly duckling, who had never succeeded in turning into a swan. Marguerite was always described as 'feminine', and wore frills and ruffles and lots of baby-pink, whereas Carmen was 'dramatic', and went in for daring outfits in bold colour-combinations like mustard and magenta, or emerald and slate. She herself had never had a label – she was simply Avril; not 'the clever one' (Marguerite), or 'the sporty one' (Carmen); not 'striking' (Carmen again), or 'elfin' (Marguerite). Or glamorous, or elegant, or fashionable – or *anything*.

She was used to that – it was the story of her childhood. But that didn't mean it was hopeless altogether. People could have makeovers – you saw it all the time: on television, in women's magazines: the unprepossessing home-body transformed into a glamour-puss. In her present situation, she had neither time nor money for cosmetic surgery, or slimming clubs, or weeks at pricey health-spas, nor was she surrounded by hordes of fashion gurus, hair-artistes, beauticians and the like. But she did have a drawerful of make-up and a wardrobeful of clothes – indeed, some of them her sisters' clothes, which she had never dared to wear. Maybe this was the perfect moment, though, to become 'feminine' or 'dramatic', and thus give herself distinction.

She rifled through the hangers to find Marguerite's fondant-pink, ruched dress, with the sweetheart neckline and the bows on both the shoulders, which her sister had bought for her tenth wedding anniversary. It was a struggle to get into it. She might be the same height as Marguerite, but not her dainty weight. Once she had managed (with grim effort) to fasten the protesting zip, she took a critical look in the mirror. The image that came to mind was of a large, lumpy, pink-iced birthday cake, encircled with a cake-frill and ludicrously over-decorated. No, she was *not* the feminine type – in fact, she looked more like a man in drag.

Having clawed herself out of the inappropriate garment (ripping it in the process), she tried on a smart two-piece that Carmen had worn to last year's Christmas office do, then discarded on a whim. She and Carmen were more similar in shape, so at least the outfit didn't strain across the bust and hips. But she couldn't carry off the way-out colours (aquamarine and purple), or the audacious style with its padded shoulders and hobble skirt. Her face looked small and wan atop the flamboyant ensemble – indeed, she had all but disappeared; outshone by the clothes themselves. They were hand-me-downs, in any case, and although hardly worn, still brought back hateful memories of wearing her sisters' cast-offs as a child. *They* got all the new stuff, while she'd made do with what they'd outgrown, regardless of whether it suited her or not. Once an adult, she had always chosen 'safe' clothes – tame, unexceptional things that wouldn't make her stand out in a crowd. Even fishnet tights weren't her usual sort of gear, especially those she had bought today: crotchless, seamed and tarty.

She ran to fetch them, removed them from their packet and eased them on with the greatest care, scared of snagging them with her newly painted nails. She couldn't really judge the effect whilst wearing Carmen's outfit, so she took it off and stood in just the tights, grimacing in instant disappointment. If fishnet was meant to be sexy, it didn't work on *her*. The tights simply made her calves bulge and drew attention to her less-than-perfect thighs. Clearly she wasn't the Sexy Type, any more than the Voluptuous Type (just solid), or even the Interesting Type. But there was no such thing as a Mousy Type or a Merging-into-the-Background Type, so, embarking on this new affair, what was she meant to *do*, for pity's sake – accept herself as she was, or try to be someone else?

Did she even have a self, she wondered with a surge of panic? Perhaps that was the whole point. Nobody had given her a label (brainy, brilliant, funny, sparky, laugh-a-minute, dreamy, deep), because she was nothing through and through. Even her name was boring. No Avril ever featured as the heroine of some steamy romance, or the star of a passionate saga. Avrils were seamstresses or parlour maids, and belonged to another age. Again, her sisters were much luckier. In fact, maybe their names had made them what they were. If you were christened Marguerite, you *had* to grow up feminine; if Carmen, then of course you'd be dramatic. Avril had no connotations, neither Spanish passion nor showy foreign flowers. Nothing, once again. Her parents had lost interest once she came along, After an eight-year gap with no babies, they'd run out of steam, run out of distinctive names, and had just let her limp along in her superior sisters' wake.

When her mobile rang, she was still standing in her old greyish bra and knickers, having dragged off the offending tights. Should she even bother to pick up? It would only be her mother, complaining (as she already had, at length) that she wasn't at all happy with the shopping: Maxwell House was shockingly expensive, compared with Sainsbury's own, and she'd specified two oranges, not a dozen tangerines.

Yet, despite herself, her finger reached for the 'on' button. 'Hello,' she muttered, disconsolately.

'Hi! It's Todd.'

Startled, panicked, she let her heart speak for her; its pounding, thumping, racing motion conveying torrents of emotion; all the thrilled, triumphant words she was too astounded to articulate.

'Am I speaking to Avril Burrows?'

She nodded, shook her head. Not only was she confused, there seemed to be a stone stuck in her throat; an iron band round her chest, pressing on her voice-box, restricting every breath.

'Have I got the right number? Is that 0791 0538 880?'

Was it the right number? Was anything right about her? Not her face, for certain. Not her legs or boobs. Not her basic shape or pallid colouring. Not her prissy name or dreary job. Not her feeble porridge-brain nor—

'Avril, is that you?'

'No,' she said, suddenly decisive, and cutting off the call. There *wasn't* any her. Why should a busy, lively, successful bloke like Todd want to be saddled with a no one?

High Speed 2

'Thank you for travelling with South West Trains. We are now arriving at our final destination, Waterloo.'

As the train shuddered to a stop, Rowena peered at her reflection in the window. Impossible to see much, with rain lashing at the glass, running down in rivulets, blurring her face to a shadowy grey mask. In fact, she had checked on her appearance several times already throughout the lengthy journey, sneaking glances in her handbag mirror to ensure her lipstick wasn't smudged, or her hair tumbling from its ponytail. Today, she *had* to look her best.

Collecting up her book and bag, she stepped down on to the platform; the sleety air a cold slap on her face after the cosy fug of the train. It had been pelting since she first set out in the chilly pre-dawn murk; driving to the station along puddled country lanes; the windscreen wipers whipping back and forth, as if expressing their vexation at the weather. Her flimsy coat was more suited to July than the middle of November, but her usual casual uniform of sheepskin and green wellies would hardly impress a sophisticate like Carl.

Just the thought of seeing him, after so long a gap, sent nervous spasms skittering through her stomach. Was it madness to have come? Should she have taken a stronger line; told him loud and clear that the affair had finished years ago and couldn't be revived? She stopped abruptly, tempted to turn round there and then and catch the next train back.

'Mind where you're going, can't you?'

A man behind had more or less run into her, and was still muttering indignantly, despite her profuse apology, and the fact it was as much his fault as hers. It was ages since she'd been to

London and she'd forgotten quite how rude a place it was. With a shrug of resignation, she let him stride on past. Why waste energy on an ill-mannered lout when she needed every ounce of it for Carl? She couldn't bolt for home – not at this late stage – leave him cruelly stranded on the station. Besides, some part of her just ached to know why he'd got in touch again, after all this time; what his expectations were, for God's sake.

'I'm flying in to Heathrow,' he'd said, his voice indistinct and muffled on the phone, as if he were speaking underwater. 'Tuesday next, first thing. So let's meet Wednesday morning. I'll see you at half-past nine, under the clock at Waterloo.'

He hadn't asked if Wednesday was convenient, or whether she could get time off work – indeed, whether she was free to meet at all. For all he knew, she could be married, tied to home and kids, or involved with someone else. Two decades had passed, with no communication between them, save for the odd Christmas card, or email, or change-of-address announcement, yet his whole attitude and tone of voice suggested they were lovers still, in constant daily contact, instead of virtual strangers to each other. And why had he suggested meeting at such an early hour, with no thought for *her* convenience? She'd managed to find a train that got in at 9.45, but, even so, it had meant getting up at five and leaving in the dark, not to mention paying double for peak-time travel. She should have objected straight away, begged not just fifteen minutes' grace, but moved the whole thing forward to some more civilized time. But his phone-call had been so disconcerting, so completely unexpected, she had simply stuttered out her astounded acquiescence.

Self-consciously, she proceeded towards the station clock, in the centre of the concourse – the same meeting-place as twenty years ago. That seemed a different era altogether; she a naïve nineteen-year-old, gauche and shy and very nearly tongue-tied on first encountering the urbane, well-dressed New Yorker who had been working with her uncle in Manhattan (to where Carl had whisked her off within the week).

She steered a zigzag path between people, luggage, pushchairs, surprised to see such crowds when surely rush-hour must be over now. Her home village boasted barely a hundred inhabitants, whereas twice that number seemed to be milling around this station. Yet she almost wished the crush was greater still, so that it would hold her back, impede her; postpone the fateful moment when she and Carl came face to face again.

But that moment had arrived. She was now within a few feet of the clock, and her stomach registered the fact by turning into a rollercoaster: hope, excitement, curiosity, careering up, up, up, while fear, doubt, agitation plunged down, down, down, down, down. Quickly, she faked a confident smile as she checked the groups of people, peering up at the indicator-boards, stretching in a long line beneath the clock. Her smile withered to a grimace, however, when she saw he wasn't there – nor indeed anywhere in sight. But then Carl had always been late. His chronic unpunctuality was one of the many reasons she had returned to England and ended the affair; tired of constantly waiting, and hurt by his assumption that *her* time didn't matter, only his. On this occasion, he had no excuse at all. He'd told her he was staying at the Savoy, only minutes from Waterloo, whereas she'd been travelling since half-past six this morning – earlier, in fact, if she counted the drive to the station. On the other hand, he might have been delayed. He was bound to be in a taxi (Carl took taxis everywhere), which could be stuck in traffic on Waterloo Bridge. Couldn't he have rung her, though? She had her mobile with her, and had given him her number, but he, of course, had failed to give her his.

Trying to swallow her annoyance, she sought distraction in the people standing next to her: a plumpish Indian matron with a large brood of sad-eyed children, and a scruffy-looking lad scrunching his way through a giant-sized bag of crisps. She envied him his trainers. Her own shoes were already hurting; cramping at the toes, throwing her off-balance with their ridiculously high heels. Was Carl really worth the effort, she wondered with a twinge of bitterness: the new clothes, new shoes, the frantic week of preparations?

She longed to rest her feet, but the few benches in this area were already occupied, and the only empty seats were in the café opposite. They should have arranged to meet *there*, of course, but Carl was, if nothing else, a romantic, and clearly wanted to replay that magical occasion back in 1987, when they had first set eyes on each other and felt instantly attracted, ending the day dizzily in love. He'd been late then, too, she recalled, but as a young, self-effacing girl, meeting a distinguished and much older man, she had accepted it as his natural right. This time, however, she intended to speak out; make a sarcastic quip about leopards never changing their spots. And he *was* a leopard, in some ways: powerful, feline, ruthless. So what did that make *her*? A leopard's prey?

For the umpteenth time, she checked the clock. If he wasn't here by ten past ten, then she would decamp to the café. It was only a few yards away, so if she sat at one of the tables on the concourse, she would see him when he did arrive.

'The train at platform 8 is the 10.05 South West train service to Weymouth, calling at Clapham Junction, Woking, Basingstoke, Winchester, Southampton Airport Parkway ...'

'The train at platform 16 is the ...'

The constant announcements on the tannoy only served to emphasize her plight. Other people were dashing to catch trains; purposeful and busy; only she aimless and rooted to the spot. And why did every minute take so long to pass? Could the clock have stopped, maybe? No, her watch said exactly the same: four minutes past ten.

An enticing smell was wafting from the kiosk next to platform 12. 'Millie's Cookies,' she spelled out, suddenly realizing she was ravenous. Too rushed to snatch a bite of breakfast, she had planned to buy a snack on the train, then changed her mind and decided not to eat until she actually met Carl. During the two years of their affair, he had always swept her off, within minutes of their meeting, to some stylish brunch, or ritzy lunch, or elaborate, four-course dinner. So why spoil her appetite by stuffing Millie's Cookies?

By 10.20, there was still no sign of him, so she marched over to the café, ordered an Americano (which seemed appropriate) and took it to an outside table, in direct view of the clock. It was colder there than in the snug interior, but she didn't intend to miss him, having expended so much effort and expense on her outfit and the rail fare, not to mention the sheer stress of anticipation.

She took slow, reflective sips of her coffee, in a bid to calm herself. Carl *would* come. He always did. Eventually. She remembered one occasion, waiting for him in the Plaza Hotel on Fifth Avenue. After half a fruitless hour, pacing up and down the lobby, she was picked up by a swarthy Arab, and was actually tempted to go off with him, just to pay Carl out. Though, in truth, New York had terrified her. Transplanted from her sleepy Devon hamlet to the shrillest city in the world had left her all but reeling: the speed, the buzz, the glitz. The tallest buildings in her village at home were the steepled church and the silage tower, whereas the overweening skyscrapers seemed to reduce her to a pinprick. And exchanging her parents' cosy cottage for Carl's twentieth-floor, minimalist apartment, over-looking Central Park, had been another culture-shock.

Even here, in London, she felt something of an alien. She was used to greeting everyone she met, be they stranger, or fellow villager, yet if she did the same on this busy, heaving station she would be locked up as a mental case. And despite the fact she was sitting close to several other customers, no one smiled; nobody made eye-contact, let alone struck up a conversation. Most were on their own, like her, save one young couple sharing a milkshake; taking it in turns to drink from the single straw. They seemed so relaxed, companionable; wiping froth from each other's mouths, giggling when they slurped or burped; even their legs entwined beneath the table. She and Carl had never been at ease like that. It wasn't just the age-gap, but the fact that he surpassed her so decisively in income, education and sheer experience of life. Yet, somewhat paradoxically, that very fact had spoiled her for all other men. Here she was, still single at the age of thirty-nine, because every male she'd met since Carl had seemed tedious and tepid, uncultivated, penny-pinching.

She spooned the melted sugar from the bottom of her cup, then, with another glance at the clock, opened the book she'd brought: a challenging novel set in eighteenth-century Moscow. Despite the long train journey, she had barely read two chapters and, once again, it proved impossible to concentrate on Russia under the Tsars, when her mind was so fixated on Tsar Carl. What she really needed was a frothy magazine. Normally, she shunned them as a waste of time and money, but she was in dire need of distraction and, if she went to Smith's next door, could buy a couple, whilst still keeping an eye on the clock.

There were more women's magazines in Smith's than she could read in a whole lifetime – every subject on display from cookery and knitting to weddings, babies, health and fitness, fashion and psychology. She stood leafing through a selection of them, surprised by the assertive tone of many of the articles: 'How to take your man in hand and demand what you want in bed'; 'Is it time for you two to part?'; 'The *Cosmo* guide to going it alone'. Clearly, she was out of touch with the zeitgeist. She should be standing up for her rights, refusing to be messed around by a thoughtless, selfish male who had no idea of time. Any woman with an ounce of pride would have stalked off after half an hour, but she, the willing slave, kept abandoning the magazines and nipping to the door, desperate for the sight of the inconsiderate bastard, who had already walked all over her, twenty years ago.

Yet her natural inclination was to make excuses for him. He might have been so jet-lagged he had slept through the alarm. Or perhaps he'd gone down with a virus – one with a sudden onset that had taken him unawares. In fact, she ought to phone the Savoy, to check if he was there still. She rang Directory Enquiries, who dialled the number for her.

'Yes, hello. I'd like to speak to Mr Carl Luzzatto. Can you try his room, please?'

'I'm sorry, madam, Mr Luzzatto left the hotel over an hour ago.'

'Oh … I see. Thank you.'

So where was he, for God's sake? If some problem *had* occurred, perhaps he'd left a message on her home phone, rather than ringing her mobile. She dialled in, to check her calls, but there was only one from the boiler-repair-man, saying he couldn't come till Friday. Boilers somehow made her think of bombs. Could there have been a terrorist attack – one involving Carl? The thought of him lying mangled amidst the wreckage of his taxi filled her with such horror, she rushed out of the shop, in search of a policeman.

She had to walk some way along the concourse before she came upon two transport police, standing by the escalators that led to Waterloo East.

'Excuse me,' she said, approaching them. 'I wondered if there'd been any sort of … incident – something that could cause a delay?'

The younger man gave a rueful smile. 'Anything can cause a

delay in London – faulty traffic lights, burst water mains, signal failure on the tube, a march or demonstration.'

'No, I meant something much more serious, like a terrorist attack.'

'You can rest assured on that score,' the other man replied. 'We've heard nothing of that nature whatsoever.'

OK, bombs ruled out. She was overreacting to a ridiculous degree. He might be waiting in another part of the station, despite his saying it must be under the clock. In fact, much the same had happened in New York. She still remembered, all that time ago, his curt instruction on the phone: 'Meet me at Regine's at one.' By three o'clock, when he'd failed to show, she went back to his apartment, half-furious, half-frantic. When he eventually returned himself, hours later, he had insisted, deaf to argument, that he'd distinctly said the St Regis bar, not Regine's.

So she had better make a tour of the whole concourse, searching every part of it – and start here, with the Reef Café, which, annoyingly, was up a flight of stairs. More punishment for her feet. Still, the terrace on the upper floor afforded a good view and, as she gazed down at the people below, she could see every shape and size and age and type – except the one she sought. Limping down the stairs again, she ventured into the Marks & Spencer food store. He might be buying her a present: truffles or champagne. For all his faults, Carl never failed to bring her lavish gifts. No sign of him, but she proceeded down the escalator to Starbucks, for no other reason than the fact it was American-owned. She found Starbucks and MacDonald's side by side, but no Carl among their customers. Returning to the concourse, she tried the Wellesley pub next – a basement joint, which meant more stairs. Venturing down, she was assailed by rackety music and flashing slot-machines, and stood recoiling from the smell of smoke, which, despite the recent smoking-ban, lingered stale and cloying in the air.

Still no Carl and, having hobbled up to ground-level once more, she saw she had reached the far end of the station. Crossing over to the other side, she started checking all the stalls and kiosks located between the platforms, most of which sold food. The Krispy Kreme doughnuts looked especially tempting: a luscious choice of maple-iced, strawberry-filled, sugar-coated, chocolate-topped. And the hot croissants on the patisserie stall lured her with their buttery smell. She was so hungry she could wolf the lot.

Trudging on past *Délice de France* and Upper Crust, she was reminded of New York, in that almost every stall was staffed by foreigners. At home, she barely saw a black or Asian face, or met anyone who wasn't smugly middle-class and white. But her two years in Manhattan had shown her a much wider world, in which every different race and nationality seemed to be flung into a gigantic potpourri. She had listened on street corners to esoteric languages; sampled ethnic foods (everything from sushi and sashimi to fried plantains, hot pastrami, polenta and pupusas); toured Chinatown and Harlem and Little Italy, intrigued by the exotic sights and sounds. And Carl himself was something of a United Nations, with his German first name, his Italian surname and his mixed Jewish and Sicilian blood. What had bowled her over initially was the intense darkness of his eyes: a potent, gleaming black, like strong espresso coffee. And his hair was equally dark: thick, rebellious, raven hair that had made her own mousy crop seem timid and half-hearted.

She was suddenly struck by an appalling thought: he'd be *grey* by now, not dark. In fact, would she even recognize a Carl of sixty-five? She should be looking for a pensioner, someone bowed and bent and slow; not the upright, agile hunk who had whisked her from her home and country into a totally new life. Absurd as it might sound, it hadn't really dawned on her till now that two decades would have aged him to a quite noticeable degree. Rather, she had clung to her belief that a man like Carl, so powerful and controlling in every other matter, would have overmastered change and time in his usual dominant fashion. But sixty-five was old by any standards – indeed, the same age as her father, who was arthritic, paunchy and very nearly bald. And what about sex, for heaven's sake? Would a guy so ancient be able to perform still, or would his former passion have petered limply out? Playing bowls or bridge was perhaps more his kind of thing now than playing skilled seducer.

The prospect of encountering a hairless, sexless, doddery, old Carl made her feel so desolate, she strode up to the counter of Pie Kitchen and ordered the largest pie on display: a crumbly beef and mushroom affair, which left her little change from a fiver. But she needed fuel – and comfort – something to plug her increasing sense of loss. For an entire two decades, Carl had remained her touchstone of male physical perfection. His character might be wanting, his virtues thin on the ground, but when it came to sheer good looks, he left most men at the starting gate. But even an Adonis could wither and decay.

Miserably, she bit into her pie, cursing as the filling spurted out and dribbled down her coat in a greasy brownish gunge. She tried to rub the stains off with a tissue, but only made them worse. Well, if Carl found her gravy-bespattered, with crumbs all round her mouth, he would only have himself to blame.

She continued munching defiantly as she approached the clock once more, now looking for a different Carl – older, greyer, wrinkled. But no Carl at all was there. Might he have come and gone while she had made her tour of the station, assuming she had given up in despair and set off home?

Well, she *would* go home. It was now a minute past eleven, which meant she had waited one-and-a-quarter hours. Aged nineteen, she would have waited half the day, of course; willing to indulge his foibles and overlook his faults, but she had changed since then, and was less patient altogether. She was particularly annoyed today to have taken time off work, only to waste it on this fruitless expedition. However, if she went back right away, at least she could retrieve the afternoon; catch up with her emails, and tackle the pile of washing-up she'd been ignoring for a fortnight. In fact, the Honiton train was due in just four minutes, she remembered from the timetable.

With a last desperate look in all directions, she finally cut her losses and ran full-pelt to platform 7, click-clacking on her silly heels, and arriving in the nick of time. She found a corner seat, kicked off her shoes and opened her book with a flourish. On the journey home, she would concentrate, read a dozen chapters; refuse to waste another minute regretting the aborted rendezvous. If truth be told, she had probably saved herself a load of trouble. Life with Carl might have been exciting, but it had invariably left her exhausted and in turmoil.

'*Welcome aboard this 11.05 South West train service to Exeter St*

Davids, calling at Basingstoke, Salisbury, Sherbourne, Yeovil Junction….'

Just as the doors were closing, she leapt to her feet, grabbed her shoes and bag, and sprang from the train in her stockinged feet, leaving her book behind in her haste. Why rush straight home and engage in tedious chores, just because some louse had stood her up? Having spent so much time and money coming up to London, she should surely make the most of the place. As an emancipated woman, she could treat *herself* to lunch, instead of waiting for a man to foot the bill. And afterwards, she could go to a museum or take in an exhibition, soak up a little culture, for a change. And if she bought a brolly and a pair of cheapo trainers, she could stride around, unhampered, and without getting wet *en route*.

Ramming on her shoes again, she tottered back along the platform, taking a final look at the station clock. No Carl, of course. That settled it. If he ever got in touch again, she'd simply bang the phone down. It wasn't a matter of mere unpunctuality. During her two years with him, she had lost her whole identity: her home, her job, her way of life. If she had displayed the slightest sign of independence, he had immediately cracked down on it. She mustn't work – it might make her unavailable – but be at his beck and call. Oh, he was generous, yes, indulgent, yes, but what she had put up with as a penniless *ingénue*, she refused to stomach now. Her present self-sufficient life was too valuable to risk.

Before leaving the station, she popped into the Ladies room, to sponge her coat and wash her greasy hands. Glancing in the mirror, she wondered just how different she might have looked to Carl, after the twenty-year hiatus. She had certainly plumped out a bit since her skinny, coltish teens, but, on the whole, she had worn surprisingly well – no grey hairs, no wrinkles. What she didn't like was the make-up. She had overdone the blusher and even the eye-gloss looked, frankly, vulgar in the cold stare of the fluorescent light. Scrabbling in her handbag, she whipped out her pack of tissues and started scrubbing off her war-paint. At home, she never wore it, and she detested this false self, which had tarted itself up to please a man who wasn't worth the effort. She would enjoy her day in London naked-faced and sensibly shod, and consign inconsiderate Carl to the dustbin of her past.

Emerging from the Ladies, she paused a moment, deciding where to go: the National Gallery, perhaps, or the Egyptian rooms in the British Museum, which she still remembered from school. Or maybe …

'Rowena! Rowena!'

Startled, she looked up, jolted by the American voice – that voice she knew so well, with its unique blend of steel and velvet; its deep, authoritative tone. Someone was striding towards her from the direction of the clock: a tall, athletic, agile man – elegant, impeccably dressed, black-eyed, silver-haired. He was carrying a huge bouquet of lilies, which he let fall dramatically (like mere impedimenta), so that he could sweep her into his arms. She struggled to resist; tried to tell him she was furious and demanded an explanation, but his kiss had lit some touch-paper deep within her body, so that she was smouldering, exploding, sending up great rocket-showers of heat and light and colour. Whatever her head might want to say, their joined lips and tongues were speaking a quite different language; renewing the acquaintance in the most outrageously sensuous fashion. She had no option but to surrender, as the whole busy, bustling station became nothing but a backdrop for the longest kiss in the history of the world.

A century must have passed before he finally let her go, and, when he did, she simply stood and stared at him. The shining silver hair (still thick and lush and vigorous) only served to emphasize the intense darkness of his eyes, while the deep-etched lines around his mouth lent him a new gravitas. All the recriminations were dying on her lips. How could she have remembered all his bad points – his rudeness, lateness, selfishness – yet blanked out the most vital thing about him: his expertise as lover?

Retrieving the lilies, he thrust them into her arms. 'For you,' he whispered. 'With all my love.'

Their swoony scent seemed to knock her even further off her guard. She should be insisting on an apology, not allowing him to purchase her submission with yet another gift.

'Where *were* you, Carl?' she stammered out, at last.

'St Pancras Station.'

'St Pancras?' she replied, confused. 'Was I meant to meet you *there*?'

'No, my gorgeous girl, you were meant to meet me here.'

'I did,' she retorted. 'I was under that clock on the dot of 9.45, and I've been searching for you ever since. In fact, I'd just given you up and was going off on my own.'

'Well, you'd better not do that, because I've got a surprise for you, sweetheart.'

'Surprise?'

'Yes, lunch in Paris, instead of lunch in London.'

'Paris?' she repeated, incapable of anything beyond parroting his words. The 'gorgeous girl', the 'sweetheart' were fatally distracting. Such endearments had been depressingly rare in the recent man-less years.

'Yes, by Eurostar. I just hope you've brought your passport, like I asked?'

So *that* was the reason for his peculiar request. Still flurried by the fact they were actually speaking on the phone, after twenty years of silence, she had assumed he must be harbouring some crazy plan to whisk her back to the States with him – a replay of 1986.

'Of course not,' he had laughed, his voice still faint and fuzzy, as if he were ringing from another planet, instead of from Manhattan. 'I just want to see your passport photo and remember how you looked when we first met.'

'Carl,' she had pointed out acerbically, 'I renewed my passport four years ago, so you'll see a woman of thirty-five, not a girl still in her teens.'

'Never mind – bring it anyway.'

'But why my passport, Carl, instead of an ordinary photograph? I mean, it's not even flattering.'

Just as he was about to answer, an urgent call came through, and he'd had to ring off almost instantly, with only time to tell her he adored her. Mystified, and still shaken to her very roots, she had complied with his demand. Carl expected orders to be obeyed.

'Well, did you bring it?' he repeated, his tall figure dwarfing hers. That distinctive height was just another aspect of his dominance; his natural superiority compared with lesser men. And it was hard to tell untruths to such a man – pretend she had forgotten all about the passport, or mislaid it altogether. Yet, despite his romantic gesture in arranging a trip to Paris, one part of her resented it. Couldn't he have asked her first, instead of simply assuming (as he always had) that she would fit in with his plans? 'Carl,' she said, at last, 'I've just *been* on a train for the last three-and-a-quarter hours. I'm not sure I want to—'

'This is another thing entirely, Rowena – in a different league. It's the first commercial Eurostar service leaving from St Pancras, rather than from here at Waterloo. I first read about the change-over in a feature in the *New York Times*, a week or two ago, and realized that it coincided with my business trip to London. And I decided there and then that you and I should go together, but I wanted to surprise you. I tried to book seats right away, only to be told there wasn't a hope. Those tickets are like gold-dust. People had written in six *years* ago, in the hope of reserving seats – train-buffs who travelled on the first Eurostar from this station, and wanted to repeat the experience from the big new terminal.'

She suppressed an impatient sigh. Why were they standing around on a cold and draughty station, discussing train-buffs, of all things, when they could be in bed together, trying out variations on that first sensational kiss? 'So if you couldn't get them, Carl, why—?'

'No, wait – let me tell you the best bit! I was watching the News in my hotel room this morning, and they were showing the whole St Pancras thing – crowds of people milling around the station, and all kinds of celebrations in full swing. And a guy came on who said they'd spent literally billions renovating the place, and how it's an architectural wonder, and that the new trains themselves are the fastest on record and go at nearly two hundred miles an hour – which means London to Paris takes a whole hour less than your trip here from Honiton! They're calling the new line High Speed 1, and ...'

High Speed 1– a rather apt description of their time together twenty years ago. She hardly remembered a day in New York when he wasn't tearing from a business-breakfast on to a power-lunch, followed by a shareholders' meeting or financial seminar, until at last he was free to race through drinks and dinner with her, before seducing her in the same urgent, headlong fashion. In fact, *all* New

Yorkers seemed to live at a frenetic pace; even speaking faster than Americans from other cities, and almost proud of being harried, as they hurtled to meet deadlines or close important deals. Carl must be jet-lagged, for heaven's sake, having flown in only yesterday, yet here he was desperate to dash off again. Her dad (the self-same age) insisted on his daily nap and would be knackered after little more than a day-trip to the coast.

'It's an historic occasion, the guy said' – Carl's voice was speeding up again as he galloped through the story – 'something to tell your grandkids. So I thought, what the hell, I'll go to the station in person and have a second shot at getting seats. I rushed straight over in a cab and found the place swarming with cameramen and newsmen. They even had an orchestra playing, right there on the platform, and people dressed in Victorian costume. Hell, I didn't waste a second – I knew I had to get us on that train. "Sorry, sir", they said – just like the first time I tried – "I'm afraid it's fully booked". But I stood at that damned ticket-window, refusing to take no for an answer, and – would you believe? – two returns came in. It seems some guy's wife had broken her wrist actually on the way to catch the train, so naturally the couple couldn't go. Well, I snapped the tickets up, of course, and the bonus is they're first-class seats, with lunch and free champagne laid on. And talking of champagne, wait till you see the champagne bar! It's the longest one in Europe, and it opened just today. So if we get moving, sweetheart, we'll have time for a quick glass before the train departs. It's leaving at 12.30, and check-in's only half an hour before.'

As he paused for breath, at last, she jumped in quickly, trying to curb the tide of words. 'Carl, I've told you already, I don't think—'

'You can't turn this down, Rowena. It's something we'll remember all our lives. There'll never be another first train, so if you refuse to go, we'll lose the chance of being part of history.'

An exaggeration, surely. As far as she could recall, Eurostar had been running for some twelve or thirteen years. Did it really make such an earth-shaking difference for the trains to depart from St Pancras rather than Waterloo? They were both just stations, weren't they, and frankly she'd had enough of stations for one day. Nor did she relish the prospect of travelling at 200 miles an hour.

Essentially a country girl, she preferred life in the slow lane. But what was that to Carl?

Sweeping the lilies from her arms, he tossed them on the ground once more, so he could press his body into hers, so tight and close she could feel its every contour. She was aware that people were watching – casual passers-by enthralled by this romance.

'It'll be wonderful,' he whispered, 'not just the train, the whole experience. We can stay in Paris as long as you like. I'll book us in at the *Hôtel de Crillon*. Their suites are just sensational, with antiques and oil paintings and fabulous wood panelling. We can lie in bed all morning, see the sights all afternoon, then back to bed for—'

Resolutely, she pulled away. 'Carl, I'm meant to be at work tomorrow.'

'This is more important than work. I just know we have to go, my love.' He ran a seductive finger softly down her cheek; down lower between the buttons of her coat.

His black gaze was mesmerizing, but she forced herself to look down at the floor. 'And, apart from anything else, I haven't any luggage with me.'

'Nor have I – my bags are at the Savoy. But we can shop till we drop in Paris. In fact, I'd love to pick out some clothes for you. Remember when we did just that in Bloomingdales?'

She nodded silently. She did remember; still had those stylish dresses, that sexy underwear – the most expensive stuff she had ever owned – kept them as a kind of souvenir. What in God's name must he be thinking of her now, with her scrubbed-clean face and gravy-spotted coat? No wonder he wanted to kit her out from some swanky Paris store.

As if tuning in to her thoughts, he cupped both hands around her face and continued his fierce scrutiny, his eyes dissolving flesh and bone. 'I haven't told you yet how beautiful you look. You haven't changed in twenty years.'

Sheer flattery, of course, and just part of his persuasion technique, yet those lavish compliments had always weakened her defences; worked on her like some potent (fatal) drug.

'Rowena, we have to get going right now! It's already eleven-thirty and if we waste another minute arguing about it, that train will go without us.'

Still struggling between reluctance and desire, she allowed herself to be coaxed into a taxi. Carl found one straight away, of course – another of his skills. However bad the weather, however big the crush, cabs magically appeared for him. Sometimes, in New York, she had imagined he could summon one by will and thought alone.

Once they were sitting side by side, desire began to swamp her doubts. His warm thigh was nudging hers, his hand had crept inside her coat again and already found her breast. Even the smell of him was exciting: that citrus-sharp *Eau Sauvage* he had always worn, in bed and out, and which had become the signature-scent of their affair.

His thumb was dawdling across her nipple in slow, exquisite circles, pausing only for a second as he urged the driver to 'Step on it!'

No cab was ever fast enough for Carl. She recalled careering down Park Avenue one evening, with him chivvying the driver, as if they were an ambulance or cop-car speeding to some emergency, rather than two lovers headed for dinner at Rossini's.

'I can't go any faster, guv,' the fellow countered, with a shrug. 'This is central London, not Le Mans.'

She hid a smile; one secret, shameful part of her hoping that they *would* be too late, then he could whisk her to the Savoy, instead of its French equivalent, hurtle her into bed, scorch her with his kisses. But that would mean chucking away a hell of a lot of cash. First-class tickets on Eurostar wouldn't be exactly cheap. And what about his longing to be part of an 'historic occasion'? For her, it *was* historic, without any special trains or renovated stations – just the fact of him beside her was phenomenon enough, when she had assumed she'd never see him in her life again. The expression in his eyes was affecting her profoundly – no one else had ever looked at her so blatantly, provocatively, as if seducing her by gaze alone. And his proud, overweening profile and sensuous, open lips were stirring the same emotions that had left her weak and willing at nineteen. And those dark hairs on his wrist, disappearing beneath the crisp white shirt-cuff, reminded her of his hirsute chest, the rough feel of it against her own soft skin; that earthy, animal side of him, so different from his elegant exterior.

None the less, the voice of caution nagged still: why start the thing again, when he would only overrule her on every single issue, just as he was doing at this moment? Paris would be no different from New York. He could keep her waiting in the *Champs-Elysées* with the same infuriating disregard as he had done in 42nd Street.

Yet the tantalizing pressure on her nipple continued to say otherwise; coming up with arguments in favour of the plan. After all, this Paris jaunt would only be a matter of days, not two tempestuous years, and she could insist on going home within the week. Besides, Carl would be on holiday and so surely more relaxed.

Although he seemed anything but relaxed right now, still harassing the driver (whilst continuing his wooing of her breast), and peering at his watch. If she did decide to go with him, then she should be ringing her boss, inventing some illness or excuse; not allowing his hand to glide across to the other breast and caress it in its turn. And still she hadn't the faintest notion *why* he'd got in touch again, or what he was expecting of her: one dizzy whirl in Paris, or a more serious commitment? He hadn't even thought to ask if she was involved with someone else – in fact, hadn't asked a single question about her job or life or circumstances. If such things were of no consequence except as they affected *him*, she'd better disabuse him fast, explain that—

'Great, we're here!' He leapt out of the taxi, over-tipped the driver, and swept her and the lilies through the station entrance. Her first reaction was a strong sense of disappointment. The place seemed nothing special – indeed, windowless and gloomy, with no sign of any awe-inspiring architecture, just the usual London crowds.

'This is where we check in,' Carl informed her. 'But we still have ten minutes to spare, so I want to show you—'

'Aren't we cutting it awfully fine?' she asked, interrupting *him*, for a change.

'Don't worry, we'll be OK,' he said, as they manoeuvred their way through the scrum. 'This part is called the under-croft, and was once used as a beer-cellar. When it was full, it could hold twenty-eight million pints. That's a hell of a lot of beer!'

She could hardly hear what he was saying for all the noise and bustle. They had now come to an arcade of shops, and, suddenly, she caught her first glimpse of the roof – magnificent, as Carl had claimed.

'Come on!' he said, propelling her up a flight of steps. 'We'll see it better from upstairs.'

At the top, she stopped dead, gazing in admiration at the huge iron struts and girders soaring up, up, up, above them, like the vault of a great secular cathedral, and painted an unlikely ethereal blue. The sheer scale of the arch was breathtaking; instantly raised her spirits, as did the triumphant music playing on the station. Building and music seemed to match: both grandiose, declamatory, uplifting.

Carl's eyes followed hers. 'They said this was the inspiration for Grand Central Station back home. I must admit I didn't know that.'

For a moment, she was transported to New York again, and they were sitting in the Oyster Bar, sharing a platter of bluepoints – the same impressive architecture, the same imposing companion, the same crowds and noise and jostle.

'Apparently, the whole of the glass roof was covered with black bitumen from the Blitz,' he explained, still acting the proficient guide. 'That newscaster was saying how it all had to be scraped off, before they inserted eighteen thousand panes of *new* glass.'

He, the New York visitor, was showing her – the native Englander – the sights of her own capital; reeling off facts and figures she ought to know herself. How had he picked up all this information in one scant hour this morning? But that was typical. Carl was always perfectly briefed, whether explaining the construction of a building, or the history of some monument. Whereas she was just an out-of-touch provincial, too caught up in petty local matters, to take an interest in the wider world of London.

In fact, she had barely digested the architecture, when he began steering her through the throng again. 'Quick! There's something else you have to see.'

They paused a moment first, to watch the orchestra – some thirty or forty string-players, the women dressed elegantly in black; the men in smart white jackets, and the dashing young conductor exuberantly waving his baton. The music was so yearningly beautiful, she longed to stay and listen, but Carl was tugging at her hand again, making for a gigantic statue of two embracing lovers. The figures veered so huge and high above her, they seemed to have transcended the mere human scale and belong to a race of giants.

'The sculptor who made this,' he said, 'wanted it to reflect the romance of rail travel. Do you think he's succeeded, sweetheart?'

Without waiting for her response, he positioned himself in the exact same pose as the bronze titan looming over them: his arms wrapped around her waist, his forehead touching hers. 'That's how big I feel,' he whispered, 'when I hold you close like this.'

What could she reply? In truth, she found the statue almost repellent. No way could she relate to such colossal beings, their faces high above her; the woman's protuberant calf muscles bulging in an unattractive fashion; her stiletto heels unnaturally large and lethal. And the man was no less cumbersome – a fatuous rucksack on his back, his ugly trousers clinging to his legs and bum, in a way more crude than sexy. Moving her head away from Carl's, she peered up at the statue again. Was it some sort of warning to her – that she was overreaching herself; didn't really belong with the superior sophisticate who had brought her to this place? She had always been a small-scale person, petite in build and height, modest in her expectations, content with a quite lowly job, and living all her life in a tiny Devon village that didn't boast so much as a pub. So what was she doing here in this city of eight million, with a man of six-foot-four, whose ambitions were prodigious (as was his bank account)?

'Perhaps it'll become like our Statue of Liberty,' he was saying. 'Something famous and iconic.'

There wasn't time to speculate. Already he was urging her on, weaving through the crowds, with her in tow. Half of London seemed to have gathered here: sightseers and tourists, cameramen and television crews, ordinary commuters, whole families with prams and even picnics.

'Three minutes to check-in,' he said, glancing at the huge station clock. 'Just time for a quick glass of *Moët*.'

She doubted it – especially when they reached the Champagne Bar and saw how packed it was. There didn't seem the slightest chance that they would be served within three minutes, let alone have time to drink the stuff. However, if she persuaded him to try; suggested they sit at one of the tables until a waiter was free to take their order, it might be as good a way as any of ensuring that they'd miss the train. Or was that downright mean?

Carl had other ideas, in any case. 'On second thoughts, we'll have a bottle – to drink in bed in Paris.'

Had he reckoned with the queue, she wondered? Yet, already, he had almost reached the front of it, not shoving in a discourteous way, but relying on his natural air of authority, which made people grant him precedence, as if it belonged to him of right. She tried to follow, with the lilies, which were in danger of getting squashed; their heady, honeyed scent mingling with his *Eau Sauvage*, and with the aroma of fresh-brewed coffee, also being served. However exquisite the bouquet might be, it was an utterly impracticable gift to lug around like this, and the delicate flowers were bound to wilt before the train reached Paris. But perhaps they were symbolical of the whole relationship – exotic and luxurious, yet fragile and short-lived.

At last, she was close enough to see into the large, glass-fronted cabinet holding the champagne, some of the bottles so huge in height and girth they seemed vulgar, like the statue. While she waited, she quickly scanned the wine list, amazed to see a Laurent-Perrier costing £900 a bottle, and a Krug Collection 1949 priced at almost £3000. She could *live* a whole three months on £3000.

Within minutes, Carl was handing over his American Express card, emerging with a bottle in his hands, although there wasn't time to ask him what it cost.

'Shit!' he said, ushering her in front of him. 'It's already five after twelve. We're going to have to run for it.'

They dashed full-pelt down the stairs, despite the fact that they were both impeded now; he by the bottle, she by the bouquet. Again, she cursed her shoes, but Carl adored high heels and she had bought them in his honour.

Once they reached the lower floor again, she panted in his

wake, passing shops, stalls, more cameramen, even a man in a bear-suit collecting money for charity. If New York had been High Speed 1, then this was High Speed 2. Already she was out of breath; her bag banging against her side; her ponytail thumping wildly up and down, as if spurring her on in this mad dash against the clock.

'Passport!' he demanded, as they swooped towards the check-in, already worryingly late and confronted by a surly-looking man behind the desk. But Carl could charm a boa-constrictor and, after a few smiles and wiles on his part, they were waved through with no objections.

The next few minutes flashed by in a blur, as they were frisked, scanned, x-rayed, questioned, checked by UK Immigration, then re-checked by the French police; every official remarking (as she had done herself) that they were cutting things extremely fine – the train was already boarding.

They dashed across the Departures Hall, making for platform 5, where they were whisked by travelator back to the upper floor, to be greeted by the sight of the stupendous vaulted roof. Again, it seemed to lift her mood, as if she herself were part of that exalted arch, leaping upwards with the soaring structure until she hit the sky. Carl had to jog her arm, to return her to reality, bring her back to earth.

The escalator deposited them right on to the platform, where the sleek, streamlined, yellow-snouted train was all but ready to depart. A dapper little Frenchman in a grey and yellow uniform ushered them to their seats and, once she'd removed the offending coat, she collapsed back in relief. It was too late now for doubts or second thoughts. Besides, some euphoric part of her was still floating a hundred feet high; no longer even caring if this was folly or good sense. Her own safe and tepid existence back home was surely not so crucial that she couldn't take a chance, for once; run a crazy risk. Admittedly, euphoria could be perilous, but – what the hell – she had to *live* a little, even if she paid for it with heartache and regret.

At 12.30 precisely, the train glided out of the station, watched by a huddle of people, some of whom waved and yelled 'goodbye!' She waved back until they'd dwindled to mere specks, experiencing a childish glee at her five minutes of fame. Then a voice with a charming French accent announced, 'Welcome aboard this first commercial service on Eurostar to depart from the new St Pancras. We would like to thank you for joining us on this historic occasion.'

'Didn't I tell you?' Carl said, with a smile, stowing the lilies and champagne in the overhead luggage-rack.

Soon more champagne was in evidence as a young woman with a drinks trolley opened a bottle of Bollinger and poured it into two glasses. Pausing a moment to let the first fizz subside, she refilled both the flutes, then presented them on a little silver tray. Rowena took hers eagerly, elated to be travelling in such style and with so distinguished a companion.

Carl touched his glass to hers. 'To my darling, unforgettable Rowena.'

Then, putting down the glass, he traced a slow and lingering circle in the centre of her palm. The gesture seemed deliciously erotic; a promise of what was to come – tonight. Though how could she wait that long? She wanted him this instant. That pressure on her palm was stirring reverberations that affected her whole body, made her dazed and dizzy, as if she were already drunk, on champagne.

'To *us*,' she said, slipping the tip of her finger into his mouth, and feeling his teeth close dangerously around it, graze slowly up and down, and …

At that very moment, the sun broke through the clouds outside. Dazzled by the light now streaming through the window, she stared out at the sky, which had changed from lowering-grey to lenient blue. The trees were burnished gold and bronze and glinting in the sun. And the tiny bubbles frisking up from the bottom of her glass made the champagne seem alive – in fact, as tingly and exhilarated as she felt herself, inside. What had happened to this morning's murk and gloom – or, indeed, to her own irritable misgivings? The rain-clouds were still there, in fact, churning beneath the white, fluffy bank of cumulus, acting as a warning that this fine spell wouldn't last. Just as the bubbles would go flat, evaporate to nothing; the lush lilies fade and droop.

But she no longer even cared. There would be *more* champagne, more lilies, more seductive summer skies, however brief and fleeting. And, right now, she intended to enjoy the sun and sparkle just as long as they might last.

Travelling Light

'Mike and I have some really exciting news.' Alison spoke with smug complacency, accompanied by a radiant smile.

'Really?' Jane asked, already aware of what was coming. Alison's previous six pregnancies had been heralded by that same self-satisfaction. 'And what's that?'

'We're expecting another baby.'

'Congratulations!' Jane trotted out on cue. The resources of the planet were already stretched to breaking point. Was it socially responsible to procreate on such a scale?

Alison paused to sugar her tea, appearing now a shade embarrassed. 'And, actually, it's … twins.'

Jane froze. The very word was perilous; never failed to rouse a flood of emotions: shame, horror, guilt, disgust.

'We're thrilled, of course, but I must admit it *was* a tremendous shock. I mean, to be pregnant at all, at my age!'

Yes, Jane thought, determined to keep her mind off twins, forty-six was more the time for menopause than pregnancy. *She*, thank God, had avoided both, so far, although hot flushes and night sweats couldn't be far off, since she and Alison shared exactly the same birthday – same day, same month, same year – a coincidence that had bonded them at school. As adults, though, they had grown further and further apart, and, once Alison started breeding, it had proved more or less impossible to maintain a meaningful friendship, especially when the kids were younger. Indeed, she had barely been able to finish a sentence without some baby bawling, or toddler wanting its bottom wiped, or bursting into tears over some broken toy (or promise). And she had watched the house itself gradually taken over, changing from an attractive adult realm into a rumpus-room-cum-nursery: pram in the hall, high-chair in the dining-room, cot and bunk-beds upstairs, potties in the bathroom, toys littered on the floor. And, even now, when three of the six were teenagers, things had not improved: raucous music blaring from their rooms, adolescent tantrums, wrangles over homework, football boots and skateboards dumped anywhere and everywhere. Miraculously, this was the first time in a decade she had found all the offspring out. The two eldest had gone roller-blading, and Mike had carted the rest off to the park – deliberately, she suspected, since she had never made a secret of her own lack of maternal instincts.

Yet, even without the children's actual presence, there was no danger of forgetting them, since they had left their imprint on the fabric of the house: paintwork scuffed, carpets stained, walls scribbled on and marked, even strips torn off the wallpaper in places. And, with Alison now starting again from scratch, the assault was unlikely to stop. The thought of just the washing made her reel. The machine was always churning away, full of dirty clothes times eight – soon to be dirty clothes times ten, along with a double load of nappies.

Alison gestured to the home-made cake, which shared the kitchen table with colouring books and crayons. 'Help yourself to another piece.'

'Thanks, I will. It's good. But *you* haven't eaten anything.'

'To be honest, it's hard to keep food down. I don't know why they call it "morning" sickness. Mine seems to last all day.'

Jane suppressed a shudder, hoping she'd be spared the details. As a result of her various pregnancies, Alison had suffered swollen ankles, violent indigestion, haemorrhoids, mastitis, varicose veins and even pre-eclampsia. Not to mention the labour itself: humiliating, undignified, and excruciatingly painful, according to all accounts.

Alison leaned forward and gave her arm a sympathetic pat. 'Actually, I do feel rather awkward bringing up the subject of twins, when—'

'It's OK,' she interrupted. 'Not a problem.'

'And I can't help worrying that once they're born, they may bring back sad memories.'

'Look,' Jane said, a shade impatiently. 'All that was years and years ago.'

'Yes, you were only seven, weren't you?'

'Nine.'

Alison shook her head in deep regret. 'It must have been quite tragic.'

'For my mother, yes.'

'But for you, the elder sister – what a dreadful loss!'

Jane stabbed at her cake with her fork. *Gain* for her, not loss. Although, of course, she had never explained to anyone – never would, never could – the sense of sheer relief she had felt to be an only child once more; no longer forced to share her parents with two disruptive intruders, or watch those tiny tyrants drain her mother's energy, her father's time and money.

'I know you don't like talking about it, but it might actually help to get it off your chest, Jane.'

Absolutely not. Inconceivable to admit to an earth-mother, of all people, that, as a child, she'd been *glad* those babies died. It was a cause of the deepest shame; a shame so acute at times, she felt debarred from the whole human race.

'I've never liked to bring it up before, not all the years we've known each other.' Alison sounded nervous, although not nervous enough, unfortunately, to drop this dangerous subject. 'But, you see, once I knew I was expecting twins myself, I've been thinking about *your* twins.'

'They weren't mine,' Jane retorted, refusing to be associated with the unwelcome interlopers who had overshadowed a whole two years of her childhood – *and* the nine months before, when her mother's undivided attention switched from her, the existing daughter, to those unborn aliens.

'Your sisters, though.'

'Not really.' From the moment they arrived, premature and sickly, the entire household had revolved around them, and *she* had been pushed out; made to feel she didn't count. A high price to pay for sisters.

'But don't you think,' Alison persisted, 'it might have made you wary of having children of your own?'

She faked a casual laugh. 'Good gracious, no! I'm just too selfish, that's all.'

'Of course you're not selfish. You've always been a marvellous friend – and so generous to *my* children.'

Jane refrained from answering. Shelling out on presents hardly counted. A form of recompense. Doing good to atone for evil.

'In fact, if anyone's selfish, it's me,' Alison remarked earnestly, 'propagating my own genes.'

Despite her inner turmoil, Jane tried to lighten the mood. 'But it's a religious thing for you, Alison. Remember what Sister Ignatius used to tell us? Once we left school, our duty as good Catholic women was to produce more souls for God.'

Alison had the grace to laugh. 'Well, I've certainly done that!'

'Do you really still believe?' Jane asked, keen to shift attention from herself.

'Yes, actually I do. Not in all the inessentials, but as far as God and Christ and the Church are concerned, I can't see any better way of living.'

Jane continued hacking at her cake, irked by the fact that she and Alison had nothing left in common. At school, they had shared a simple childish piety, a love of horses, an interest in athletics, but nowadays they were miles apart in their beliefs, ideals and whole way of life. So why did she still bother calling round, wasting precious Saturdays with someone who upheld irrational concepts like virgin births and three persons in one God? She already knew the answer: it was for their mothers' sake. Those mothers had been close friends since early childhood and, both widowed now, had moved to the same sheltered housing complex. And each asked her daughter regularly, 'How's Alison?' 'How's Jane?'

'Well, Mum will be pleased,' she said lamely, finally reducing the cake to a mass of sticky crumbs.

'She's delighted. *My* mum told her yesterday and apparently, she's already knitting bootees!'

The silence was uncomfortable. Jane guessed they were both thinking the same thing: had the twins survived, her mother might have been knitting bootees for *their* babies, instead of Alison's. 'I suspect she's never quite forgiven me for pursuing a career and depriving her of grandchildren.'

'You could have had both, you know. Look at Caroline – mother of three, and a C.E.O. already!'

Caroline. Another dutiful alumna of St Joseph's Convent School for Girls. 'Yes, and she spends her whole time trying to juggle home and job, and risking a heart attack in the process. I saw her a couple of months ago and she looked absolutely whacked. She was fretting about some survey or other that said working mothers spent only nineteen minutes a day with their kids. And you should have heard her, laying into herself, because she reckoned *she* spent even less. I've told you, Alison, I'm too selfish for all that breast-beating.' People found the concept of selfishness easier to accept – and it was certainly more tactful as far as Alison was concerned. How could she admit to a mother of six – *eight* – that the very thought of pregnancy filled her with revulsion? Once pregnant, you lost all vestige of control; your body swelling inexorably as some alien life-form took up residence inside it; snaffled your food, leeched away your vitamins, prevented you from sleeping, kicked you in the ribs, and finally split you apart in its struggle to get out. She had seen it as a child; watched, appalled, while her mother's slender figure expanded and ballooned, and the once-energetic woman, who used to race her to the shops and take her swimming, skating and cycling, disappeared completely, transformed into a beached and breathless invalid.

'I suspect you're in denial, Jane, my love. It's a basic instinct for women to want children.'

'One that's dying out,' Jane snapped, angered by this extended conversation. 'More and more women, these days, make a careful, considered decision to stay childless.' Her own decision had been arrived at rather earlier – somewhere between the age of nine and ten. 'Yet it's still regarded as shameful, like admitting being gay was, twenty years ago, or Americans letting slip that they never go to church. Sometimes, when people ask me – and they still do,' she said pointedly, with a resentful glance at Alison, 'I'm tempted just to lie and pretend I wasn't *able* to conceive. I'd get sympathy then, not blame.' She sprang to her feet, strode over to the sink, and banged her cup and plate down on the draining-board. 'Anyway, I'd better go – I need to do some errands.'

'I'm sorry, Jane, I've upset you.'

'Not at all,' she muttered, although vowing to herself to avoid all future visits. In nine months' time, those twins would be a living, breathing reality, stirring memories she was too terrified to face. Yet how could she end a friendship that had lasted forty years, or

– worse – explain the breach to her mother? Alison was the daughter her mother would have liked to have had herself.

'Don't get up. I'll see myself out.'

'I wouldn't hear of it!' Alison gave her a hug – one of genuine affection. That was part of the trouble. Her friend's natural, inbuilt decency made her own vile nature seem all the more despicable. Would Alison continue to hug her if she could see into her mind?

Parcelling up the remainder of the cake, Alison insisted she took it home with her, then lumbered out to open the front door. 'Oh, look!' she said, 'here's Mike back, with the gang. You'll just have to stay a bit longer now, and say hello to them all.'

Jane let herself in to her smart, uncluttered flat with an overwhelming sense of relief. No destructive children had ever wreaked their havoc *here*. Her white walls were still immaculate, the cream carpeting unscathed, and there was not the smallest chip or crack in her elegant bone china. Her home was an oasis in comparison with Alison's, and, indeed, such perfection was essential for her basic peace of mind. To have a neat and tidy flat seemed as crucial a requirement as untainted food or unpolluted air. Every surface must be clean and clear, and no shred of flotsam and jetsam allowed to foul the tide of her ordered adult life.

Having put away the cake, she hung her jacket in the cupboard and stowed her bag on the shelf. Glancing in the mirror, she couldn't help but contrast her face and figure with Alison's. The six pregnancies had taken their toll; left her friend with saggy breasts and a flabby, protruding stomach. And the strain of bringing up six kids had etched deep frown-lines into her forehead, whereas *she*, thank God and Botox, was completely free of wrinkles. In six months' time, Alison would be vast, if her last pregnancy was anything to go by. That baby had been a ten-pounder, and, of course, twins would be still worse.

Suddenly, a plan hatched in her mind: why not ensure she was out of the country when the twins were due in September? It would be the perfect time for a holiday abroad: the resorts less crowded, the heat less intense, and the risk of encountering families with children considerably reduced. One of the perks of childlessness was freedom: freedom to go away whenever one chose; not restricted to school holidays or child-friendly destinations. And, even more important, the freedom of travelling light. Holidays for Alison involved tons of paraphernalia, and, with two babies on the way, it would be back to carrycots and pushchairs, baby-baths and booster-seats, feeding-bottles, sterilizers and piles of disposable nappies. Not to mention all the older children's clobber: roller-blades and scooters, cricket bats and swimming gear, stacks of toys and games, clothes and shoes and picnic stuff and a veritable first-aid chest – wagonloads' of baggage that had to be transported, along with the actual tribe.

The thought of her own vacation, with one small, streamlined suitcase, was definitely appealing, especially as she hadn't been abroad since the autumn before last. In fact, she could probably take a good four weeks, since she was owed the leave left over from last year. She would need to time it carefully, of course, to ensure she was at least 2000 miles away the first weeks after the birth, when Alison would be bloated still, her colossal breasts leaking milk and padlocked to a crumpled, red-faced monster; a bawling, burping bundle of appetite and need.

Having retrieved her bag and jacket, she went straight out again, heading for the travel agent. Best to book well in advance, to allow the widest choice of dates and destinations. Besides, having been stuck indoors with Alison half the afternoon, she hadn't had a chance yet to enjoy the rare spring sunshine. So far, March had been continually wet and blustery; more raging lion than gambolling lamb. Only today had the wind died down and the sun resumed its role of coaxing green from brown. She decided to take the long route, through the park, and see if the horse chestnuts were in leaf.

Not quite. The fat, sticky buds were swollen and distended, but no fluttery green sprays had yet opened like the fingers of a hand. The blackthorn was in flower, though, having changed from last week's mourning into a froth of white confetti. Ironical, she reflected, how even here, in the park, she couldn't escape from procreation. Birds were hatching their young; frogs copulating in the pond; catkins puffing pollen-clouds on every passing breeze; the whole of nature burgeoning and breeding. Still, she was feeling distinctly better, out in this soft, scented air and enjoying the sense of relaxation engendered by the weather. Now that winter's grip had loosened, people were coming out of hibernation like butterflies or bees, basking beneath benevolent blue skies. Some were walking dogs, others flying kites, several simply lazing on the grass.

She took the path that led past the large lily-pond, on towards the bandstand, through the rockery and rose-garden and eventually out to the High Street, keeping up a brisk, determined pace. She hated being idle, even at weekends; preferred to stick to a timetable; have some goal in mind.

All at once, she stopped, riveted by the sight of two babies in a pushchair – twins – *her* twins; the twins who had died at two years old, yet alive and resurrected. She continued staring in amazement, although uncomfortably aware that their wary mother, a slip of a girl, in a garish purple anorak, was eyeing her suspiciously – as a potential baby-kidnapper, perhaps. Quickly she averted her gaze, but, too shaken to walk on, sank down on the bench beside the girl, so she could watch the twins surreptitiously. The likeness was astounding and all the more extraordinary, considering how rare that particular colouring was: the rich, gleaming, red-gold hair – not carroty, not ginger, but genuinely titian – and the distinctive eyes, a brilliant speedwell-blue. As an insipid-looking child herself, with mousy hair and drab grey-nothing eyes, she had been jealous of those hated babies' sheer glamour and appeal. How horribly unfair it seemed that no one ever stopped to ogle *her*, exclaim about her beauty or joke about the droves of men who'd be queuing up to date her. She was simply overlooked: the plain, boring, elder sister, not worthy of a second glance.

Again, her gaze strayed back to the twins. It was as if she were looking at the photograph which still stood in pride of place on her mother's mantelpiece: the same mop of auburn curls, the same delicate, porcelain skin; even the same listless air, as if the babies were over-tired or ill. She knew from Alison's family that most toddlers were tornadoes – explosive, irrepressible – yet these particular two sat slumped passive in the pushchair.

'How old are they?' she asked their mother, suddenly.

'Just coming up to two. But they're small for their age. You see, they haven't been too well....'

Desperately, Jane tried to close her ears; couldn't bear to hear the details: the slow decline, the death, the parents' lifelong mourning, while she, the sister, silently rejoiced.

'Chantal has a problem with her breathing, and Melanie's not eating as she should.'

Fancy names. Of course. Exceptionally beautiful children must have names to match. Her mother's two had been Rosamund and Bella. Another painful contrast. Plain Jane was considered good enough for her.

'Do *you* have children?' the girl asked, thawing now a little.

'No.'

'Actually, twins are quite a handful.'

Jane gave the curtest nod, aware she must seem rude. 'Yes,' she repeated, her voice indistinct and shaky. 'I know.'

'Why? Do you have twins in the family?'

The silence seemed to stretch for ever. 'I had twin sisters,' she blurted out, at last. 'Just like these, in fact. The same hair and eyes and … but I, er, lost touch with them.'

'You mean, when you grew up?'

'No, as a child. Very early on.'

'Gosh! How awful.'

'It wasn't, actually.' She was appalled by the words escaping from her lips. She must be losing her grip. As a rule, she would no more confide in strangers than run naked down the street.

'Could I *hold* them?' she asked, barely recognizing the person making so unspeakable a request. The very thought of touching the twins brought her out in a sweat.

The girl bit her lip, clearly on her guard again. 'I'm sorry, no. I told you – they're not well. In fact, I really ought to get them home.' She stood up, grabbed the pushchair handles, made to walk away.

'No, wait! Don't go! This is desperately important. You see, I … I never held my own twins.'

The girl swung round, with a frown. 'But you said you didn't have children.'

'I was lying,' she whispered, almost to herself. 'They *were* my twins, but I … lost them.'

'Look, are you OK? You sound a bit – well …' The sentence petered out.

Jane said nothing. Had she *ever* been OK?

'Maybe you ought to see a counsellor…. Anyway, must dash!'

Gone. Vanished in a trice. With no warning, no goodbye. Exactly like the first time. Men in black, called undertakers, swarming through the house. Two tiny coffins, shock-white against the black. Stiff wreaths; their blooms distorted; pins stuck through fragile flower-heads; evil scarlet roses bleeding into white. Her father's cold, stern, hurting hand, shackled to her own hand throughout the funeral. Yet, even long years afterwards, she had never got her parents back. Her mother remained chained to the dead twins, shrouded in black-marble grief, and her father buried his loss in overwork, escaping day and night from the dark morgue of the house. While *she* grew up, alone.

Tears streamed down her face. Furiously she brushed them off. She *never* cried, let alone in public. And, even now, she wasn't mourning the babies – that was well beyond her powers. Rather, she was weeping for her childlessness: the childlessness imposed on her by terror and resentment, and meted out as a due punishment for murder – murder in intent, at least. And she was weeping for the fact that, wherever she might go, on whatever 'adult' holiday or 'perfect' trip or tour, she could never travel light.

And never had.

Prickly Pear

Louise blew the dust off the blue-silk padded cover, with the tooled inscription, OUR BABY'S BOOK, and the picture of a stork holding a cradle in its beak. She opened the first page.

> Our baby was born on ...
> Our baby was born at ...
> Our baby weighed ...
> We called our baby ...

All the entries had been filled in by her father, in his distinctive, flowing copperplate. She sat staring at the writing, so familiar from his countless letters, or lists of jobs he left around the house, or instructions laboriously copied out for workmen – although wasted on them, really. Such impressive penmanship should be preserved in a museum, under a glass case.

As the phone rang for the umpteenth time, she dragged herself out of her chair. It had been mostly kindly neighbours, commiserating, offering help, but she had fobbed them off, so far. It seemed imperative to be alone – as she very rarely was these days.

'Hello ... *Who?* ... Oh, the dentist ... I'm sorry, I'd no idea he had an appointment this morning ... No, he isn't ill ... Yes, I know he should have cancelled it, but it wasn't actually possible.' A nervous laugh escaped her – a vulgar squawk, wildly inappropriate, which she quickly tried to turn into a cough. 'He, er, passed away – yesterday.'

'Passed away' – loathsome phrase. Lily-livered. Euphemistic. Muffling the dark, dread shriek of death.

'Thank you,' she said to the receptionist, who was giving little bleats of sympathy, before launching into an involved account of her own father's sudden death.

When she had finally rung off, Louise went straight back to the baby book. Why blue, she wondered, stroking the plush cover? Had they wanted a boy? And, if so, why had they never tried again; produced a second child? Maybe they had tried, though, and failed. So many things she didn't know – would never know, now that he had gone. Gone for ever. She couldn't grasp it yet; kept expecting to hear his key in the door and his cheery cry, 'Louise, my love! How good of you to come.'

Turning the pages of the album, she peered closely at the tiny photographs – black and white, of course, since they dated from the fifties. The first showed her as an infant, bundled up in her father's arms in this very sitting-room, which had changed little over all that time. Her parents were so frugal and old-fashioned they had seen no reason to replace the existing furniture and furnishings, as long as they were serviceable. Admittedly, most of their stuff had faded and deteriorated but, over the years, *they* had also faded, and perhaps began to feel an instinctive bond with the rickety and obsolete. So different from her own generation, who had insisted on the up-to-date, the fashionably contemporary.

Something fell out of the book on to her lap: a small brown envelope, dated 2 May, 1955. Inside was her first lock of hair, cocooned in tissue paper, with a note added by her father: 'Louise's hair is turning slightly darker. Originally, it was the colour of clover honey, but now it's more like butterscotch. Although the texture's very fine, there's a definite hint of a curl.'

It amazed her that he had found the time for all this detailed record-keeping but, knowing his perfectionism in matters of calligraphy, he had probably refused to allow her mother to inflict her messy scrawl on the book. And actual photos of her mother were noticeably rare, since she had always shunned the limelight and tended to disappear on some 'urgent' kitchen mission, if any of their relatives showed up with a camera. It was her father who was pictured, year on year, giving her a bottle, or feeding her as she sat in her high chair, or using his bent, braced knee to help her stand, as a wobbly but determined toddler.

Reluctantly, she closed the book. It was sheer indulgence to be wallowing in nostalgia when there was such a lot to do. Although all she had managed to achieve so far was to cover the old hearth rug with mementoes of her father, which she had collected from around the house: his shabby, Velcro-fastening shoes, misshapen from his bunioned feet; the *TV Times*, with his favourite programmes highlighted in marker-pen; the ancient, rusting, long-bladed, lethal scissors he had owned since God knew when; his stout wooden box of tools, containing not just hammers, pliers, chisels, but a bag of Creamline toffees and – strangely – a child's skipping rope. She had also found a shopping list, impeccably penned, of course, but pathetic in its meagreness: 'toilet roll, tin of Irish stew'. She couldn't chuck such objects in the bin. They seemed part of her inheritance, to be treasured and conserved.

She got up again as the doorbell rang: Miss Mays from number six: a small, bird-like creature, with fragile skin, parchment-pale, and watery blue eyes. She had lived next door for close on half a century; been part of their life in a vague and distant sort of way; someone they helped out in emergencies, or chatted to over the fence about the weather, or the National Health, or the black-fly on the roses; someone whose smelly, manic spaniel she had played with as a child.

'How are you, Louise, dear?' she asked, in her thin reed of a voice. 'I wanted to come and pay my respects. Your father was such a lovely man – a real gentleman, in fact.'

'Thank you,' Louise murmured. She had been thanking people all day – although rarely with true gratitude: her father's brusque and businesslike GP; the pompous, prune-faced registrar; the ridiculously young undertaker, with his soft fuzz of a moustache.

'It must have happened very suddenly.' Miss Mays edged a fraction closer on the step, obviously keen to hear the saga.

'Yes,' said Louise tersely, herself shrinking back a little. 'Look, it's good of you to call, Miss Mays, but forgive me if I don't ask you in. I'm up to my eyes at the moment.'

'You always were a busy one. It was go, go, go, with *you*, my dear, even from the age of eight or nine!'

Louise flushed. The trouble with living in the same small street from birth to the age of twenty-one was that people got to know you far too well. So she had always been a restless type, impatient to get on, but was that any worse than idling away her existence? It had been a relief, as well as a wrench, to move to Inverness, and to a house set on its own, without the musty breath of neighbours exhaling in her face. 'I could pop round in an hour or so, if that's convenient, and fill you in on the details.'

'Lovely, dear! I'll put the kettle on. And you must try a slice of my lemon sandwich cake.'

Once she'd closed the door, Louise stood leaning against the table in the hall, trying to gather her strength. The energy she'd possessed aged eight, and, indeed, most of her adult life, seemed to have deserted her entirely – the worker-ant now turned into a sloth. All the things on this morning's long 'to-do' list, she had carried out in so inert a fashion, it was if she were groping through a dense and choking fog.

'Full name of the deceased?' the registrar had asked, and she'd actually forgotten her own father's middle name. And when she had come to sign the papers, to obtain the death certificate, her hand had shaken so badly, her signature looked spastic as it tottered across the page. Then, sitting in the small, stuffy room at the funeral directors', she had tried to choose a coffin from the brochure. They all looked so pretentious, and she knew her father would vehemently object to lying on white taffeta, or being buried in a box that went by some highfalutin name such as Herald or Balmarol.

Worst of all was viewing the body: his face frog-cold and waxen; his nails a grisly bluish-mauve; his hands clasped across his chest in a reposeful, pious manner, quite alien to his character. Equally untypical was the dreadful, eerie silence. Never had her father been uncommunicative. Normally he took the lead, if there was something to be organized, gave orders, spoke his mind. So why wasn't he complaining about what he'd call this 'carry-on', insisting they bury him in the garden in a nice, strong cardboard box, beneath his favourite bush? And, no, he didn't want a wreath – lugubrious things, and a scandalous expense. And, as for a hearse, what was wrong with the old wheelbarrow?

'Open your eyes,' she had whispered desperately. 'Take an interest. Tell them who's the boss.'

She had left the place two hours ago, feeling disoriented and drained, and had been mooching round the house since then, failing to complete a single task, but drifting indecisively from one thing to another. She must choose a job and stick to it – perhaps start in the kitchen and clear out all the cupboards.

Having found a couple of packing cases in a corner of the cellar, she began removing all the crockery and stowing it away, first wrapping it in sheets of her father's unopened *Guardian*. She had better take this china to Oxfam, although the stained and pitted saucepans and rusting baking tins were fit only for the dump. And the mincer and the jelly-moulds were in little better shape, and clearly hadn't been used since her mother died. No way would her father make jellies or mince meat.

She stood holding the rabbit jelly-mould, recalling her childhood birthday parties: the trembly red rabbit, sitting on a bed of chopped-green-jelly grass; its tail a blob of whipped cream; its whiskers strips of angelica, and the grass itself sprigged with whipped-cream daisies. Although the mould was badly dented, she laid it on the hearth rug in the sitting-room, along with all the other things that couldn't be thrown out.

Hardly had she got back to the kitchen, when the phone rang yet again. It still seemed wrong for her to answer it and, every time she picked up the receiver, she looked nervously around, as if expecting her father to come rushing in from the garden to take the call himself.

'Yes, hello. Mr Chandler's house … Oh, Graham, it's *you*! I told you not to ring.'

She listened with increasing impatience to her husband's halting croak – all he had left in the way of a voice now. He was distressed about the new carer – unfriendly and unkind, he said, and as much use as a blue peapod.

'A blue peapod,' she repeated, with her usual irritation at his misuse of the language. Once, he had been skilled with words, employing them with rigour and respect.

'What time will you be back, Louise? I can't manage here without you.'

'Graham, I've only just *come*! The flight didn't get in till ten … Yes, I know I left at six, but we were held up at the airport … No, I can't fly home tonight – I've told you that already.'

Shameful to be sharp with him and so lacking in compassion, but her normal reserves of sympathy appeared to have dried up overnight. If Graham hadn't had his stroke, she wouldn't have neglected her father for an interminable six months, or failed to realize that he, too, must be ill. And it was Graham who'd put paid to his usual frequent visits, because he hadn't wanted anyone, not even his own father-in-law, to witness his infirmity.

'Look, I'm sorry you're not feeling good. Why don't I ring Melanie and get her to come over?' Unfair to blame her husband, when it was just as much her fault. She'd been so horrified, so shaken, by Graham's sudden, dire decline from an independent work-horse to a complaining, clingy invalid, she had barely spared a thought for her poor father; simply rung him once a fortnight and accepted it as gospel when he assured her he was fine.

'Graham, you *must* remember Melanie! She came just last week – tall, with reddish hair.' Strokes were so insidious, blitzed not just language and mobility but memory and mind. The man she had loved for thirty years was now damaged goods, a wreck. Sometimes, passing the bin of marked-down products in the local corner-shop, she imagined Graham lying there amongst broken packets and dented cans – forlorn, unwanted objects, reduced for clearance and finally thrown out.

'Yes, she's very nice. You liked her. I'll phone her now, and ring you back the minute I get hold of her. OK?'

Melanie was out, of course, but she left a message on the answerphone, then, returning to the kitchen, began sorting through the cutlery drawers, wrestling with self-pity – despicable yet difficult to shift. She had barely come to terms with losing Graham – as husband, helpmate, friend – and now she was faced with her father's death. Even Jake had disappeared, deciding to take a sabbatical in Kenya – presumably his way of saying that he simply couldn't cope with a depressed and drooling father in a wheelchair.

Angrily, she filled the second packing case, only to stop, with half-a-dozen fish-forks in her hand. What on earth was she about, clearing out the crockery and cutlery, when she'd need it for the funeral reception? Her father would want it to be held here, as had happened when her mother died. What she *should* be doing was drawing up a guest list and getting in touch with everyone, to inform them of the date and time. She simply wasn't thinking straight. Her mind kept sneaking back to that claustrophobic funeral parlour, to plead again with the cold and stiffening corpse: 'Come back. Sit up. Get out of that vile box!'

She jotted down a few random names on the back of an old envelope – Miss Mays, Aunt Nora, Jim and Janet Slade – then sat staring into space, aware how weak and empty she felt. She had eaten nothing since the news of her father's death, nor wept a single tear. The two appeared to be connected. While her eyes remained perversely dry, it was her stomach that had expressed her grief by going into painful spasm and rumbling audibly.

As she put the kettle on, she heard his usual admonition chiming in her head: 'Don't forget to warm the pot'. He had been saying it for decades, as if he hadn't quite grasped the fact that she had actually grown up, and now ran a home of her own. Obeying his silent instructions, she went to fetch the tea-strainer, which, in deference to her mother's rules, he insisted that they use. And the all-important tea cosy – a weird, multi-coloured monstrosity knitted by her thrifty mother from bits and pieces of wool.

Once the tea things were assembled, she raided the fridge for milk, shocked by what she found. The slab of cheese had sprouted a fine blue mould; the slices of ham were a translucent, slimy green, and the sole pot of yoghurt had separated into curdled solids and greyish, watery ooze. My tears would look like that, she thought, as she poured the liquid down the sink – festering and sickly, tainted by an excess of grief.

But why was all this produce way past its sell-by date, when yesterday morning her father had been still alive? Had his eyesight failed to the point that he couldn't even see the mould? Or had he been so gravely ill that he could no longer eat at all? But, if so, why the shopping list? In any case, Dr Hayes had told her just this morning that, as far as he knew, her father was in reasonable health.

But, of course, he avoided doctors on principle. 'Don't trust the buggers, Louise. They'd kill you soon as look at you.' And he wouldn't want to worry the neighbours – or worry anyone, for that matter. His attitude had always been, 'Don't make a fuss. Don't ask for help. Soldier on regardless.'

Yes, soldier on through death.

Opening the back door, she hurled the offending foodstuffs into the dustbin, then stopped a moment, glancing up at the cloudless azure sky. It seemed little short of an insult that summer should be preening in the garden, when it was winter in her mind.

Back inside, she made a tour of her father's bedroom, hunting for some clue – perhaps a packet of aspirin he'd been taking for high blood pressure, or a letter in his jacket pocket admitting he wasn't quite as well as he'd made out. If there *was* such a letter, maybe he'd been planning to post it before he finally collapsed, as a last-ditch cry for help. But all she found in his pockets was a tube of glucose sweets, an old, brown, shrivelled conker, a tiny, well-thumbed photo of her mother, and a few crumpled handkerchiefs.

She sank down on the bed, still holding his best grey suit, the one he'd worn for her mother's funeral. She pressed the fabric against her face, trying to recapture his vital essence. But the only smell was mothballs. Her mother's antipathy to moths had rivalled his aversion to the medical profession.

The phone shrilled through her thoughts. She prayed God it was Melanie, and not Graham in distress again. Gingerly, she picked up the receiver.

'Who? … Oh, Miss Mays … No, of course I haven't forgotten. Could you give me a bit longer?'

Stupid to have promised to go round, with all the things outstanding on her list: her father's bank and insurers to contact, his electricity and gas suppliers, BT, the Inland Revenue; his credit cards to cancel, his outstanding bills to pay, his library books to be returned, his milk and papers stopped….

In need of consolation, she went to fetch the large, square biscuit tin with the picture of Prince Albert on the lid. Every day of her life, until she left home to get married, that tin had made its appearance after supper, as adjunct to her parents' post-prandial pot of tea. The biscuits rarely varied: mostly plain digestives and falsely named 'Rich' Tea. And, even after his bereavement, her father honoured the traditions of frugality and thrift, and would no more return from Sainsbury's with fancy chocolate fingers or extravagant real-butter shortbread than invest in new clothes or replace the fraying bed-linen. In fact, the only way he had managed to cope was to carry on as if his wife were still alive; buy the brands she had bought herself, and keep strictly to her timetable and to her watchword of economy.

She dipped a stale digestive into her mug of milkless tea. The milk in the fridge was semi-solid, and stank, but at least the mug was comfortingly familiar – as old as she was, in fact, and part of a boxed Peter Rabbit set, including a plate and bowl, which had been one of her Christening presents. Sadly, the plate and bowl had broken, but the mug had stayed the course, outliving both her parents.

The frieze of bunnies leaping in a circle round the top rim of the mug looked enviably fit and frisky. Rabbits had always figured in her childhood: rabbit jellies, rabbit books, even a natty rabbit-skin coat and – somewhat paradoxically in light of the coat – a whole series of rabbits as pets.

'Dad,' she said out loud, 'remember Thumper and Snowy and their twenty-seven babies?'

No answer but a shrill peal on the doorbell. Surely not Miss Mays again, when she'd just spoken to the poor old soul?

'Hello,' she said uncertainly, disconcerted by the sight of a broad-shouldered, burly man standing on the step, dressed in a brash blue suit and garish purple tie.

'May I offer my condolences,' he murmured, eyes respectfully downcast.

Condolences – another odious word: over-formal, hollow at the core. 'Thank you,' she responded, 'but, er, have we met? I presume you're a friend of my father—'

'I'm afraid I didn't have that pleasure. I've only just moved into the road, less than a fortnight ago. Johnny Johnson's the name.' He thrust out a hot, perspiring hand and shook hers with jovial force. 'I was informed about your tragic loss by my neighbour across the street. She told me your late father had lived here over fifty years, and ...' – he cleared his throat, continued in a rush, 'I was wondering if you had plans to sell the house?'

'Well, yes,' she frowned, 'at some point, but—'

'I do hope I'm not intruding. I realize it's a delicate time. But, you know, I could save you a lot in estate agents' fees, if we settled the matter privately between us. Thing is, my business partner wants to move much closer to me, and this house would be ideal for him and his young family.'

'Mr Johnson,' she said icily, 'I'm not in any state at the moment to discuss property transactions, let alone—'

'Do call me Johnny,' he interrupted. 'Everybody does. And you're Louise, I understand. Now look, Louise, have you any idea how much these estate agents rake off for themselves in commission?'

Pink with indignation, she slammed the door in his face. The *cheek* of the man – to try to wrest her father's house away when the corpse was not yet even buried!

She collapsed into a chair – the one where she'd left the baby book – and held the small, square album close against her chest while she wrestled with her feelings. She was probably overreacting, as she seemed to have done for the last thirty-six hours. Insensitive the man might be – certainly premature in his approach – but he might genuinely wish to save her trouble and expense. After all, it was part of her duty as executor to put the house on the market, and it would surely help to have a purchaser ready and willing to move in. Apart from anything else, it would save her constant treks down south to see prospective buyers, all of whom might renege on the deal just as it appeared to be going through. Which would mean she could put Graham first, instead of continually leaving him in the hands of so-called carers.

Yet she felt sickened by the thought of giving up this place to someone else. Indeed, so painful was the prospect, she began a sort of pilgrimage, wandering into every room to pay her last respects to it, and ending up in the kitchen – the old-fashioned, gloomy kitchen, with its broad-shouldered, bulky cupboards and stained, well-trodden lino. Any typical new owner would rip out the old appliances, replace them with streamlined fittings; repaint the sludge-green walls (chosen by her mother as 'unlikely to show finger-marks') in a dazzling, heartless white. The whole house might be remodelled; all traces of her parents lost beneath fresh plaster; her entire childhood and past history blitzed by callous strangers who cared only for modernity. And her father's garden, with its rows of runner beans and the special bed he'd given her, as a kid of five or six, to grow catmint and nasturtiums – still preserved in tribute to her – would be 'landscaped' into conformity and lost beneath smart paving-stones.

But what was the alternative? To keep the place for ever, as a shrine and a memorial, and commute from Scotland every week to polish up her memories?

Despondently, she returned to her armchair, wishing she were better at decisions, or at least far better organized. She shouldn't even be thinking about the problem of the house, until she had sorted out the details of the funeral: which hymns to choose, and readings; what food and drink to serve at the reception. Yet every time she applied herself to such pressing practicalities, it was like trying to build a structure from sawdust and Scotch mist, as if she, as well as Graham, had lost some vital component of her mind.

Closing her eyes, she let herself be comforted by the steady, rhythmic ticking of the clock. It had ticked throughout her childhood, measuring out the days; signalling getting-up-in-the-morning time, catching-the-school-bus time, homework time, suppertime, biscuit-time, then bedtime. How consoling all those rituals were; the safe and orderly structure provided by her parents, where no one ever overslept, or turned up late for anything, or skimped on work, or forgot their roles and duties. In her present life, such rigour had capsized. Graham had lost all sense of day or night; lost his previous way of life, with its timetable, its schedules, its strict delineation of weekdays and weekends. Now, every day was a weekend, in the sense that he was continually at home – jobless, workless, aimless – and she, too, had lost her job, or at least taken on a new one, as unpaid minder and nursemaid.

With a sigh of resignation, she began flicking through the baby book again, pausing at the heading, 'Our Baby's First Words', printed in italic script. 'Dad-Dad' was the first entry, of course. What else? And 'Singing brush' the second. Singing brush – how weird. The sort of peculiar phraseology Graham might come up with; in fact, akin to a 'blue peapod'.

Leafing on through the album, she found herself, as a tot of two or three, preening almost coquettishly in her glamorous rabbit-skin coat. 'Hollywood star!' her father had written underneath.

The next photograph, in contrast, showed her dressed in a drab pinafore and scowling at the camera, her eyes narrowed in ill temper and her bottom lip stuck out.

'Prickly Pear', the caption read – the name her father used for her when she was fractious or ill-tempered. How extraordinary that she had forgotten it entirely. Or blanked it out deliberately, perhaps. Because she *had* been fractious – and often, she recalled now to her shame. In fact, only at this moment did it dawn on her how difficult she must have been: an obstinate and self-willed miss, subject to mercurial moods, and with lofty, but quite contradictory, ambitions – to be an astronaut, a gangster, a Black Belt and the Queen.

Yet, whatever aggravation she had caused him, her father had always been her rock: the one she ran to with scraped knees or broken toys; the one who took her swimming, taught her how to fly a kite, spent hours explaining decimal points, or the proper use of adverbs, or the life-cycle of frogs – frequently mugging up the facts beforehand from a stack of library books. He had even prepared her bottles, the first three months of her life, taking unpaid leave from work, so as to be there in the daytime, and getting up several times each night. (Her mother, a martyr to depression, couldn't – wouldn't? – breastfeed.) And, judging by the record of her weight – from 6lb 7oz at birth, to 13lb at three months – he had done a creditable job.

She continued staring at the petulant child, its arms rebelliously crossed, and one bare foot twisted round the other – the very image of prickliness. Is that how Graham saw her: as spiky and sharp-tongued, and bristling with resentment? And had their only son removed himself to Kenya not to avoid his stricken father, but to escape his stroppy mother? And, of course, prickly pears were cacti – desert plants inhabiting an arid, parched terrain. Was she a *human* desert: stony-hearted, sterile, and too barren and dried-up to dispense any but the most meagre drops of the milk of human kindness?

She was aware that she was blushing from the unspoken accusations; even her biased-in-her-favour father admitting she could be a 'trial', and not only as a child. When he had last stayed with them in Scotland, a good seven months ago now, she had snapped at him for nothing; been overhasty, querulous, and with no excuse whatever.

Did he even like her, she began to wonder now, desperate at the thought that the close father-daughter bond she had so arrogantly assumed to be a keystone of her life, might be built on a delusion? Just because he'd championed her against hostile teachers, or cruel or feckless friends, didn't mean he admired her as a decent human being. All her faults and failings seemed to have taken solid form and were being projected on giant movie screens in the multiplex of her head, to a soundtrack of cacophonous reproaches, some from decades back.

'When he tried to stop you smoking as a teenager, you refused to listen and flounced out of the house.'

'Even on your wedding day, you made a fuss because you didn't approve of his suit. Couldn't you have let him be him*self* – a simple man who hated pomp and show?'

If only she had apologized – on her wedding day, and *every* day on which she might have caused him pain. And couldn't she have thanked him for his lifetime of loyal service; explained how much it meant? Now it was too late. Yet, despite the sting of that stark fact, still she couldn't cry, as if all her grief had solidified into a black, strangulating boulder, damming up her throat.

She slammed the album shut, no longer able to bear the sight of her own peevish, screwed-up face, and terrified she was about to lose her grip. She had no one else to help her – no husband, son or sibling – so it was imperative to keep control.

She shut her eyes, slumped back against the cushions, fixed her whole attention on moving further back in time – to those hushed nights in the nursery, when she was too young to have emotions except hunger sated, bliss restored, as she lay cradled in her father's arms.

Slowly, almost guiltily, she let herself relax; saw, through half-closed eyelids, bars of dappled moonlight silvering the nursery curtains; shadows of the cot-bars flickering on the wall.

Yes, she was there again, serene again, in her smocked night-gown and soft shawl; no sound except her father's heartbeat, slowing the wild tempo of the world. Her adult burdens had faded with the light. Death and grief were meaningless, and Graham was dissolving to a mere shadow of a shadow. Both he and Jake were only possibilities in a distant, far-off future – a future unimaginable and of no interest to an infant. There were only two people in existence now: her father and herself. Inverness and Kenya were no longer on the map. This modest, compact terraced house comprised her sole geography. Of *course* she couldn't sell it, or fly back up to Scotland. As a babe-in-arms, she didn't have the power; was too vulnerable, too small. She must stay here with her father, learning to crawl, to stand, to walk – him beside her always; his bent, braced knee the pillar to her universe.

The pair of them were quite alone, she sheltered by the bulwark of his body, and staring up intently at his face – a face young again, unlined again, fresh and firm and healthy again, and crinkling in his familiar smile as he whispered, 'Prickly Pear!'

At last, she understood. However sharp the spines of the pear, he had always known – and was even now assuring her – that underneath was sweet and succulent fruit.

River Heights

'And this,' said Toby, opening the door with a flourish, 'really is a view to die for.'

Lauren followed him into the spacious lounge, with its dark-oak polished floor, its twin white leather sofas, solid-marble coffee-table, edgy modern sculptures. Before admiring the view, she stopped and gazed around the room, wondering if this could actually be *her* – a failure and a nobody – viewing such a ritzy flat? The whole scenario didn't seem quite real, as if she were playing a part in some lavish Hollywood movie and, at any moment, the director would shout, 'Cut!'

As she walked towards the floor-to-ceiling windows, she seemed to be level with the sky, about to burst through all that acreage of glass and go skedaddling across great banks of rolling clouds. And, however sullen those rain-swollen clouds might look, in no way could they dampen her elation.

Toby led her on to the balcony, with a grand gesture to the impressive panorama, began directing her attention to several landmarks. 'I'm afraid it's a bit nippy today, but just imagine this in summer!'

Who cared about the cold? From this amazing altitude, she could see the broad curve of the river stretching out below, and a great swathe of London on the opposite bank, sweeping all the way from Westminster to Chelsea. If she took the flat, she could stand out here in every kind of weather, charting the river's ever-changing moods; the wind flirting with her hair, and gulls soaring in white flurries past her head. Looking down from such a height gave her a sense of near-omnipotence, as if *she* had built those bridges, laid out the embankment; even controlled the tides. She had loved the Thames since childhood, when her three elder brothers had taken her canoeing, taught her how to beachcomb, how to catch an eel – brothers who disowned her now.

'Cool,' she said, 'having the Thames as your front garden!'

'Yes, I understand from head office that you particularly want a river view.'

She nodded, unwilling to say more. It would sound pretty naff to start babbling about the symbolism of water – the renewal and regeneration that were part of her new start.

'And as high up as possible.'

She mumbled her assent. Height, too, was symbolical. She had left behind her low life, her grotty basement slum, all those grubby, grim relationships with losers.

'You can even entertain here. The balcony's quite big enough. And these chairs and table are solid oak, so they're completely weather-proof.'

As he spoke, a speedboat lasered across the water; two drunken-looking cormorants bobbing on its choppy, churning wake. She imagined her guests sitting in the stylish chairs, watching all the different craft: pleasure cruisers, sailing dinghies, the harbour-master's patrol boat in spanking black-and-white, great lazy, lumbering barges, towed by sturdy tugs.

'But once you close the windows,' Toby told her, 'you won't hear a sound, Miss Armitage. The entire flat's triple-glazed. And air-conditioned, of course.'

'Do call me Lauren.' Only fair, when he had volunteered his Christian name the moment they'd first met. He seemed entirely different from the sharp-suited estate agents she had dealt with up to now. In fact, he struck her as eminently fanciable, in his black polo neck and tight black jeans, and, if she hadn't vowed to put an end to all one-off entanglements, she might have put a teasing hand on some part of his anatomy, or made sure their bodies touched when he was pointing out a feature of the flat. As it was, she was determined to be businesslike; act the part of a wealthy, well-established woman – however fraudulent it felt inside.

'Right, let's go and see the bedroom now. I know you're going to love it.'

Yes, she loved it – and partly for its size. Just that one room was bigger than the whole of her previous flat and, instead of being a cluttered mess of jarring styles and colours, was furnished totally in white: elegant white counterpane on the imposing queen-sized bed; floor-length, white linen curtains; white, fluffy, deep-pile carpet; white marble bedside lamps; white ceramic vase holding tall, white, hothouse lilies, whose cloying, musky, insistent smell seemed to seep into her skin, as she were wearing some exotic scent herself. White was totally impractical, of course, but, as she stood amidst the subtle shades of pearl and snow and ivory, she felt herself being effortlessly released from the smut and grime that had characterized her life to date. This whole block was newly built and newly furnished, with no stains or smears from previous tenants to mar its white perfection – the ideal place for a rebirth.

Toby was pointing out the variety of lights: strip-lights in the wardrobes; concealed spotlights in the ceiling, fluorescent panels set into the dressing table, and a whole range of dimmer-switches by the bed.

'And the bed itself is adjustable,' he said, pulling a lever to demonstrate. 'It also has a built-in massage function. Just press this knob and ...'

As the mechanism purred gently into action, she pictured herself reclining on the freshly laundered sheets, being sensuously kneaded and pummelled at the end of every high-achieving day. She added Toby to the picture – a Toby stripping off his clothes and stretching out beside her, doubling all the delicious titillation. 'For Christ's sake!' she muttered to herself. 'You've finished with those sordid one-night stands.' If she had a new relationship, it must be with someone worthy; different altogether from the pick-ups she'd made do with in the past.

As he showed her the en-suite bathroom, her inanely grinning face was reflected in the gleaming mirrored walls. Quickly she switched off the smile, tried to look nonchalant and blasé, as if the glamour of this flat was very much the norm for her, something she'd grown up with all her life.

'I understand you're an author, Miss Armit— er, Lauren.'

She gave a self-deprecating shrug. It still felt bogus to call herself an author, instead of a waitress or a barmaid, or, latterly, a nightclub hostess. Although, in fact, she was surprised that he didn't know her name, which had been splashed all over the papers when her book came out four months ago. The publishers classed it as a 'misery memoir' – a term she disliked intensely. The word 'misery' seemed too downbeat for all the drama and sensationalism she had revealed about her family: her father's racketeering, her mother's drink and drugs, her brothers' sexual advances to her when she was a kid of twelve or so. Such disclosures had caused a furore, and an uproar from the relatives, who had united in trying to rubbish her, claiming that the entire 300 pages was nothing but a pack of lies. Which had only increased the sales, of course, shot it to the bestseller list, and resulted in her present two-book contract, with an advance so high, she could afford to rent a flat like this and still have money over for new clothes and a car.

'Yes, I'm working on a couple of things at the moment.' That was true, at least. Her new prestigious publishers had not only commissioned a second instalment of the memoir, to bring her story up to date, but also an erotic saga, drawing on her life again, but fictionalized this time. The second memoir was going at a cracking pace, as if all the scandal and hysteria, the fury and acclaim, had acted like a spur, goading her into still more revelations. 'One's a sort of life story, which is already three-quarters done, and the other one's a novel, but that's only at the planning stage.'

'Really? I'm an avid reader. You don't write thrillers, do you?'

'No,' she laughed, distracted by the taps: slim silver dolphins, spouting jets of water as Toby turned them on. 'The novel's more a family drama, but told from the viewpoint of a girl of twenty-three.' She had decided to make the protagonist exactly her own age, mainly because it was easier to write. She couldn't imagine being forty, with a bunch of grotty kids and nothing much to show for them but saggy breasts and stretch-marks. Worse still being sixty: a withered crone, with no more men or sex, no more hope of conquests.

'She's never settled down, and had a really lousy childhood, living with these freakish parents and three brothers who abused her. But then she meets an American guy and—' She shook her head, broke off. 'Look, if I give away the plot, I won't be able to write it. And, anyway, the other book's more urgent, because they want to try to capitalize on the success of the first volume, so I'm working to a deadline. Which reminds me, Toby, I have to meet my agent in less than half-an-hour, so we ought to get a move on.' She liked trotting out that phrase 'my agent'; relishing the kick it gave her.

'How do you get an agent?' Toby asked, apparently more interested in the literary world than in completing the deal on the flat. 'I was reading just the other day about some guy who'd made a million on a book deal, and I was rather tempted to have a bash myself. The problem is, I haven't a clue as to how to start.'

Lauren hesitated, having only a vague idea of how the system worked. In her particular case, her future agent, Hugo, had wandered into her nightclub, semi-drunk, and she'd encouraged him to buy champagne (as she did with all the guys – the most expensive brand, of course). Only when he spelled out what he did, did she tell him about the pile of scribbled pages stuffed in her bottom drawer – pure dynamite, she'd said. From that one evening, her life had taken off. She no longer earned her living chatting up the punters who came to Funky Joe's, but sitting at her new, state-of-the-art computer, when she wasn't hobnobbing with famous authors in Hugo's Chelsea pad.

'Actually, it's difficult to find an agent who'll agree to take you on. In fact, it's as hard to get an agent as a publisher. You see, hordes of would-be writers are dying for a share of the action and sending in their stuff, but the great majority haven't got a chance in hell. Only a fraction of the manuscripts ever get read at all – the rest are sent straight back, or land up in the waste-bin.' Which made her own success all the more astounding. She had Lady Luck to thank for that and, of course, her monstrous family.

'Well, you've obviously done well,' Toby remarked, a touch of envy in his voice, 'But, look, I mustn't keep you if you're pushed for time. I'll just show you the kitchen, then I think we're done.'

The kitchen had the spotless, streamlined efficiency of an operating theatre, and the same battery of complicated machines. Not that she could cook, but it would be a definite advance to own so many gleaming gadgets and a sleek, split-level oven, instead of the single basic gas ring she had made do with up till now.

'What's this?' she asked, peering at a stainless-steel cabinet that resembled a large safe.

'A rather snazzy drinks-cooler.' Toby returned to his role of lettings agent, as he explained the mysteries of the built-in water-dispenser and integral, high-speed ice-maker, the temperature-control system and—

'Toby,' she interrupted, 'I'm going to take the flat. I've made up my mind – this minute!' In fact, the drinks-cooler had clinched it. Such gloriously superfluous extras seemed even more desirable than the sumptuous pad itself. 'It's far nicer than anything I've seen.'

'Brilliant! I know you won't regret it. It's perfect for a writer – the whole ambience feels right.'

'I'm afraid I haven't time to go through all the paperwork right now, but if you can hold it till tomorrow, I'll come in first thing and do the necessary.'

'Great! I'll expect you in the morning.' He ushered her to the door, first presenting her with a large, laminated brochure, listing the selling-points and specifications of luxurious River Heights – the brochure itself as heavy as a hardback, and so glitzy in its general presentation, it did emphatic justice to its subject. 'Just let me lock up, then I'll escort you down in the lift.'

As they descended thirty floors, she experienced a curious sensation: instead of going down, she was soaring up, up, up – up into the clouds again; up into the dizzy heights of her spectacular new life.

'Quiet, please!' Hugo commanded, raising his voice above the buzz of conversation, so he could be heard by the whole gathering. 'I want us all to raise our glasses to Lauren. She's already had a huge success with *Rock Bottom* and I predict an equal triumph for her next two books.'

'To Lauren!' fifty voices echoed, followed by a cry of 'Speech!'

For a moment, she stood dumb, unable to believe that this was really happening; that film producers, scriptwriters and the top brass at a top publishers could actually be her guests. When Hugo first suggested the flat-warming, she had wondered who on earth to ask – certainly not the girls from Funky Joe's, who would only get rat-arsed, nor indeed her waitress friends, who would lower the tone (and might even nick the silver), nor Nathan, Greg or Brian, whom she'd buried in her unsavoury past and had no wish to resurrect – except in the pages of her second memoir. As for her family, forget it. Far from joining in the celebrations, or saying even a brief 'Well done!', they simply shunned her as traitor and a slut.

'Leave it to me,' Hugo had said. 'We'll make the party a publicity exercise, invite the whole media pack, especially the gossip columnists and all the big guns in telly, and a few select but major players from the movie world. Though we won't bother with the snooty literary editors – they'll only damn the book with faint praise, or ignore it altogether.'

'But what about the food and wine?' she'd asked, alarmed at the prospect of catering for big shots, who'd only turn up their disdainful noses if she laid on plonk and crisps.

'Don't worry – we'll use a caterer. In fact, I know this marvellous woman who's an absolute whiz when it comes to upmarket nosh. Even her canapés are works of art. And she's pally with a guy who owns a couple of vineyards in the Dordogne. Just relax, my sweet, and let the pros get on with it. All you have to do is wear something svelte and slinky, and be sure to schmooze the guests.'

'Lauren!' Hugo hissed, bringing her back to the present with an urgent nudge in the ribs. 'We're waiting for you to speak.'

In search of inspiration, she gazed out through the panoramic windows at the lights of London reflected in the water. Churches, bridges, cupolas were laid out below, as if some kindly architect had provided little toys for her diversion; sent catamarans and cabin cruisers chugging up and down the river purely to amuse her.

'W … welcome,' she stammered, suddenly overcome with nerves. She had never made a speech before, let alone to such a swanky gathering. But Hugo's strong, supportive arm was still pressing into hers, acting as a prompt. 'It's great to have you here,' she said, smiling round at the assembled company. 'This block is called River Heights, which isn't very original, I know. But actually I like the name, because I feel I've moved from living at *"rock bottom"'* – she emphasized the title of her book – 'to a place not far from Heaven!'

Surprised by the ripple of laughter, she continued with more confidence. 'When Hugo told me we were going to go to auction, I didn't understand. You see, I thought only paintings or furniture were auctioned.'

More laughter. How extraordinary. As a child, she'd been instantly shot down if she dared to open her mouth, but these people were laughing when she hadn't been remotely funny, and seemed to be hanging on her every word. 'But it was me that was going to be auctioned, Hugo said, or at least my two new books, so you can imagine just how scared I was! It turned out all right, thank God. In fact, it was the only time I remember in my life when men – and even women – were fighting tooth and nail to possess me.'

Guffaws now. She relished them; gloried in the fact that nobody was telling her to shut up, pipe down and stop making an exhibition of herself. Her parents had always sought to muzzle her, but with an audience like this, she felt she could talk for ever and the whole of teeming London would stop its frenetic life to listen.

'Say thank you,' Hugo whispered.

God, she'd totally forgotten! She was meant to be expressing gratitude to Piers Pemberton, the publisher, who had outbid all his rivals and 'bought' her for his stable.

She began voicing her appreciation and, all at once, the legendary P.P., alarmingly high-born and seriously rich, pushed forward to embrace her – an overpowering figure, built like a boxer with broad shoulders and a burly chest. He kissed her on both cheeks and she seemed to drown a moment in the heady scent of cigars and Dior *Homme*, as the entire rapt room exploded in applause.

She paced up and down the lounge, dragging on a cigarette – the first since she'd quit, officially, at the beginning of the month. But this was an emergency: a severe case of writer's block. At first, she had put it down to a hangover resulting from the flat-warming, but no hangover would last for four whole weeks. Since the morning after the party, she had deleted every sentence she had typed, as being, stupid, ungrammatical or just boring, boring, boring. She had even ditched the computer and tried writing in a notebook, as she'd done with her first book, but that had proved worse still. The messy scrawl looked so childish and unprofessional, she'd finally tossed the notebook in the bin.

'Look, get a grip,' she told herself. 'You need a cup of coffee, that's all – something to wake you up.'

She stole into the kitchen, daunted, as always, by its steely, cold perfection. Ignoring the complicated coffee machine (which still baffled her, with its strength-selector, milk-frother and rows of different buttons for Espresso, cappuccino, lattes and the like), she unscrewed the jar of Nescafé and tipped a good three spoonfuls into a white bone-china cup. Then, taking her coffee back to the lounge, she sat staring at the computer screen, still frustratingly blank. She had reached the point in the memoir when she had first moved in with Nathan, and there was enough drama in that period to fill a dozen books: the violence, the affairs, the risks he took to fuel his crack-cocaine habit. Yet still the words refused to come.

She glared at the prissy cup, feeling a pang of nostalgia for the chipped, stained Snoopy mug that had been her constant companion throughout her writing career to date – indeed had become a magic talisman. So long as she used it for her endless cups of coffee, it kept the words cascading out and imbued them with real power. Whereas this namby cup and saucer was useless in the extreme, and seemed even to disapprove of her raw and brutish memoir. 'You're mental!' she muttered irritably, 'blaming a cup and saucer for your own lack of inspiration.'

Jumping up from her desk, she lit another cigarette and continued her restless pacing – back and forth, back and forth, from the pompous, pallid sofas to the glass-topped dining-table and its uncomfortably pretentious chairs. This expensive, showy furniture was beginning to seem unnatural, if not downright alien, and, in fact, only now did it dawn on her that there was not a single item she had actually bought herself. She had deliberately trashed her former stuff as being cheap and shoddy and thus forbidden entry into prestigious River Heights. But, without her things, she felt her whole identity slowly crumbling into nothing.

The flat didn't appear to want her here, as if its own insipid pallor recoiled in sheer distaste from her jolt-blue nail-varnish and wildly hennaed hair. Never, in her former pad, had she felt stagnant or slow-witted. Vivid scenes and characters poured pell-mell from her pen, in their haste to be immortalized, but here the high-flown atmosphere acted like a censor.

Stubbing out her cigarette, she marched into the bedroom and grabbed her coat and bag. She was going out – to buy another Snoopy mug. And a fake leopard-skin rug to lend a bit of tarty life to those immaculate twin sofas. And a nice, fat, bouncy beanbag, so she could sit cross-legged on the floor, as she had always done at home.

'This *is* home,' she reminded herself. 'You've left Tottenham for good.'

Could you really miss a squalid basement flat, with damp walls and peeling paint and the whiff of cats and cabbage seeping through the ceiling from the weird old trout upstairs? Yes, you damned well could.

Having banged her fortress-like front door, she stood waiting for the lift. Even that was pointlessly grand: carpeted and spacious, marble-clad and mirrored. Once she'd stepped inside, she averted her gaze from the glass, avoiding the sight of her pale, drawn face and the dark circles under her eyes. It was proving impossible to sleep in that vestal-virgin bedroom, beneath a stiff white shroud.

The foyer was deserted, save for the smugly plashing fountain and the veritable Kew Gardens of exotic, jungly plants. Most of these flats were corporate lets, rented by faceless City types who spent most of their time at work. And the upmarket boutiques and restaurants, planned as part of the complex, hadn't yet been built. Though even when they *were* built, she would still hanker for the corner shop right opposite her former flat, run by Pakistanis who treated her as family and even gave her credit; still miss the friendly newsagent a few paces down the street, the grungy caff and shabby launderette.

'You don't need a launderette,' she said out loud. 'You have your own washer-drier, as well as a dishwasher, a microwave and an elaborate juicer-cum-blender you haven't even used yet.'

Yes, but the launderette was company, a place to meet the

locals, have a chat, share a joke, cadge a cigarette. As were the café and the newsagent's. At River Heights, there was not a soul to talk to.

'Which is why you're talking to yourself.'

Christ, she'd better watch it! If she carried on like this, she'd be locked up as a lunatic. Already the concierge was glancing at her oddly. Which was hardly any wonder when she was wearing purple leggings and bright green plastic flip-flops underneath her coat. He, of course, was all dolled up in his smart blue livery and ridiculous top hat, and looked like an extra from some TV series on Dickens and his World.

Before venturing to the shops, she decided to take a walk along the river. The languid way it was rippling and meandering might help to calm her down, but, of course, it had nothing else to do all day but slowly sink and rise in obedience to the tide, and open its obliging arms to fish and flotsam, birds and boats. She buttoned up her coat, wishing she'd brought gloves. The November day was cold and overcast; the pigeons on the promenade fluffing out their feathers; the water itself pigeon-coloured: a sombre, brooding grey. As a child, she had always used her blue crayon to colour in a river, but the Thames was never blue – rather shades of shale and slate.

The tide was out and she stopped a moment to watch the scrum of hungry gulls pecking for food in the mud bank. Birds were lucky in that they didn't live alone, but in flocks and throngs and colonies. Still, it was probably her own fault that no one phoned or visited. She'd cold-shouldered all her former friends, assuming she'd gain entry into her agent's own charmed circle, mixing automatically with the cultured types she had met at his smart soirées. But although they'd fêted her short-term as Hugo's latest protégée, they'd subsequently ignored her; never following up with an email or a phone-call, and probably regarding her as scum, because she hadn't been to Oxbridge and didn't read the Literary Review. But just give her time and she'd show the rotten snobs. Once her two new books were published to critical acclaim, they'd be queuing up to kiss her arse.

She spread the tartan rug across one of the white sofas, and stood back to judge the effect. Yes, a definite improvement. Fake leopard-skin had been impossible to find, but at least the zingy reds and greens made the flat more colourful, lessened its severity. And the giant-sized scarlet floor-cushion would be perfect to sit on while she wrote. She had bought a Snoopy notebook and a near-twin of her old Snoopy mug – a double dose of magic, bound to yield results. She planned to return to the computer once she was in full flow, but for now she'd trust to pen and paper. According to a piece she'd read, writing by hand was more natural altogether. The hand, it said, was connected to the arm, and the arm to the rest of the body and thus to the brain and heart, which meant the process could produce effects denied to soulless technology.

Settling herself with her new notebook and new mug, she jotted her provisional title at the top of the first page. Then, biting her lip in concentration, she continued where she'd left off a good four weeks ago.

'Nathan,' she wrote, taking care to make her scrawl more legible than before, 'was a cross between a peacock and Rottweiler – vain and self-regarding, but also savage, aggressive, destructive and obstreperous.' She chewed the end of her pen, wondering if it was true. Who cared? The important thing was to get the words on paper. If Nathan sued, that would be a problem for the libel lawyers and, in any case, might even help her sales.

Except she mustn't think about sales. The publishers were building such high hopes on her, she was terrified she'd let them down. Suppose this second memoir bombed? Would they blame her, send her packing? When she'd written her first book (scribbling it as therapy rather than as literature), she'd known absolutely nothing about royalties, advances, foreign rights, book-club deals and all that sort of stuff. Now she felt overwhelmed by the expectations resting on her shoulders: would she sell serial rights to the *Express* or *Mail on Sunday*? Get a big American deal?

'You won't get a bloody thing if you don't write the fucking book!'

She was startled by the sound of her own voice. She was talking to herself these days almost all the time. Could it be a sign of something sinister? If she lost her marbles, that would put the kibosh on any future as a writer.

'Don't overreact,' she told herself. 'You're just not used to being on your own.' In her previous jobs, she had always interacted with the public, nattering non-stop to customers or clients, and spending barely any time alone. Talking to herself was simply a harmless substitute.

'I first met Nathan,' she continued, trying to concentrate on the task in hand, 'when I was working at the *Brasserie Chantal*.' God! The thrill of that encounter; the audacious way he'd looked at her, holding her gaze for an insolent two minutes flat, as if challenging her to lose her nerve and look down, look away. Instead, she'd stared back blatantly; told him with her eyes that she'd go as far as he liked – and further – do anything he pleased. But how could she put that meeting into words; make the prose rampage and throb with the sheer frenzy of that evening; the move from passion and elation to fury and despair? She sat sucking the end of her pen, conjuring up odd phrases in her head, only to abandon them as tepid. No words seemed quite to capture the emotions of that desperate, electric night.

Maybe she was hungry – she'd had only toast for breakfast and half a nectarine. With some decent lunch inside her, the creative juices might begin to flow. Having mooched out to the kitchen, she stood examining the array of foods in the cupboard and the fridge. She had set up an account with an organic delicatessen, in an attempt to change her diet – in fact, embark on a total detox, by giving up booze and cigarettes. No more junk food or unhealthy snacks or greasy takeaways; only fruit and vegetables and stuff awash with vitamins. Just last week, she had taken a delivery of so-called superfoods, but already she was tiring of bilberries and wheat germ, probiotic yogurt, adzuki beans, alfalfa. Bamboo shoots, in her opinion, were better left to pandas; hemp-seed was canary-food, while only vegetarians would enthuse about five-lentil salad – or any kind of lentils, for that matter. What she really fancied was a cheeseburger and chips – and would it really hurt? After all, she could order a burger as easily as hemp-seed, simply by picking up the phone. She had the cash and standing now to summon anything she pleased, be it a bottle of Smirnoff or a hundred cigarettes. She had probably been too hard on herself, banning every pleasure, and all in one fell swoop. Most writers had their vices – needed them, in fact. While she waited for the burger, a vodka might actually help, loosen her up, cure that dreaded block.

Three drinks later, she struggled up to answer the bell. The delivery man looked really rather gorgeous, with olive skin and tousled jet-black hair. Why not ask him in, if only to hear another human voice? She could invite him to share her lunch; even embark on a harmless flirtation – nothing heavy, just a bit of fun.

But, having handed over the package, he froze in mute embarrassment when she touched his chest provocatively, then turned tail and fled to safety. Well, bugger him – she didn't care; didn't even want his rotten food. In fact, the reek of grease and onions made her feel quite queasy, on top of all the booze. What she did need was a nap. Nobody could write when they were knackered, and she had barely closed her eyes these last few weeks. She was so used to sleeping on a narrow, lumpy divan, her new, ultra-large, ultra-comfortable super-bed made her somehow restless and uneasy. And, of course, it only emphasized the fact that there ought to be a bloke beside her. A singleton in a double bed was a glaring sign of failure.

She removed the rug from the sofa and laid it on the bed, in place of the white counterpane. That was another problem: the overload of white. If her memoir had a colour, it was shrieking, flagrant scarlet, so was it any wonder that the damned thing wouldn't work in this chaste, unspotted sanctuary of a flat?

When she woke, the room was pitch-dark. She groped out her hand for the light-switch and peered groggily at her watch. Half-past two – in the morning – which meant she'd been dead to the world for nearly thirteen hours. Well, that was a minor triumph in its way, compared with her recent insomnia. In fact, now that she'd had some sleep, her brain would probably function. She must go straight to her computer and stay there for the rest of the night; seize this chance with both hands. The new notebook hadn't worked, so it was back to the keyboard for some punchy, powerful prose.

She turned over on her back, listening to the silence. The triple glazing blocked out every sound, but instead of welcoming the peace, it increased her sense of isolation. Was there anybody else awake in this whole vast apartment block? Anyone alive? She had never heard the slightest noise from any of her neighbours, never even *seen* them, for God's sake. Could she really be the only living tenant in a complex of 500 flats? Perhaps all the rest had vacated the place, or simply lain down and died. Perhaps the whole of London had suffered an apocalypse.

Dragging herself from the tangled sheets, she stumbled into the lounge, desperate to see the city lights and prove there hadn't been a meltdown. The floodlit buildings reassured her instantly, as did the lighted squares of windows in the adjacent blocks of flats. And the river pulsed with light – lights along the bridges; lights along the embankment; the illuminated London Eye gazing down from its lofty vantage point.

She switched on all the lounge lights, creating her own private blaze from spotlights, desk-lamps, table lamps and chandeliers. Great – she'd banished the darkness, and next she'd banish the block. Hugo didn't even believe in writer's block; dismissed it as another name for laziness or fear. Actually, she suspected he was tiring of her. He seemed more edgy these days, and had even told her not to phone so much. Well, she certainly couldn't phone him in the middle of the night, so best to stop faffing about and have another crack at writing. She caught sight of herself in the mirror: a total wreck, with crumpled, slept-in clothes and unkempt hair. Still, she refused to waste precious time making herself presentable when there was no one to impress. Even the gulls had gone to roost.

She turned on the computer, welcoming the tiny fanfare as it carolled into life, and the mechanical voice informing her, 'You've got mail.' That cheery voice was comforting. She just wished it had a slightly larger repertoire. Why not 'You've got inspiration', instead of the endless 'You've got mail', or, better still, 'You've got a *male*'? Yes, a big, hot, sexy bloke in her bed would do her very nicely, thanks. Although emails themselves would have to wait until she'd produced at least a thousand words – and brilliant, blistering words at that.

Half an hour later, she had written half a paragraph. Nathan himself seemed to be acting as a stranglehold on any creative burst. The shame and fury she'd always felt on his account not only tied her into knots but kept posing awkward questions. Could she blame him entirely for the horrors of the relationship?

Or was it partly *her* fault? Blame had fuelled her first book and she'd had no hesitation in attacking mother, father, brothers and her whole extended family. But now doubts had started niggling and throbbing like the pain from a deep cavity in a slowly rotting tooth. And, far-fetched as it might sound, it was the judgemental flat itself that seemed to be forcing her to face the truth. But what *was* the truth, for Christ's sake? Fact and invention were now hopelessly entangled; indeed, in the months since publication, invention had become the truth. The interviewers and chat-show hosts had all regarded what she'd written as totally authentic and, as sympathy increased for her dire, disastrous childhood, that childhood grew more horrific still. If you repeated something often enough, even to yourself, it became so familiar, it was difficult to know if it had started out as true or not. And, of course, she'd been more or less compelled to add extra twists and traumas, to feed the growing hype.

Yet, sitting here alone, further stabs and twinges of doubt began shooting through her head, undermining her victim-role. Her mother *wasn't* an alcoholic, not in any strict sense of the word, even less a druggie – in fact, the only drugs she ever took were Mogadon and Stelazine, prescribed by her GP. And was it really fair to call her father's scrap-merchant business 'flagrant racketeering'? OK, he turned a blind eye sometimes to distinctly shady deals, but he wasn't the shameless conman she'd described.

'Get lost!' she hissed to her invisible accuser – an accuser who dwelt here in the flat, as if embodying its sanctimonious character. Since the day she'd first moved in, that shadowy persona had been bent on gagging her writing-voice, as her parents had gagged her child's voice.

'Except they didn't, Lauren, did they? That was just another fabrication. You screamed blue murder most of the time, and no one could have silenced you, even if they'd tried. You always won by yelling louder.'

'Piss off, I said! You just don't understand. Any memoir-writer is bound to exaggerate a bit – it's part of the whole process.'

'But you claimed quite categorically that all three of your brothers repeatedly abused you. That's more than exaggeration – it's a gross distortion of the facts.'

'Listen, if I'd shrugged it off as a bit of childish horseplay, there wouldn't have been a story. The word "abuse" sells books, and I have to think about sales, if only to please my publisher.'

'You didn't *have* a publisher when you concocted all those lies. You were acting out of revenge, because your brothers were successful, while you were just a nobody.'

'Yes, but now I'm the toast of London! Fans worship me, you know. A lot of them write in and say how much I've helped them, just by being frank about all the shit I've had to take.'

'Being frank? Lying through your teeth, you mean.'

'Stop using the word "lie". All I did was add a bit of emphasis.'

'It's hardly "adding emphasis" to depict your brothers as sex-crazed criminals. If they'd decided to sue, you'd have been done for libel.'

'Look, if you really want to know, a libel lawyer read the book, prior to publication – every single page of it – so what's the fuss about?'

'And what did the lawyer conclude? That it *was* a risk – a serious one. Yet your publishers went ahead, regardless. With you cheering them on, of course.'

She fled to the front door and slammed it furiously behind her, refusing to listen to another word. The ghostly presence in this flat had become an accusing judge, a narrow, strait-laced prosecutor, determined to evict her because she didn't have the cachet expected of its tenants. And it knew nothing whatsoever about writing – how you were forced to embroider the truth, otherwise your memoir would read like *Mary Poppins*. OK, she'd gone a bit too far, but it had paid off, hadn't it? Piers Pemberton himself had called her 'a sensation'.

Too overwrought to wait for the lift, she began running down the stairs, her bare feet slipping and hurting on the cold, uncarpeted stone. After eleven flights, she was forced to stop to catch her breath, leaning on the banister in a state of near-despair. What the hell could she *do* the rest of the night? Prowl up and down the corridors, in the hope of finding someone else awake?

She stole along the passage of this unfamiliar nineteenth floor, stopping to listen at the door of every flat. No music, no voices, no sound of any night-time life. If she hadn't left her mobile on her desk, she could have phoned Hugo, claimed it was an emergency and asked to sleep on his sofa. Or rung her friends, to get a bit of support. What friends? They'd all deserted her – or she'd deserted them. Anyway, how could she admit to such a crisis, when she was meant to be a dizzying success?

Best to call on a stranger; invent some story about being mugged on her way home from a club – that would explain her dishevelled appearance, her lack of shoes and coat. Yes, a gang of thugs had assaulted her, nicked her Chloe handbag and her best black leather jacket; even her Jimmy Choos, for heaven's sake. An attack on that scale would win her instant sympathy. She might be offered a brandy – tea and comfort certainly.

Plucking up her courage, she chose a flat with two 3s in its number, and rang the bell as long and hard as she could. Three was lucky, wasn't it, so how could two 3s fail?

No answer. Well, whoever lived there was probably fast asleep; would need a bit of time to shake himself awake, fumble for his dressing-gown. It *was* a man, she'd bet. She *needed* a man – someone she could cling to, someone she could charm.

She rang again, louder still. All at once, the door was flung open by a stout, silver-haired matron wearing a long-sleeved nightgown and an expression of such fury, Lauren simply fled – back along the passage and headlong down all nineteen flights of stairs. When she reached the foyer, her feet were sore, her heart pounding through her chest, her lungs bursting from the unaccustomed exertion. And, although her body gradually quietened, her mind continued spinning and sparking like some manic Catherine-wheel. She must get help; find some cool, calm person who would damp her down, douse the freakish firework she'd become.

'Larry!' she thought, limping along to the night-porter's desk. He had his back to her and was sorting something out in the cupboard opposite. But when he turned to face her, she saw it wasn't genial Larry but the other porter, Ivan, an odious piece of work. She and Ivan had almost come to blows last week, just because she'd asked him to change a fucking light-bulb. OK, she'd lost her rag and sworn, but he shouldn't have tried to pass the buck and tell her to call Maintenance.

'Can I help you, Miss Armitage?'

She shook her head, stalked out through the main doors, wincing as the winter air pounced on her and nipped; whipping through her pathetic purple leggings and filmy cotton top. And, as she picked her way, barefoot, along the river-path, the ridged paving stones felt pitilessly rough. The whole place was deserted – no one out at this hour – certainly no one fool enough to brave the late-November night without a coat and shoes. But nothing would induce her to go back to the flat. She just couldn't be herself in such a prudish, disapproving place.

But did she even *have* a self? If her memoir wasn't true, then all that money and attention had been grabbed on false pretences. And she could hardly continue with the second volume without more pangs of conscience. She had planned to paint Brian in the blackest possible hue; make Greg half-pimp, half-gangster, and reveal all Nathan's vices, even throwing in some extra, to spice things up a bit. You had to pile on drama and sensation, Hugo told her constantly, to keep your readers coming back for more.

It was *his* fault, in a way, for taking her on in the first place. He had described her as a 'hot property': sexy, young and streetwise, but he should have known she couldn't really write and that her success was just a fluke. Making it as an author was largely a matter of luck; some brilliant writers languished, whilst crap ones hit the jackpot. And *she* was crap – that was clear enough. No wonder Hugo had told her not to ring. He had obviously seen through her, at long last; realized she had lost the grain of talent she might have had a year ago, and was now burnt out as a writer, finished and washed up.

Finished as a *person*, come to that – with no job, no home, no friends, no family. Christmas was only a month away, but where in God's name would she spend it, when her brothers barred their doors to her and her parents had changed the locks? Well, not in her apartment – God forbid. The dizzying block reared haughtily above her; her own flat indistinguishable amidst the acreage of glass. River Heights – what a laugh, when *she* was in the depths. Instead of moving to this lordly tower, she should have crawled into some rat-infested cellar.

She leaned against the railings, staring down at the river; the glittering lights of London reflected in its surface. That was a lie, along with all the rest. Beneath the dazzle was mud. She had seen it at low tide – sludge and silt and sediment; endless centuries of history crumbling into gunge. Wasn't *she* like that, as well: the glittering surface concealing filth and lies? Is that why Nathan had left her, Brian betrayed her and Greg refused to speak to her again?

But there was a way to save herself, save the second memoir. A plan was forming in her head – audacious and yet foolproof. If Hugo took the chunk she'd written (200 pages, roughly), and added a sort of postscript of his own, he could ensure the book was published to even greater interest and acclaim. *He'd* know what to say; how to keep it brief but tragic: the author had suffered so appallingly, she'd had no recourse but death, and had decided to drown herself in the river she adored. Thus the memoir, although incomplete, had been completed by the act itself – an act that spoke volumes about its subject's gruelling life. She could already see the headlines; hear the buzz, the hype, the sobbing of her fans. It would be a *tour de force*, a masterstroke, so long as it was done with due drama and panache. Death, like any memoir, had to be theatrical. No good wading in to this deserted stretch of river and waiting till the water dragged her down, with no witnesses, no public shock and outrage. Her bloated body would sink unseen, like a broken branch, a piece of mouldy trash. No, she must make her fateful leap from the centre of the bridge, in full view of the traffic. Even at this time of night, the traffic never ceased, so every eye would be focused on the frail, courageous figure in flimsy clothes, with bare and bleeding feet, plunging to her doom.

As she limped along the embankment to the bridge, she imagined one of the drivers rushing to her rescue – the sort of decent, brilliant bloke she had always longed to meet. And, as he dragged her from the water's cold embrace, she would realize there was hope still – hope of love, commitment, a future free from pain.

'But suppose he doesn't reach you in time?' she asked herself aloud, teeth chattering as she spoke.

'You'll just have to take that chance, Lauren. What's one more risk, when your whole life's been a gamble from the start?'

She was shivering now from fear as much as cold; her feet smarting on the pavement; her hair blown about by the unforgiving wind. None the less, she turned on to the bridge with a sense of almost triumph.

Because, however it panned out – tragic death or tumultuous love – it would make the perfect ending to her memoir, the perfect (honest) ending to her life.

Pecking Order

'By the way,' Gerald said, putting down his coffee cup. 'Henry died. Yesterday.'

'Who?'

'Henry.'

'Sorry, I'm not with you. Do we know a Henry?'

'We did.'

Eileen watched her husband, noticing how tense he seemed, buttering his toast with unnecessary force, the blade buckling under the strain. 'When?' she asked. 'How long ago?'

'Ages.'

'What's that supposed to mean? Why are you being so mysterious?'

'I'm not being anything.' He shook his head impatiently. 'I'm just surprised you don't remember.' Wrenching the lid off the marmalade jar, he heaped a glistening dollop on to the spoon. 'Henry ...' – he paused, the name hanging in the air – 'is – *was* – Samantha's husband.'

She choked on her coffee, and began to cough and splutter, almost welcoming the paroxysms, which allowed her time to calm her instant reaction: jealousy, distaste and fear.

'How ... how awful for her,' she said, finally. The news demanded sympathy – an outward show, at least. 'Although I suppose she must have been expecting it,' she added, trying to sound casual, unconcerned. 'He was quite a bit older, as far as I recall.'

'Yes, twenty years. But that still makes him only sixty-one. Which is extremely young to die, these days. It was a heart attack, apparently – mercifully quick. Anyway, I'm going to the funeral.'

'*We're* going, don't you mean?' she said, instinctively sensing danger.

'No, just me.' He snapped a small piece off his toast, and fired it, like a bullet, into his mouth.

'But surely I'll come, too?'

'I don't think it's appropriate.'

'Gerald, we always go to funerals together. People will think it very odd.'

'What people?'

'Well, the other guests.' And Samantha herself, she didn't add. Too painful even to mention her. In her own personal scheme of things, the woman herself was dead; had been for the last two decades.

'Eileen, for heaven's sake, I won't know anyone there.'

You'll know Samantha. Again she didn't say it, just sat staring at the label on the marmalade: '*Rhapsodie de Fruit.* The natural flavour of hand-picked oranges is carefully conserved through long-established French country traditions ...' Why, she thought, with sudden irritation, couldn't Gerald settle for common-and-garden marmalade? But then he had always had a taste for the exotic. Hence Samantha, of course.

'When *is* the funeral?'

'Next Tuesday.'

'But that's the day of your meeting with—'

'I know.' He cut her off; shot a second toast-bullet into his mouth.

'You can't miss that meeting, can you?'

He shrugged. 'Seems I'll have to. But I can't discuss it now. I'm already late as it is.' He pushed his chair back, disappeared upstairs.

Mechanically she began to clear the table; swilled his untouched coffee down the sink; saved the toast crusts for the birds. Within minutes, he was down again and giving her his goodbye kiss: brief, though on the lips.

Don't go, she all but pleaded. Don't leave me on my own.

She was so used to leaving *with* him, catching the same train, heading for her own office, while he walked north to his. In the last two weeks, she had become a fifties wife, waving off her man, then embarking on the household chores, while he toiled in the Big, Bad World Outside. She ought to don a frilly pinny and a submissive, simpering smile. In fact, she resented her enforced redundancy – this morning more than usual. The whole structure and routine of work would have stopped her dwelling on Samantha; distracted her from the awkward questions seething in her head. How had Gerald *known* that Henry was dead? The man wasn't a public figure, so there wouldn't have been an obituary – a line or two in the *Telegraph*, maybe, but her husband didn't have the time to peruse 'births, marriages and deaths' columns. Besides, if the death had occurred only yesterday, any notification was unlikely to have appeared yet. Could Samantha herself have somehow been in contact with him?

The very thought made her guts churn, as if she had gorged on tripe and onions for breakfast, instead of nibbling half a slice of toast. Back in 1988, after the woman had discarded Gerald – ditching him at the altar, more or less – she had innocently assumed that the pair had never seen each other again. And, certainly, since he'd married *her* (on the rebound, she suspected), Samantha's name had never passed his lips, not in nineteen years. It had been taken for granted that the subject was a painful one – for both of them – and thus best kept firmly buried in the past. Which made it all the more extraordinary that Gerald knew the details of the heart attack ('mercifully quick'), as well as the date of the funeral.

She slumped into his chair at the still messy breakfast table and grabbed the jar of marmalade by its smugly slender neck. Its very shape annoyed her – not the usual dumpy jar, but elegantly tall, as Samantha was herself. And distinctive, like Samantha; three times the price of basic Golden Shred. On the one occasion she'd met the woman, she'd been struck by her air of natural superiority: the mane of honey-coloured hair rippling to a tiny waist; the long, coltish legs, tanned a glowing bronze. And her clothes were both original and daring: an exclusive designer top in damson-coloured silk, teamed with a tatty denim junk-shop mini-skirt. She had carried off the combination with enviable aplomb – the same 'I'll-do-as-I-please' audacity that had caused her to dump Gerald, while retaining his engagement ring. Henry was the catalyst – a much older man, who happened to be seriously rich, with a flat in Paris, a couple of villas-in-the-sun, and fingers in numerous lucrative pies. Had the marriage worked out, she wondered now, exactly as she used to in the past? Did Samantha have a brood of healthy children, and her own equally healthy bank account? She would still be only forty; pre-menopausal, fertile; dangerously attractive. Worse – she was suddenly available, a widow maybe hungry for a playmate.

She slammed the jar back on the table, angry with herself now. She was jumping to conclusions without a shred of evidence. Henry's body was barely even cold. Samantha would be mourning him, not already on the lookout for a substitute. And, as for Gerald hearing about the death, some old friend from the past might well have given him the news. Her wisest course would be to arrange a little diversion for Tuesday, to keep her mind off the funeral – perhaps lunch with a friend, followed by a shopping spree. In fact, she was lucky to be spared a long and probably tedious church-service. Far more fun to sit sipping wine in a restaurant, before splashing out on a pair of silly shoes.

'Goodbye, darling.'

'Goodbye. Take care.'

Gerald took a sudden step back in to the house, and, with uncharacteristic tenderness, clasped her hand in his. 'I'm sorry all your arrangements fell through.'

She shrugged. 'It's worse for Kay. That's the second time this year she's gone down with tonsillitis.'

'Well, try to do something else. You could ring Roberta and see if—'

'No, Roberta's away this week. But don't worry – you get off.'

As he walked towards the car, she tried to see him through Samantha's eyes. Despite being forty-nine, there was no trace of middle-aged spread, and his few grey hairs only served to emphasize the darkness of the rest. *She* had been less fortunate, and was two years older anyway, with thinning hair and a thickening waist. She just hoped he wouldn't compare her with the Girl Who Got Away, who was bound to be still slim. And honey-coloured hair would certainly look striking against the black of widow's weeds.

'What time will you be back?' she asked, following Gerald out to the car.

'Difficult to say. You know how these things drag on – first the church bit, then the burial and the reception and what-have-you. And it's quite a drive, in any case.'

'Well, don't forget to ring me.'

'I *always* ring you, Eileen.'

True. He was a model husband in that respect: considerate and reliable, although admittedly a man of few words; emotionally distant, however much she might try to draw him out. She stood watching the blue Volvo back into the road, accelerate along the street and finally disappear around the corner. She didn't wave – nor did he. She mustn't build this whole thing up – it was little different really from him leaving for work, as normal. What she needed above all was to find another job herself. Retirement didn't suit her, and, because almost all her friends worked, she wasn't in the habit of having girlie lunches or forays to the shops. And since her plan for just such an outing had been scuppered by Kay's tonsillitis, she ought to use today to re-think her life and future. It certainly wouldn't hurt to ring a few employment agencies and discover what her chances were of finding a new line of work.

Having fetched the Yellow Pages, she made a shortlist and rang the first: Reed Recruitment.

'Yes, I do have good computer skills ... Mm, my previous firm was involved in a cost-cutting exercise and made half of us redundant ... My age? Fifty-one ... Is that a problem, then?'

It *was* a problem. For Brook Street, too. And for Acme Appointments. Apparently, fifty was over-the-hill – indeed, not far off senility. However, two other (less ageist) agencies suggested she call in, and although it was now sheeting down with rain, she decided to brave the interviewers, along with the hostile elements. She would also go to Waitrose, since she had planned a special dinner to welcome Gerald back. He liked proper, well-cooked meals, not the sort of itsy-bitsy snacks on offer at most funerals. She might not have a wasp-waist, nor a cascade of blondish hair, but she *was* an ace in the kitchen, whereas Samantha (so the rumour went) couldn't so much as boil an egg.

*

Having already turned the oven down at least a dozen times, she finally switched it off and removed the casserole. It was clearly over-cooked; the meat beginning to shrivel, the sauce reduced by half. This was Gerald's fault and, in fact, the entire meal would be ruined if he didn't show up soon. Again, she calculated the timings in her head – a futile exercise, since she'd been doing it all after-noon, yet was still none the wiser as to the cause of the delay. He had left at ten this morning, for a service at eleven, which would have lasted, say, an hour. Another hour for the burial (at most), then back to the house for drinks and snacks and chat – three hours at the outside. That would bring the time to 4 p.m. Add an hour's drive back, and he should have been home by five. It was now getting on for nine.

Odder still was the fact he hadn't rung. And each time she had tried to reach him on his mobile, she'd been greeted by the same frustrating message: 'The Vodaphone you are calling has been switched off. Please try later.'

If he'd had an accident, wouldn't she have heard? The police contacted next-of-kin immediately, once they'd identified the victim. She closed her eyes a second; saw not his bloodstained corpse but his naked body, very much alive; clamped to Samantha's in threshing, thrusting ecstasy.

'Gerald, darling, I never thought we'd do this again.'

'Nor me, my sweet. Christ! I've missed you desperately. Never for a single moment have I forgotten how it was for us. And it's every bit as thrilling now as then.'

'Can you ever forgive me, Gerald? I made a stupid mistake, let myself be blinded by Henry's age and money. He seemed so mature, so solid, to a girl just pushing twenty. Yet you were the one I only ever loved.'

Such things could happen – easily. He might never have intended making any sexual move; just stayed behind till the other guests had gone, so that he could talk to her in private, and find out what had happened in the intervening years. It would be Samantha, the seduc-tress, who'd have used her wiles to get exactly what she wanted. And, of course, he was much more of a catch now, than he had been twenty

years ago: well-established, prosperous, still in good shape, and with
no children to tie him down. In fact, if Samantha had kids of her own,
that might double the attraction, since she would welcome a ready-
made stepfather to help her bring them up. And Gerald would relish
the role, as the next best thing to being a real dad. Although why stop
there, when he and Samantha could go on to have their *own* kids? It
wasn't him who was infertile, after all.

The very word brought the usual stab of curdled grief and
shame; every bit as strong now as during those futile years of tests
and drugs and scans – in fact, stronger, when she compared herself
with Samantha: not only ten years older, and less pretty and viva-
cious, but lacking in the key component of womanhood. A barren
woman was so much damaged goods.

Putting down the phone, she stood staring at her casserole,
wondering why she'd bothered. Why expect him back for dinner if
he was busy making babies? And could she really blame him if he
left? He had probably only stayed so far, because he'd continued to
keep hoping – even through her forties – that she would finally
conceive. But the menopause had dashed such hopes; every hot
flush and night sweat seeming spitefully to underline the point.

'My wife's no fun now, Samantha. She's always getting
headaches, or some tedious pain in her joints. And she disturbs me
every night, getting up to change her pyjamas because they're
soaked with sweat.'

Samantha wouldn't wear pyjamas, but a baby-doll-style nightie
that showed off her astounding legs. And Samantha's joints would
never ache.

'Let's do it with my feet up on your shoulders. I love that way –
it makes your cock feel so snug inside me. No, of course it doesn't
hurt, Gerald. I'm as supple as a piece of India rubber. In fact, if you
want to try a really wild position ...'

Eileen marched into the dining-room, where the elegantly set
table seemed just more wasted effort, as did the impressive
hazelnut gateau she had made as a dessert. Although one of her
husband's favourites, it wasn't exactly a staple on the menu, since
it was extremely time-consuming, not to mention fiddly. Gerald
had probably glutted himself already, on oysters and champagne,
in bed, so why would he want dessert?

'Yes, she is a good cook – I'll give her that. But I could just as well hire a housekeeper. What's important in a marriage is what goes on between the sheets, not what's on the dinner table. I want to eat your glorious pussy, darling, not my wife's confections.'

Again she tried his number. 'The Vodaphone you are calling is …'

Where *was* he, for God's sake? And why had he switched off his phone? There was no one else she could contact to discover what was going on. She didn't have Samantha's number, nor did she remember Henry's surname, so she couldn't try Directory Enquiries. And Gerald had failed to give her an address, only the name of the village and the church – a deliberate oversight, no doubt, and one that seemed increasingly suspicious. In fact, reflecting on their marriage, hadn't it always been somewhat enigmatic, full of guesswork on her part when it came to Gerald's sentiments? They had been declared one flesh, back in 1989, but a similar meeting of minds had never quite occurred. Rather, they proceeded along parallel lines that very rarely touched or intertwined, and it even felt at times as if her husband was a foreign country, with her, the would-be explorer, left baffled and excluded, without a guide or map – never more so than right now.

She turned on the radio to check the travel news, but there were no reports of accidents, hold-ups or road-closures. The earlier heavy rain had stopped; the weather settled into relative quiescence, with no fog or snow or sleet or gales to cause problems for a motorist. *She* was the one who was storm-tossed; out of touch with the season. It might be April outside, but, here at home, it was stark November.

Peering out of the window, she watched other cars drone past in the street, but no sign of their blue Volvo. Perhaps it had broken down, although that seemed highly improbable when it had been serviced just last week. Gerald was an efficient type, who ensured his precious vehicle was in first-rate running order, and his mobile fully charged. And, anyway, it was even more unlikely that both car and phone would conk out simultaneously.

Suddenly decisive, she returned to the table, rammed the knives and forks back into the drawer; returned the glasses to the sideboard, re-corked the wine and refolded the lace tablecloth. Gerald wouldn't eat at this hour – elaborate meals, consumed late on in the evening, tended to give him indigestion. And her pork, prune and Armagnac casserole could hardly be called plain. Maybe they could have it for tomorrow's dinner – *if* he were back tomorrow. He might never come back; never phone her; just disappear without trace, like those chilling stories featured in the tabloids.

'Look, get a grip on yourself,' she muttered. 'You're behaving like a lunatic.' Would any woman, even a bitch like Samantha, really fall into bed with another man on the day of her husband's funeral, let alone run off with him? The house was probably full of grieving relatives, many of them staying over, so the widow and the hostess could hardly sneak away to some steamy little love-nest.

Actually, she ought to be more sympathetic – widowhood was bleak, especially at so young an age. However, sympathy wasn't easy towards someone who'd cast a shadow on her life; forever underlining the point that Gerald's first and natural choice of wife was a woman utterly different from herself. Indeed, if she hadn't chanced to meet him within a week of his broken engagement, when he was stunned and thrown off-balance, he probably wouldn't have married her at all. There was no denying the fact that she was hardly a worthy substitute – old for a first marriage (thirty-one to Samantha's girlish twenty), and not in the same class in terms of physical attraction. In truth, that sense of being second-best had affected her profoundly, made her feel insecure, wife almost by default. Yet, here she was, still married, after nineteen years, and although Gerald was uncommunicative – unable constitutionally to lay bare his inner soul – he seemed happy enough with his second choice, or had been up till now.

All at once, a wave of all-consuming heat stampeded through her body; scorching from her chest to her neck, her face, her upper arms – her fifth hot flush this evening, *and* the most intense. Flinging open the window, she inhaled a few deep breaths, but, despite the cold night air, her hair was already wet with sweat, and beads of perspiration were trickling down her back. As she leaned far out, still gulping air, she saw the vile Samantha roll triumphantly on top of Gerald: her skin cool and fresh against his naked limbs; her long hair soft and fragrant, rather than wet and coarse and sparse; her flesh firm to the touch, with no unattractive bulges.

Slamming the window shut (and the bedroom door, to boot), she forced herself to settle down and watch the News at Ten. The succession of disasters – mass slaughter in Darfur, atrocities in Kenya, rioting and bloodshed in Belgrade – helped to put her own plight in perspective. She might have an errant husband and a few menopausal symptoms, but she was neither dead nor wounded, nor living in a war zone. Although she was, in fact, ravenous, having eaten nothing since breakfast. (The dearth of jobs at the agencies had temporarily quashed her appetite.)

Slouching over to the sideboard, she hacked a large chunk off the cake. Too bad that Gerald hadn't seen it in all its finished glory. She had decorated the top with three circles of whole hazelnuts, interspersed with curls of bitter-chocolate and piped rosettes of cream. The decoration alone had taken the best part of an hour, not to mention the time she'd spent grinding up the hazelnuts (used in place of flour), then making the *crème patissière* that sandwiched the six layers, and finally the praline topping.

She ate standing up, hardly bothering to chew, just stuffing in great fistfuls of the stuff, despite the fact that it was exceptionally rich. She had probably gone overboard, putting praline on top, as well as cream inside. But it had been a deliberate bid to pull out all the stops in an attempt to outshine her rival. Samantha might be 'rich' in other crucial respects – looks and sexual wiles – but the wife at home could compensate with her extravagant cuisine.

Doggedly, she continued eating, although her enjoyment of the gateau brought diminishing returns, since she was depressingly aware it would only make her fatter. Samantha, in her imagination, was still as thin as a knife-blade, as delicate as a chocolate curl, and weighed little more than a swirl or two of cream. Besides, how had she managed to kid herself that the way to a man's heart was through his stomach? Admittedly, Gerald loved good food, but advanced, elaborate sex would be much more of a novelty; something he didn't get at home.

She shovelled in more cake, although disgusted by her greed and by the revolting way she was eating. Now, in addition to her bedraggled hair, there were smears of chocolate round her mouth, sticky crumbs adhering to her blouse, and her hands were covered with cream. Half the cake was already gone; the rest a mangled mess. She had not only destroyed her handiwork, she'd made herself gross in the process. Yet somehow she had to prove that her gateau was worth eating; that her long hours in the kitchen hadn't been a total waste of time.

As she forced in one more chunk, she heard the sound of a key in the lock, and froze in shock and embarrassment. Gerald mustn't find her like this: slatternly, dishevelled; a glutton on a feeding frenzy.

Having dashed into the kitchen for a quick wash at the sink, she tried to calm her breathing as she went to confront him in the hall.

'Whatever happened, Gerald? I've been out of my mind with worry.'

'I'm sorry.'

Two words – nothing more. No excuses, explanations, convenient alibis. Thrown by his strange silence, she took a step closer, to check if there were blonde hairs on his coat, or perhaps a whiff of women's perfume clinging to his skin. No – none that she could see or smell. In fact, he looked exhausted; his complexion noticeably pale against the severe black of the suit. The accusing words shrivelled on her lips. This man seemed a stranger; not the Gerald who had left this morning. 'Are you all right?' she asked.

He nodded, although giving the impression of someone knocked off-balance – as he had been twenty years ago, after the bust-up with Samantha. But, of course, a febrile reconciliation might be just as overwhelming.

'Can I get you something to eat?'

'No, thanks. In fact, I think I'll go and have a shower. I feel completely bushed.'

Bushed from *what*, she'd like to know? But before she could open her mouth to retort, he had disappeared upstairs. He hadn't even removed his coat, which was odd in the extreme. It was part of his routine to hang it on the hall-stand as soon as he came in. Then he would pour himself a drink and sit and talk a while. Although strictly unforthcoming on matters of emotion, he never failed to share with her the details of his day. Yet tonight he hadn't said a word about the funeral, his lateness, or the fact he hadn't rung. And why on earth should he want to take a shower the very second he got in? To wash off Samantha's traces, or simply to escape? Perhaps he *had* to remove himself because the contrast was too great: the fat, infertile, messy wife dispelling his treasured memories of the slimly fecund mistress, sleek even in the sack.

Furious, she strode back to the kitchen, seized the casserole, took it out to the dustbin and tipped the entire contents in among the empty tins and tealeaves, the potato peelings and other sorts of trash. The vegetables went the same way. Why had she gone to so much trouble braising chicory and fennel, poaching carrots in butter, making potatoes *Lyonnaise*? She should have known he'd have no appetite – sated on Samantha. In fact, she was beginning to wonder if there'd been a funeral at all. Perhaps the whole thing was a smokescreen; part of a complicated web of lies that, for all she knew, might have been going on for months.

Deliberately she banged about in the kitchen, taking out her anger on the dirty pots and pans, scouring them with unnecessary force, before ramming them back on the shelf. Let him stew upstairs, reliving in the brothel of his mind all the disgusting things he'd done with his ex-fiancée – no longer 'ex' at all, she'd bet. *She* intended staying down here – all night and every night – staying where she belonged as the skivvy and the kitchen-maid. Unless she grabbed a carving-knife and stabbed him through the heart.

All at once, she heard his feet on the stairs, and stood gripping the sink for support, as he came in to the kitchen, now in his pyjamas, his hair still wet from the shower.

'Aren't you coming to bed?'

'Bed? What, straight away? Gerald, I can't just settle down to sleep when I don't know what the hell's been going on. I know you're not exactly a chatterbox, but this really is a bit steep – I mean, not so much as opening your mouth when—'

'I'm not feeling all that marvellous.'

'But why? What's wrong? If you're ill, I ought to know.'

'I'm not ill – just whacked. I'll tell you all about it in the morning.'

'You'll be at work in the morning.'

'Before I go, I mean. I'm knackered now. It's late.'

She damned well knew it was late. And why did he keep stressing his exhaustion? The adventurous sex had taken its toll, no doubt. She should demand an explanation – *now*.

'Does Samantha have children?' she asked, instead, standing, arms akimbo, at the sink.

She saw him hesitate; prayed to God – to all the gods – that the answer would be no. It was actually quite possible. Samantha was the sort who wouldn't want to spoil her figure – a superficial creature, who'd be more concerned about droopy breasts and stretch-marks or the risk of a Caesarean scar, than about the joys of motherhood. 'Well, *has* she?' she persisted.

'Yes,' he said. No more.

Already she was reduced to racking jealousy. 'How many?' she demanded.

Again he paused, which only stoked her fury.

'Gerald, what's wrong with you, for God's sake? You stay out for hours and hours, and don't even bother phoning to tell me where you are, then, when you *do* come back, you refuse to say a word.'

Picking up the pepper-mill, he began examining it studiously, only to put it down again. 'Four,' he said. 'Two boys and two girls.'

His voice was soft, quite different from her own aggressive tone, yet the words were like a punch in the face. *Four*! For a woman of only forty. And they were bound to have been at the funeral, so Gerald would have seen them for himself: two beautiful, blonde daughters; two enchanting little boys. Perhaps they'd bonded with him instantly, desperate for a father.

He reached across and put his hand on her arm. 'Do come to bed, darling. You know I hate sleeping without you.'

The 'darling' and the gentle touch were merely guilt-induced, as was the specious stuff about wanting to sleep beside her. Now that he was home, he was beginning to feel uneasy and trying to make recompense – that was clear enough – yet the fact remained he expected her to acquiesce in his mysterious behaviour, and without any further probing on her part. Any woman with an ounce of pride would cross-examine him, not settle for evasions, and even she, the accommodating wife, was tempted to force a showdown for once; tell him loud and clear how his refusal to communicate was an insult, an affront.

Yet, all at once, she slumped against the sink, remembering her status. There was such a thing as a pecking order; a strict hierarchy, set in stone, impossible to overturn. A mother of four was inherently superior to an older, barren female, who was washed-up and expendable, without so much as a job – and Gerald's second-choice, of course; wife only by default. So, if she wanted to preserve her marriage, she couldn't afford to chivvy him or challenge him, or even beg him to engage with her, confide and open up. As side-kick to Samantha – strictly B-list to her rival's starring role – she couldn't actually afford to say another word.

Instead, she must simply follow him upstairs and go to bed – to sleep.

On the Road

Derek rang again, louder. He had booked in advance, for heaven's sake, so the least they could do was let him in. Yet, not only was the front door locked, all the windows were dark; no light except the dim lamp in the porch. That seemed odd in itself. Surely there must be other guests; folk who hadn't yet gone to bed?

He turned up his collar against the bullying March wind; cursing his own folly in not opting for a better class of establishment. But, by staying at the cheapest dives, he could pocket the difference between the small amount such places charged and his official hotel allowance. And, if ever he got the chop (a prospect depressingly likely), he would need every damned penny he could save.

VACANCIES, the notice on the door read, so they must be open for business. Admittedly he was late – much later than he'd said – but his first customer had kept him waiting hours, which had set him back all day.

'Third time lucky,' he muttered to himself, as he pressed his thumb, hard, against the bell-push.

Ah – footsteps! His salesman's smile was now so automatic, it switched itself on without him even willing it. The woman who'd taken his booking had sounded old and crotchety, so he was expecting a bad-tempered crone to come limping to the door. But, there, standing in the doorway, was a small, slight girl, with flame-red hair, an elfin face and a profusion of freckles that masked her milk-white skin.

'G … Gemma,' he stuttered, all but reeling in astonishment. Decades had passed since he'd seen her, yet here she was, restored, revived, regained.

She gave him a blank stare. 'My name's Stacey,' she said, with undisguised hostility.

Flushing with embarrassment, he stammered his apologies. What in Christ's name was he thinking of? Gemma would be fifty now: grey and lined and, most like, menopausal, whereas this girl was barely out of her teens. 'Sorry,' he mumbled again. 'I … I was confusing you with someone else.'

She was still regarding him suspiciously. No wonder.

'You're Mr Baines, I take it?'

'That's right. Sorry I'm so late, but—'

'Yeah, we'd given you up.'

'Sorry,' he said, fourth time. 'Always apologize' was one of his personal mantras, even when he wasn't in the wrong, although he was definitely overdoing it right now. But the uncanny resemblance between Gemma and this girl had completely knocked him off his guard. 'I was held up on a call. I did try to ring, to warn you I was running late, but no one answered the phone.'

'Mum must have switched it off. It's *her* who runs this place, but she's gone down with a stomach bug, so she's left me in charge – worse luck! Anyway, come in. Your room's all ready. Shall I take you up?'

'Actually, I wouldn't mind a drink first,' he said, putting his case down in the hall, to signal his intention of not moving from her vicinity.

'Sorry, the bar's closed.'

'Any chance of some food?' OK, he was pushing his luck, but he just had to feast his eyes on her. It wasn't food and drink he craved, but her face, her voice, her presence. Now that she'd switched the lights on, he could see she was shorter than Gemma, and had a different shape of mouth and slightly smaller breasts. None the less, she was stirring deep emotion in him; wild, tempestuous memories.

'We don't do meals – only breakfast.'

'Well, could you make me breakfast?'

'What, *now*? It's ten past midnight.'

He risked a jovial laugh. 'Don't they call it "all-day breakfast"? I would be grateful, honestly. I haven't eaten anything since six o'clock this morning.'

The girl looked dubious. 'I could make you scrambled eggs, I suppose. Or egg and beans and sausage. But I'm not doing the full works – not cereal and toast and stuff.'

'Egg and beans and sausage would be great. And maybe some fried bread.'

She ignored his last request. 'The dining-room's this way.' she muttered, leading him past the reception desk into a small, shabby room, over-stuffed with ugly fake-wood tables and an assortment of mismatched chairs.

'Tea or coffee?' she asked, her tone suggesting that both were forms of poison.

'A pot of tea would be perfect. If you're sure it's no bother.' Of course it was a bother – she was making that perfectly plain. Yet, however sullen she might be, he still yearned to take her in his arms, crush her close against his chest, beg her never to leave him again.

'Why don't you wait in your room till the food's ready? I'll give you a shout, OK?'

'No, I'd prefer to stay down here.' Quickly he took off his coat and sat at one of the tables. How could he miss this chance of watching her come in and out; that lithe and lively figure he'd assumed he would never see again? However, she shut the kitchen door with what sounded like a petulant slam, leaving him with no company save the cutesy kitten gazing at him beseechingly from a picture on the wall.

Slowly he took in his surroundings. Kitten apart, there was little in the room that wasn't past its prime: old-fashioned, faded wallpaper; scuffed, grey vinyl floor; limp, half-hearted curtains that didn't quite meet in the middle. Even the table-top was smeary, and the red plastic tomato standing guard by the salt-and-pepper-set was oozing drools of congealed and crusted ketchup.

'Please wait to be seated' ordered a notice on the wall – a request that underlined his solitude. He tried to picture the room full of cheery diners, queuing for a table, but failed to make the imaginative leap required. This hotel was in a backwater and off the beaten track, and it was giving him the feeling that it was a ghost hotel, or hotel in a dream, and that no guest but him had ever ventured here. Maybe even Stacey had vanished into the stratosphere and he would continue to sit, abandoned and alone, throughout the long night hours.

He reached out for the pepper-pot and gripped it in his hand, just to anchor himself to something real and solid. Perhaps the girl was avoiding him deliberately. It must have seemed peculiar, the way he'd called her Gemma, or she might even have regarded it as some sort of clumsy chat-up line. He fumbled in his pocket for his wallet. A tenner (maybe a couple) might work a minor miracle; change her mood from aggressive to amicable.

Just at that moment, the door burst open and she barged in with a tray. Once she'd unloaded the tea things, he slipped the notes surreptitiously into her hand; his fingers tingling from the shock of meeting hers. 'I realize I'm keeping you up late, so here's a little something for your trouble.'

'Gosh, thanks! Fantastic! And it *isn't* any trouble – honest.'

The cash had softened her up, but who was he to object? He knew all too well how money made the difference between battling on in life, or giving up.

'Great cup of tea,' he enthused, although the brew was weak and pallid; a single teabag floating in the chipped brown earthenware pot.

'Mum says I can't make tea to save my life. Normally, she never lets me near the kitchen.'

A definite advance. Information offered in a congenial tone of voice. 'Are any other guests staying at the moment?' he asked, keen to take advantage of the truce.

She shook her head. 'Mum's been ill – not just the stomach thing, but – you know – other problems ...' The sentence petered out.

Poor kid, he thought. If business was so bad, the mother might be forced to sell up; even land in the bankruptcy court. The sense of insecurity, the constant dread of ending up with nothing – they were *his*, as well.

'Must dash, or I'll burn your egg.'

He'd gladly risk a burnt egg – indeed, a completely charred and ruined breakfast – for the privilege of keeping her in view. But she had already disappeared, although her pale, slender legs continued jouncing in his mind. He knew those legs – the silky feel of the skin; the two special, star-shaped freckles on the inside of the left (and luscious) thigh.

Within minutes, he heard steps approaching, and racked his brains for some wise or witty overture. Somehow, he must charm her, gain her interest, prove he could be trusted. But, as he opened his mouth to speak, he saw not Stacey, but a young gangling man slouch into the room.

'Sorry,' the stranger muttered, wiping his hands on his dirty denim jeans. 'Didn't know anyone was here.'

'That's OK,' said Derek, speaking to empty air. The youth had gone as swiftly as he'd come.

He spooned more sugar into his tea, to add a bit of flavour, although aware that every spoonful increased the calorie-count. When he'd first met Gemma, he'd been as slim as a swordstick. Now, he was developing the male equivalent of love-handles – something of a misnomer, since he'd made love to no one else in all those barren years; years he called his exile, in the sense of lifelong banishment from the one woman in the world who had been his hope and haven.

He jumped as Stacey banged back in. 'D'you want your egg soft or hard?'

Would *he* be hard, he wondered, if he were back in bed with Gemma? The very thought sent a flutter through his groin.

'Did you hear what I said?'

'Sorry – yes. Hard! By the way, a guy popped in just now. Was it your brother, by any chance?'

'No!' She gave a nervous giggle. 'I'm an only child, worse luck! That was Steve, our handyman.'

'He's working late.'

'Yeah, we had a ... problem. But he's fixed it now, so he'll be leaving in a jiff. Listen, I've done you some fried bread.'

'Wonderful! It's one of my little weaknesses – fried bread. D'you find you have certain things you just can't do without?'

'Yeah,' she said. 'A decent night's sleep.'

'OK, don't rub it in. Look, the minute you bring me my break-fast, I'll gobble it down double-quick.'

'Don't worry – only kidding! Anyway, the sausage isn't done yet. I had to get them out of the freezer, and they're in this huge great catering pack. It took me ages to hack one off from the rest. In fact, I almost lost a finger!'

'I'm sorry.' Sixth apology. They must somehow move from sausages and 'sorrys' to something more profound. 'Do call me Derek,' he urged, hoping to strike a more intimate note. 'And do you mind if I call you Stacey?'

'Not bothered.' She gave a dismissive shrug, although at least she made no move to go. 'So what line of work are you in?'

I'm a 'champion', he all but said, a 'hero'. Those were the terms bandied about at sales conferences, in an attempt to flatter conference-members that they were venturing out to win new lands, like the pioneers who had conquered the Wild West. In point of fact, most salesmen were despised, and with some real cause, he felt. There *was* something rather creepy about employing all the social graces not for genuine friendship but just to make a profit.

'Well,' he replied, 'you'll laugh at this, in light of what you said about your sleep, but I work for a company that manufactures Sleep-Sound beds. They're a totally new concept in sleep-health. Each bed has a memory-foam mattress that reduces pressure on the joints, and our double-deluxe model is electrically adjustable and comes complete with a built-in massage function. Or, if you upgrade to our top-of-the-range bed, you'll get an integral stereo system that plays hypnotic "sleep-well" CDs and—'

God, he thought, he was lapsing into sales patter, purely from force of habit. And, far from seeming impressed, she looked a shade alarmed. Perhaps it wasn't very tactful to have broached the subject of beds so early in their acquaintance. And 'massage' sounded worse, with its sleazy connotations.

'I bet they're pricey,' was all she said.

'Yes, I'm afraid even our standard single would set you back six hundred, and our most expensive king-size costs a cool three grand.'

'So who buys them, then? Rock stars?'

Who indeed? He could spend hours with potential customers, demonstrating every last detail of the beds, only to be told, 'We'll think about it', or even have the door slammed in his face. Or they might ask him to return tomorrow, when he'd driven miles for *today's* appointment. Or totally forget that he was coming, and go out on a shopping trip, like Mrs Watts this morning, who had eventually returned, loaded down with packages, pretending *he* had got the time wrong, although he'd phoned her only yesterday, to confirm. But, whatever the provocation, he must never lose his cool, but be unfailingly polite, upbeat and positive. His time didn't matter, only theirs. Indeed, he hardly even existed as a person. He was just a smile, a spiel.

'OK, I'll get your nosh now.' The girl had clearly lost all interest in the buyers, or non-buyers, of his beds.

'Thanks,' he said. 'And bring a second cup, so you can join me for a cup of tea.' He was probably being way too forward, but it was all he could do not to clamp his body on to hers and keep it there by force. He should have done that with Gemma, he realized now, with hindsight. The love of his life, lost to some phoney artist – and one called Tristram, for God's sake. What chance had a lowly Derek Baines against a Tristram Trelawny? The slimy ponce had not only stolen Gemma, but used her as a life-model, as if she were a slapper who stripped off for anyone? He should have killed his rival in cold blood, instead of slinking away to lick his wounds in private. Yet he was sick and tired of 'might-have-beens' – his companions now for close on thirty years.

When Stacey returned with his food, he pulled out the chair beside him and patted it invitingly. But she ignored the gesture and remained standing where she was. If only he was skilled at conversation and could enthral her with some exotic traveller's tale, or launch into a discussion about the Meaning of Life or the Riddle of the Sphinx. But all he could manage was sales-talk, and he would hardly sweep her off her feet with an account of 'Sleep-Sound's flame-retardant mattress-covers, or their 'no-quibble' five-year guarantee.

'Eat up! It's getting cold.'

What she really meant was that he was keeping her from sleep. He would gladly whisk her to her bedroom, cuddle up beside her, demonstrate his skills in a different, wordless way. Instead, he cut slowly into the rubbery fried egg. It was so small, a wren must have laid it; possibly a sparrow. The frilled edges of the white were overlaid with globules of fat and flecked with black specks from the sausage, itself afloat in a greasy pool of beans. Who cared? It was enough that she was *here*, so that he could flash back thirty years and imagine he and Gemma were breakfasting together after a night of passionate love.

'So where d'you live?' she asked, perhaps finding the silence oppressive – as indeed he did himself – or maybe feeling duty-bound to earn the cash he'd slipped her.

Again he hesitated. Walsall sounded so unappealing, on a par with Slough and Scunthorpe. He was tempted to say Land's End: the most romantic spot on earth, because he'd met beloved Gemma there – and romantic in its own right as the last land before America, wooed by clamorous waves. He rarely went on holiday, either then or now, but a pal had talked him into a fishing trip, and he'd caught not bass or mackerel, but a slender, red-haired beauty, who had nibbled at his bait, threshed and plunged as he hooked her; become even more tempestuous as he reeled her in and netted her; as wild as the wild waves themselves.

'My territory's the West Midlands,' he said, at last, hoping the word 'territory' might compensate for the 'Midlands'. And for a moment, yes – he'd exchanged the fishing-boat for a trusty steed and was galloping full-pelt across the prairie, with Gemma flung across his saddle, and the far horizon beckoning him on to adventure and escape.

'Yes, but where's your actual house?'

Flat, he corrected silently. What he hated about the Midlands (West or East) was its sheer distance from the sea. He had always longed to live on the coast – indeed, he and Gemma had planned to stay in Cornwall and buy a cliff-top cottage. He remembered wandering hand-in-hand with her along the wind-whipped strand, and the thunderous waves breaking on the shore had been so unrestrained, explosive, they had seemed an apt expression of his love. Later, when he'd lost that love (*and* the hoped-for cottage), he had walked the same unhappy beach; the strident seagulls mocking him, as they screeched out Tristram's name.

'So is this your full-time job?' he asked, keen to drown memories of Tristram, and also shift attention from the location of his flat. 'Helping run the hotel?'

'No fear! I can't wait to get away.'

'And what then? Do you have plans?'

A dreamy look came over her face. 'Oh, yes! I want to see the world. Swan off somewhere exciting; trek across the desert or maybe climb the Himalayas. Actually I don't care where it is, so long as it gets me out of this hell-hole.' She gave an embarrassed laugh. 'Shit! I shouldn't have said that, should I?'

'Don't worry. It's good that you have ambitions.' His own ambitions had died along with Gemma. After that doomed encounter, he'd become panicky and paralysed; no longer daring to spread his wings or take the slightest risk. He still lived close to his birth-place, as if any other part of England was dangerous, even disastrous. And although his life was spent on the road, every day was trammelled; yoked to rigid appointments and unremitting sales-targets, with no scope for breaking out.

'You're not eating,' Stacey said. 'Don't you like it? I must admit, I'm not the world's greatest cook.'

'It's delicious,' he said, biting into the sausage, which, although burnt both ends, was still semi-raw in the middle.

'I don't want to rush you, Derek, but I have to be up at the crack of dawn tomorrow.'

'Sorry,' he repeated. He'd lost count of the times he'd said it. Although being apologetic never really paid. Brash, bold blokes were the ones who got the girls. Still, at least she had used his name, which was definitely encouraging. 'I won't say another word, I promise. I'll just concentrate on eating.'

He scooped up a forkful of beans. The sauce was thin, yet unpleasantly sweet and a brilliant orange in colour, as if it had been watered down with orange squash. And, as he cut into the fried bread, a yellow pus of grease spurted on to his chin. He didn't mind in the least. Gemma, too, had been a lousy cook. They had lived on love – and chips.

'D'you mind if I clear off the tea-things?'

'No, go ahead,' he mumbled, through a mouthful of cold egg. He hadn't even succeeded in pouring her a cup of tea, and she'd already whisked away the second cup. Why was he so backward? A slow learner. A slow eater.

At last, he put his knife and fork down, feeling slightly nauseous. The excess fat had congealed on his plate into a semi-solid phlegm. Yet he'd happily drown in blubber if only he could

watch her dainty hands again, picking up the teapot and the milk
jug. He yearned to be the sugar-bowl, so that he, too, could feel that
close caress. He suspected she was lingering in the kitchen just to
get away from him. Yet, however knackered she might be, she'd be
duty-bound, in the absence of the mother, to show him to his room.
Could he delay her there, perhaps – say he needed extra blankets;
pretend he'd forgotten his toothbrush and ask if she could find him
one?

'OK, ready?' she asked, zooming back in, and locking the kitchen
door with pointed emphasis.

'Yes, but I'm wondering if I should move the car?' If she followed
him outdoors, he might manage to waylay her by pointing out the
constellations. Except he didn't have a clue how to distinguish
Mars from Venus, let alone Orion's Belt from the Plough. And,
anyway, there *were* no stars – the night was too overcast.

'Why? Where did you leave it?'

'In that little space by the side of the house.'

'It's OK there. No problem.'

She seemed in such a rush, there was little chance of dallying in
the moonlight. Instead, she all but shoved him into the hall.

'Your room's on the first floor. I'll just go and get the key.'

As she turned her back, he gazed at her legs again. Her skirt
was provocatively short – little more than a cake-frill – which
meant he could admire the full expanse of milky, freckled flesh; the
seductive curve of the thigh, disappearing beneath the—

'Got your case?'

'I left it somewhere here.'

'Ssshh! Don't wake Mum. She sleeps on the ground floor.'

And where do *you* sleep, he longed to ask, as he followed her up
the stairs, riveted by the wiggle of her bottom as she took the steps
two at a time. That energy, that verve – so similar to Gemma's.

'I'm afraid it's not exactly the Ritz,' she said, unlocking the door
of a small, low-ceilinged room. An expert when it came to beds, he
knew this one didn't rate at all, although at least the lurid counterpane matched the frilly curtains – more or less.

As she held the door for him to enter, he was tempted to pick her
up bodily and deposit her on the bed. Then he'd—

'Shower's in here,' she said, opening the door of what looked like a dark cubby-hole. 'Though the water won't be hot at this hour. Oh, shit – the bathroom light's gone!'

Good, he thought, now you'll have to fetch a replacement.

'Do you *need* the bathroom tonight?' she asked, a note of desperation in her voice.

'Well, yes, I ...'

'Thing is, I don't know where the sodding light bulbs are kept.'

'Don't worry,' he said, suddenly taking pity on her. 'I can always prop the door open. The light from here will be quite enough to see.'

'Great! That's really decent. Thanks a mill. Goodnight.'

She couldn't wait to get away, rattling down the stairs even faster than she'd climbed them. He crept after her surreptitiously, to see where she was going; watched her zip along the corridor and disappear into one of the ground-floor rooms. She was obviously dead-tired, desperate for some shut-eye. Young girls probably needed loads more sleep than fifty-something males, although he wouldn't really know. His entire experience of girls – young, old or middle-aged – had been restricted to Gemma, which only went to show what a total wimp he was. *Other* men knew how to handle females. Kevin, his Sales Manager, had slept with strings of women, whereas he was still an almost-virgin at the age of fifty-three.

Heaving his case on to the (patently substandard) bed, he unpacked his few possessions. The wire hangers in the wardrobe had rusted slightly and felt sticky to the touch. He only hoped they wouldn't stain tomorrow's clean white shirt. In the drawers he found a Bible, a dead moth and a bent hairpin. Sitting on the bed in his underpants, he began leafing through the Bible; every verse he read seeming to threaten retribution. He saw God as very similar to the 'Sleep-Sound' C.E.O.: remote, vindictive and tyrannical; bestowing rewards and punishments at whim. Gemma's God was different – female and benevolent.

What had happened to her, he wondered, as he'd done umpteen times before? Had she stayed with Tristram and produced a clutch of kids; celebrated her Silver Wedding and be aiming for her Golden? Was she even at this moment knitting bootees for a grandchild? The world was built round families, yet, apart from those few months with her, he had always been alone. And his job only served to emphasize his solitude. Despite the fact he spent his days with customers, they were strangers, more or less, and, as he motored from one town to the next, the very streets seemed alien. There was no sense of being 'at home', and, when he did return to his flat, he would eat and sleep (and plan and dream) on his own.

Having put on his pyjamas, he cleaned his teeth in the dim and shadowy bathroom, squinting at his reflection in the mirror. He wasn't actually fat – 'well-covered' was more the term he'd use – and at least he still had hair, quite decent hair, in fact, though admittedly more grey than brown. Some women preferred older men, valuing their wisdom and experience. Stacey hadn't mentioned a dad. Perhaps the old boy had passed away, which meant she'd need a father-figure, someone solid and dependable. In fact, the more he thought about it, the more he realized her life was rather similar to his. She was trapped, as *he* was; tied to a sick mother and to a wreck of a hotel; her hopes and dreams frustrated. And if the mother was seriously ill, the poor girl might soon be orphaned and completely alone in the world. She'd said she was an only child (like him), so she'd have no brother to turn to, no sister to offer refuge. But *he* could take her in; help her find her feet. And gratitude did sometimes turn to love. OK, the age-gap was huge, but he often read in the paper about blokes in their fifties shacking up with nymphets. Granted, such men were usually rich and famous, but love must feature sometimes – genuine affection; a bond between twin souls.

'Don't be so ridiculous,' he muttered. 'You're fantasizing, as usual.'

Turning off the bedroom light, he groped his way to the bed. A bedside lamp hadn't been provided, or indeed a fire. The radiator was obstinately cold, and its valve so stiff he couldn't move it an inch. He shivered as he eased his body between the clammy nylon sheets. Forget memory-foam mattresses – this one felt like horse-hair. As he edged his legs down, he suddenly encountered a rip in the sheet, only to tear it further as he tried to extricate his foot. The thing was paper-thin, probably rotting from years of laundering. Couldn't the invalid mother even afford some decent bed-linen?

Wearily he dragged himself up again, deciding to remake the bed and use the ripped sheet as the top one rather than the bottom. He switched the light back on and stood inspecting the damage. The tear was eighteen inches long, for heaven's sake! Surely he had every right to demand a serviceable sheet? Stacey was probably still awake, so if went down now, he'd catch her. From what he gathered, women took an age before they actually settled down to sleep; doing mysterious female things such as creaming their faces or putting their hair in curlers.

Flinging on his dressing-gown, he descended the stairs as quickly as he dared, although being careful not to wake the mother.

His heart was racing as he paused outside Stacey's door, and not from the exertion. This might be all it needed – a ripped sheet leading to romance. He must handle the situation with the utmost care and tact; forget his own base desires and focus on her needs. It was sympathy she lacked; tenderness, devotion. For all he knew, she might be weeping at this very moment, distraught about her mother's fate – her own fate. He must treat her very gently; clasp her in his arms only to console her; not to sate his lust.

He cleared his throat, smoothed his hair, wishing now he'd sprayed himself with aftershave. But no way was he retreating. He might lose his nerve if he delayed a second longer, so, screwing up his courage, he tapped softly on the door.

No answer.

Maybe she was in the bath. An image of her naked body leapt into his mind; the white flesh gleaming seductively through a haze of foamy suds – although recalling what she'd said about there being no hot water caused the vision to collapse. No, she was probably crying, as he'd thought at first, and embarrassed to be seen with red eyes and tear-stained face.

'It doesn't matter, darling,' he rehearsed in a soft purr. 'You're still beautiful to me, however red your eyes.'

He knocked again, louder, but no response whatever. Maybe she *was* asleep, and sleeping very deeply. Was it fair to wake her?

Yes! He could always soothe her back to sleep, once he'd explained about the sheet, and – more important – explained his rescue-plan. In fact, she'd sleep much sounder when she knew there was an escape-route, and that his little flat awaited her, as lovers' nest and haven, should death or heartless bankruptcy blitz her world to shreds.

His own life seemed poised on a knife-edge as he wrestled with himself. One part of him was tempted to creep cravenly back to his room. He wasn't the type of bloke to pound on women's doors, or drag them rudely out of bed. Yet, if he didn't act incisively, for once, he'd lose this precious second chance – a chance, he knew, that would never come again. If things worked out between them, she might actually bear his child – a whole brood of children, even. He'd not only be a husband, he'd be a family-man – a fully paid-up member of the human race. He'd no longer feel inferior to those younger, keener colleagues who all had wives and kids; all earned higher commission; drove superior cars. With Stacey in his life, he could sell a million beds; sell beds to sleepaphobics, even sell them to the *dead*.

'Yes, go for it!' he muttered, clenching both his fists and only hesitating a second longer before beating them against the door. The loud drumming noise was a shock to his whole system, yet a triumphant shock, bordering on euphoria. At last, he was acting like a champion, a hero. And his courage was paying off. He could hear movement from inside the room, footsteps approaching – closer – and, all at once, the door was flung open.

'What the bloody hell do you think you're playing at?' yelled an outraged voice. A deep voice. A male voice. A voice like a tornado. And there, standing, arms akimbo, was Steve, the handyman – no longer in his soiled blue jeans, but naked save for a towel. And crouching on the bed behind him (a double bed, a lovers' bed) was Stacey, also naked, although half-covered by the duvet.

He turned and fled, each step he took ageing him a good five years, so that when he limped back into his room, he was a panting, breathless pensioner, a laughing-stock, a dotard. How could he have imagined that a young girl in the springtime of her life would choose to mate with winter – brave its thin, bare, cold embrace, when she already had hot summer to melt her into surrender? He saw their agile limbs entwined; their thrusting, youthful bodies coupling in abandon. Steve was rightly called a handyman – he'd be handy with his *cock*, of course. She had lied to him; told him Steve was 'leaving in a jiff'; pretended she was tired, desperate for her beauty sleep, when, in galling fact, she was desperate to be rid of him, so she could rush to her lithe lover.

He paced up and down the small, cramped room, beside himself with humiliation. How ever could he face her in the morning? Indeed, she was bound to be the one who'd cook his breakfast: more wishy-washy tea and beans; more charred and greasy lies.

Impulsively, he seized his case and started hurling in his things at random; tossing his dressing-gown and pyjamas on the top. Then, naked in the unheated room, he dressed with feverish haste; unable to endure the sight of his blubbery stomach and grizzled old-man's chest.

Grabbing his coat and suitcase, he dashed headlong down the stairs. Too bad if he woke the mother. For all he knew, she wasn't ill at all; maybe in bed with her *own* lover. And certainly Steve and Stacey wouldn't hear a thing. They'd be making too much noise themselves: whoops of passion, moans of desire, wild bellowings of lust.

He unbolted the front door, slammed it shut behind him and raced across the tarmac to his car. Accelerating away, he drove at perilous speed along the winding lane; hit the main road and hurtled on towards the M5 and home. His sole aim was to reach the safety of his flat; hole up there and hide his shame; never show his face again, or brave the mocking world.

As he turned on to the motorway, he pressed his foot down, hard; the breakneck pace reflected in his body: heart thwacking like a sledge-hammer; dizzy blood careering round his veins. Shadows formed and reformed; headlights dazzled, glared; the ghostly glow of distant towns diminished to a blur. Other cars were mere insubstantial shapes, to be overtaken, swallowed up. Nothing else existed but his own frantic sense of motion, as bridges, pylons, hazy landmarks went streaking, flashing past. Even the road-signs failed to register, until, suddenly, the words 'West Bromwich, Walsall' struck him with such force he all but skidded to a halt.

Hardly aware what he was doing, he veered left off the motorway, scorched along the slip-road and on towards the round-about, and there did a total turnaround, until he was no longer driving north but south. The squall and storm of emotions churning through his mind had banished all clear thought; reduced rational decisions to so much airy moonshine. Since the moment he'd glimpsed Stacey naked on that double bed, he'd been acting on blind impulse; his usual common sense and caution thrown completely to the winds. Yet, strange as it might seem, it was the girl herself who had wrought this crucial change; made him see that he couldn't stay a moment longer landlocked in the Midlands; kowtowing to his customers; cringing to his boss; tied down by schedules, shackles. All that was in the past. No way was he returning to stagnation and surrender, servility, defeat, but now setting his sights on space and scope and freedom – yes, heading down to Cornwall and the last, storm-tumbled outcrop before the ocean stalked the shore; the very furthest limits of the land.

He allowed the shocked speedometer to hit the ninety-mark, as if it shared his own impatience for a new, untrammelled life. Yet, despite the whirlwind speed, his breathing and his heartbeat began gradually to slow, and his tense, angry grip loosened on the steering-wheel. Even his injured pride was fading in significance. Why fret and fume about one small indignity, when ahead was independence, a new start? However mortifying her methods, Stacey had released him – and before it was too late.

Already, he seemed to hear the brazen waves booming forth their message on the shore: that he could still find love, find purpose; that he wasn't just a piece of flotsam to be battered by the tide. And, overhead in the dark night sky, a flock of gulls went soaring up to a vaster, clearer realm – a more radiant sphere, bordering on infinity.

By dawn, he would reach Land's End. Food and sleep must wait, while he rushed straight out to walk the eager strand, feel the sea-breeze stroke his face, see the gulls for real – triumphant gulls, not crying in derision now, but screeching out a hymn of praise to the lonely but courageous man who had broken free.

At last.